The drink tantalized, honeyed yet tangy—

It was like her relationship with Rann, sweet and bitter at the same time, tempting her to touch, while knowing that to touch was to be hurt.

"More?" he asked.

"No, thank you." Storm shook her head. It was not more to drink she craved. "Save the rest for when Krish and Le come back," she suggested.

"They won't be back for some time yet," Rann replied with quiet certainty as his arm encircled her waist, drawing her toward him.

"They might be back early because of the ivory," she babbled as he bent his head.

"The elephant bells will warn us in good time." His lips silenced her protests... and her heart rejoiced, ignoring the clamoring warnings of her mind.

SUE PETERS
is also the author of these

Harlequin Romances

Many of these titles are available at your local bookseller.

For a free catalogue listing all available Harlequin Romances and Harlequin Presents, send your name and address to:

HARLEQUIN READER SERVICE
1440 South Priest Drive, Tempe, AZ 85281
Canadian address: Stratford, Ontario N5A 6W2

Man of Teak

by

SUE PETERS

Harlequin Books

TORONTO • LONDON • LOS ANGELES • AMSTERDAM
SYDNEY • HAMBURG • PARIS • STOCKHOLM • ATHENS • TOKYO

Original hardcover edition published in 1982
by Mills & Boon Limited

ISBN 0-373-02501-7

Harlequin Romance first edition September 1982

CHAPTER ONE

Storm!

She had been born during one. She was named after one. And a tropical storm had just done its best to wreck her career. She might yet manage to salvage it, Storm thought hopefully, even if there was no hope of salvaging the plane she had chartered, the smoking remains of which lay in a nearby creek bed. She could still complete her journey to the coast in time, if only this unfeeling stranger confronting her would behave like a human being, instead of a piece of unsympathetic granite.

'You *must* help me,' she insisted desperately. 'The ship leaves Kulu for England in two days' time, and I've simply *got* to be on it. There won't be another vessel leaving for six weeks.'

She wished, irritably, that he would sit down. It was almost impossible, she discovered, to demand instant obedience from someone who towered so far above your head that you had to crick your neck to look up into his lean, tanned, and totally unco-operative face.

His eyes seemed to bore right through her. They were glacier green, and noted with icy exactness her short, black, and wildly dishevelled curls, the liberal smudges of soot that smeared her face almost as black as her luminous dark eyes, and came to rest, with a look that was curiously like contempt, on the small carved ivory elephant pinned to the lapel of her jacket.

I wish he'd look somewhere else. Her fingers rose in an unconsciously nervous gesture to touch her brooch. It was faultlessly carved, and had been fiendishly expensive, but it made a perfect souvenir of her holiday in this tropical paradise that was only now beginning to reveal its drawbacks.

Perhaps he's got a thing about elephants. . . . His eyes seemed to be riveted to the brooch, noting every detail of the exact carving; noting her nervously touching fingers.

5

With an effort she pulled her hand away. It did not do to betray nervousness to an adversary. Instinctively, she classed this man as such.

'I've already told you, I can't spare the men to take you to the coast.' He did not look as if he enjoyed repeating himself, and he controlled his patience with an obvious effort.

'I don't need men. Not even one man.' Her withering look said, particularly not the man confronting her. 'I can drive myself. All I need is a vehicle. Surely you can lend me a Land Rover, or something? *Hire* me a vehicle, if you must.' She had no money, nothing, with her. She had only what she stood up in, and after the the events of the last few hours that was not in particularly good condition, she acknowledged ruefully. Her appearance was as dishevelled as her temper, and not conducive to arousing trust in a prospective hirer of vehicles. Her faultlessly tailored trouser suit looked, she thought without humour, as if it had just survived a plane crash. Which it had. But even the dimmest intelligence should be capable of realising that if she could afford to charter a plane, she could afford to hire one of his wretched vehicles.

'I can make arrangements with one of the banks at Kulu, to reimburse you.' She scorned to accept charity from this arrogant creature with hair the rich colour of a lion's mane, and brilliant green eyes that glared at her with hostile unwelcome.

'There aren't any vehicles here.'

'Do you really expect me to believe that?' she flashed back hotly. 'One minute you tell me you're here in charge of a timber operation for extracting teak from the jungle, and then you try to make me believe you haven't any vehicles. You must use *some* form of transport.'

'There are only three kinds of transport this high up in the jungle,' his voice hardened perceptibly. 'We use elephants, canoes, or Shanks' pony. The logs are floated downriver to the mills on the coast, and the only wheeled vehicles we've got are down there.'

'Then I'll hire a canoe,' she interrupted him eagerly, cutting short his explanation. She was not interested in what he did with his teak logs. He could sit astride them and paddle them downstream himself, for all she cared. All that she wanted at this moment was to remove herself as swiftly as possible away from the scatter of huts that she supposed constituted the local version of a village, and the wild, bottle green wilderness of mountainous jungle that surrounded them. And, she told herself hardly, as far away as possible from this male chauvinist whose work made the wilderness his home.

He was handsome—she glanced at him covertly from under the shelter of her curling black lashes—supremely handsome. In her own profession, his looks alone would have turned him into a star overnight. If the colouring of his hair resembled the king of beasts, his looks surely made him a king among men. But they did not make her predisposed to like him. Maybe he thought they should. No doubt he was accustomed to having girls fall over themselves to do his bidding, she told herself scathingly. Well, she, Storm Sheridan, nationally acclaimed actress, and already on the ladder to stardom, was not inclined to join the queue!

It was not her fault that the plane she had chartered to fly her overland in a do-or-die attempt to catch up with the ship at Kulu should hit a sudden tropical storm, break a fuel line, and crash-land on the edge of a creek close to the clearing that held this man and his bungalow. Not only crash-landed, she remembered unhappily, but burned itself out, and her luggage with it, leaving her with only what she stood up in. Both she and the pilot were lucky to escape with only a few minor bumps and bruises as souvenirs of their adventure, but the fact that they were comparatively unhurt did not excuse this stranger's frank unhelpfulness, she told herself unforgivingly.

The brown-skinned men, dressed in ragged shorts and little else except for weapons slung across their shoulders, who appeared like magic when the plane crashed, had shown more concern, and steered herself and the pilot to within sight of the nearest habitation before melting back into the jungle like wraiths, without even waiting for her to say 'thank you', she thought regretfully. She wished fervently that they had steered her into more hospitable company before they disappeared.

'I can't spare a man to do the paddling.' The note of
finality in his voice raised the level of Storm's temper several notches higher, until she began to feel as if at any
moment now she would bubble over.

If he says that again, I'll scream! she promised herself.
Aloud, she said with as much calm as she could muster,
'I needn't borrow one of your men. All I need is a
canoe. I can hire a man from the village to do the paddling for me, or even the pilot, he may know how to handle
a canoe, and he can't want to remain here any more than
I do.' Unrepentantly she let the tawny-haired stranger
know that she shared his own aversion to her presence in
his jungle village.

'If you hadn't hired a middle-aged drop-out for a pilot,
with a rickety plane that was likely to fall apart at any
moment, you wouldn't be here at all,' he retorted with
blunt impatience, and Storm's cheeks flamed.

'There wasn't any other transport available, I'd got no
choice but to hire him, or miss the boat,' she said shortly,
and wondered for the hundredth time what evil spirit had
managed to persuade her to linger for that fateful extra
two days, sunning herself on the most beguiling beaches
in the world, only to discover that the third day started a
national holiday, and the train service she was relying on
ceased altogether for the next three days, just long enough
to make her miss the last ship for weeks back to England.

'Your choice doesn't seem to have achieved its object,'
he observed drily, and Storm's eyes snapped.

'No one can control a tropical storm,' she justified her
action swiftly, 'and how do you know the pilot's a drop-
out, anyway? He might be just as capable of handling a
canoe as one of the local men.'

'I doubt it,' he retorted maddeningly. 'The whole of
the Kheval Province knows Mac.' His tone implied that
he did not consider the knowledge to be in any way a privi-
lege. 'The only liquid he's accustomed to comes out of a
bottle, so if you're considering trying to walk out, and
using him as a guide, forget it,' he advised, his eyes keen
on her mutinous expression. 'It's an arduous journey at
best, across mountainous jungle and swamp, and it's over

ninety miles to Kulu.' He looked as if he, personally, would make light of such minor impediments to his progress, Storm thought sarcastically, but,

'You're hardly equipped for such an adventure,' he warned her, with a straight glance that took in her slight figure and thin-soled slip-on sandals, 'and neither is the pilot.' His tone became steely. 'Mac's more accustomed to propping up a bar than taking physical exercise. He wouldn't be capable of making the journey. It'd be suicidal to even try.' His own lean, hard-muscled frame was the antithesis of the pilot's grossly overweight figure, but the contempt in his voice stung Storm to retaliate.

'The pilot lost his plane trying to get me to Kulu. At least *he* tried to be helpful!'

'Spare your sympathy,' the stranger advised her curtly. 'I doubt if the plane belonged to Mac anyway, and if it wasn't his, the loss won't bother him. He's a rolling stone who never sticks to anything for long. To my knowledge he's been using the plane as a local air ferry for the last couple of years, so he was probably looking round for something different to do anyway. The Far East's full of such men,' he shrugged.

'Then I'll hire a man from the village,' she used her last resort. Anything to get away from this odious creature, she told herself hotly. He was as callous as he was unhelpful.

'All the able-bodied men of the village who'd be capable of paddling a canoe are working for me,' he crushed her hope remorselessly. 'We need every pair of hands we can get for the work we're doing here, and every hour is urgent,' he told her flatly.

'Surely a couple of days can't make all that much difference to a load of timber?' she cried disbelievingly.

'We're not extracting timber . . .'

'But you said . . .'

'I've temporarily withdrawn all my men from felling and dragging teak, to cope with a local emergency,' he interrupted her impatiently. 'Even the working elephants and their oozies have had to be pressed into service, the need is that urgent.'

'My need's urgent, too.' Storm took his raised eyebrows

as a sign that he was at least listening, even if he was not interested in her need, and rushed on, 'I'm due to play the lead role in the best musical to hit the West End this decade. Rehearsals start in a fortnight's time.'

'A stage play is hardly a matter of life and death,' he cut in dismissively.

'It's a matter of life to me,' she burst out angrily. 'It's the best part I've ever had. It's what I've worked for and dreamed about for years. I might never get another chance as good as this,' she hammered at him desperately. 'If you won't help me to get to the coast in time to catch the ship when it sails, you could destroy my career,' she declared passionately. 'Deliberately destroy it,' she accused him.

'A very convincing performance.' He was totally unmoved, utterly indifferent. Storm's temper boiled over.

'I'm not acting now!' she shouted at him. She had never felt less like acting in her life. Suddenly she had never felt so close to tears. She gulped them back. They would be lost on this man. He was as hard as the teak he extracted from the jungle, she told herself furiously, and just about as unyielding. Instead she turned her anger into an armour, and lashed at him furiously. 'What's so urgent about *your* job, and *your* work, that you're prepared to wreck my career rather than help me?'

'My work's had to take second place to the needs of these villagers, and yours will have to do the same.' She quailed before the sudden fire that flashed in his strange green eyes. Jungle eyes. They pierced her armour with ease, laying bare her innermost thoughts, her ambitions, and her dreams. And discounted them, she saw furiously, as being frivolous, and totally unimportant. Unworthy, even.

'What needs can the villagers here have that are so desperately urgent?' she enquired with biting sarcasm. 'Nothing can be *that* pressing, stuck here miles from any-where, on the edge of the jungle . . .'

'The villagers need to eat. They need to drink. They need to live their lives free from fear.' He spelled it out for her baldly, in curt, concise words. 'Sit down and listen, and then maybe you'll get your sense of values straight.'

Before she realised what he was about to do, he grasped the top of a hard wooden chair with lean brown fingers and pushed it against the back of her knees. His action caught her unawares, and her knees folded, obliging her to sit down whether she wanted to or not. She stiffened angrily and immediately went to jump up again, but he sat down himself on the edge of a table, so close in front of her that she could not get up without physically pushing him aside. She measured him with angry eyes, and the urge to try died swiftly within her.

'You must have heard of the recent earthquake?'

She nodded, silently. Who had not? she asked herself shudderingly. At the mere mention of it she felt cold. Its scale and ferocity were such as had never been recorded before, and it turned the rest of the world numb with horror at the consequences. But. . . .

'The Kheval Province isn't in the 'quake zone.' Her eyes accused him of lying, of using even that excuse for his stubborn unwillingness to help her. 'The 'quake was at the other end of the country from here.' Did he not think she read the newspapers? Perhaps he was among the ranks of those who thought the acting fraternity were devoid of intelligence.

'The 'quake itself devastated the other end of the country,' he agreed curtly, 'but earth tremors spread out from it, and affected a large area.'

That was true, Storm remembered grudgingly. Subsidiary tremors had even been felt so far away as central Europe.

'The tremor that touched the Kheval mountains set off a huge landslide,' he went on in a clipped tone before Storm could speak. 'It brought down a large part of the watershed that marks the northern boundary of the Province, and blocked off a prong of the river that divides into two at that point, and spreads fanwise to irrigate the land around this area where the villages are congregated,' he waved a comprehensive hand at the scatter of huts visible from where they sat on the veranda of the wooden bungalow that appeared to be his home, 'and it also waters a big game reserve on the other side of this particular patch of jungle.'

'I don't see what that's got to do with not providing me with transport to get to the coast,' she butted in angrily. 'A couple of bulldozers would soon get rid of your landslide. If you can't get them here by normal transport, surely you could have them air lifted by helicopter?' He was simply using the emergency as an excuse, she told herself cuttingly.

'The slopes are too steep to make the use of machinery possible,' he brushed aside her suggestion, and went on, 'the only possible way to clear the landslide is to use men to do the digging, and elephants to move the heavy boulders and tree trunks. It'll take every man we've got, and every animal, working against time, to unblock the watercourse and get the prong of it that waters the game reserve flowing again before the area dries out.'

'The dry season doesn't start until March. That's another three months or more yet.' He should see she was not totally ignorant of the tropical seasons, she told herself triumphantly.

'So far as the game reserve's concerned, the dry season's already started,' he contradicted her grimly. 'Unless we can clear the landslide, and unblock that water course to get it running again in time, there'll be nothing left for the animals to graze on long before the dry season proper starts. One elephant alone needs six hundred pounds of green fodder a day, and the game reserve supports a large, wild herd, as well as the countless smaller grazing animals which need fodder as well.'

'I still don't see. . . .' she began stubbornly. She did *not* see. Bewilderment and frustration and fury showed clear in her mobile face. 'What has animal fodder got to do with the villagers—with my career?' she demanded to know.

'Just this.' He edged forward on the table, and instinctively Storm shrank back in her chair. He noticed the movement, and a thin smile played momentarily about his well cut lips, but it died again almost immediately, and he went on tersely, 'Without the river water, the land will dry out, and the green fodder it contains will wither. It's already beginning to wither,' he emphasised, 'which is why every hour of labour in unblocking the watercourse is of vital importance. Without fodder, and without water, the animals on the game reserve will be forced to trek out and find another source of supply, or they themselves will die.' He paused, but Storm remained silent, and he continued forcefully,

'Denied their own feeding grounds, the grazing animals, and that includes the large herd of wild elephants, will seek the nearest alternative source of food and water available, which means the villagers' crops, and the prong of the river that irrigates their land.'

'So?' The logic of his thinking was inescapable, but it did not lessen her own plight. She made her voice deliberately disinterested, and she saw his face tighten, but she did not care.

'So, what is worse. . . .'

Could anything be worse, from her point of view? she asked herself in near despair, and forced herself to listen as he went on.

'What is worse, where the grazing animals go, the gazelle and their like, the predators will surely follow.' His voice carried a new dimension of looming fear, and in spite of herself, Storm shivered. 'What until now has been a reasonably peaceful co-existence will soon turn to war between the animals and the villagers, and where their food is at stake, there'll be no quarter given on either side. The grazing animals will raid the crops. The villagers will have to retaliate or face hunger themselves, and the predators, the big cats,' he paused again to punctuate his meaning, 'the predators will reap their own grim harvest, which will put the lives of every man, woman and child in the villages at risk, as well as those of the big cats' natural prey. I intend to see that does not happen,' he told her harshly, 'no matter what it costs,' he added for her benefit, and she stared up at him in stunned silence.

Looking at the granite set of his lean, tanned features, she wondered if he would really care if the green fodder in the game reserve *did* wilt. She was unsure if he would mind all that much if the villagers *did* retaliate in order to defend their crops. But she felt one hundred per cent certain that he would care very much indeed if he did not get his own way.

'Which is why I don't intend to waste the time of two
of my men on a jaunt to the coast, simply to accommodate
your career aspirations,' he said with crisp finality. 'The
last thing I need right now is two extra people to bother
with.' He made his own feelings unflatteringly plain. 'But
since you're here, for a week or two at any rate, here
you'll have to remain.'

'Thakin! Thakin!'

He broke off, and was on his feet in one swift, fluid
movement that reminded Storm irrisistably of the powerful grace of the big jungle cats themselves.

'Thakin. . . .'

'Here. . . .' He swung down the veranda steps to meet
the small boy who burst from a cluster of huts thirty or
forty yards away, and came racing across the dusty ground
towards the bungalow, while bedlam broke out behind
him among the village huts. Children screamed. Women's
voices shouted. A baby bawled lustily, and Storm thought
she heard a terrified yelp from a dog that was quickly cut
short. Suddenly, without quite knowing how she got there,
Storm found herself at the bottom of the steps as well,
and racing in the wake of the tawny-haired man and the
child as they ran towards the village huts. A tremendous,
metallic clatter rose above the shouts and cries, and as she
burst between a gap in the huts she had the confused
impression of a flat area like a compound, full of women—
tall, graceful, brown-skinned women wearing long,
brightly coloured cotton skirts, and all banging madly at
what, to her startled eyes, appeared to be a miscellany of
metal cooking utensils, and shouting at the tops of their
voices.

The crowd of women parted to let the tawny-haired
man in, and through the resulting gap she saw it—a
crouching, snarling shape that slunk from behind one of
the huts. The man saw it at the same time, and he gave a
tremendous shout and leapt forward, and the broad, flat,
furry face turned towards him, its ears plastered down
and its eyes glinting with rage. And in its mouth . . . Storm
gulped, and suddenly felt faint . . . in its mouth it carried
something long, and limp. . . .

Even as her shocked eyes fastened on it, the creature

dropped whatever it was it carried, and turning leaped away, and disappeared into the undergrowth. It was gone so quickly that if it had not been for the excited, chattering women shepherding their children into the safety of the huts, Storm would not have known whether she had actually seen it or not.

The tawny-haired man stopped. For a wild moment she thought he might give chase, but instead he turned and vouchsafing only a single comprehensive glance at whatever it was the creature had dropped, he shrugged and strode back across the compound, speaking to the women in a firm, calm voice, and in a few moments it was all over, and the compound emptied as the women went back about their daily chores, and it was as if nothing had happened.

But it had happened. Storm had seen it with her own eyes. And the animal, whatever it was, had nearly carried . . . something, she dared not let herself think what, away with it. It was only the man's shout, and the awesome threat of his presence, that had made it drop its prey. Why didn't someone go to what it had dropped? she asked herself frantically. Why didn't someone check to see if anything could be done to save it? But the women had disappeared into their huts, and the man was walking back towards her across the compound. She looked up and met his eyes across the empty, dusty space, and suddenly she felt sick.

'It only killed a pi-dog—this time,' he said significantly.

And apparently pi-dogs did not matter. His callous indifference to the animal's fate sparked her anger afresh, and she stiffened.

'Surely wild animals are a natural hazard of living on the edge of the jungle,' she retorted sharply. She was determined not to allow him to see how badly the incident had shaken her. Even now, she felt weak with relief that it was a pi-dog, and not a child. She trembled violently, and only by a supreme effort of will did she manage to erase the tremble from her voice when she spoke.

'It's a hazard the people cope with under normal circumstances.' His voice was as curt as her own. 'But already there's almost double the concentration of wild animals in the area because of the lack of water on the game reserve. Already the big cats have discovered that pi-dogs make easier picking than the wild deer—what happened just now ought to convince you of that,' he said grimly. 'It can only be a matter of time before one of them discovers that a child is even easier to grab than a pi-dog.'

Storm stumbled. While he had been talking they had reached the wooden bungalow, and suddenly the shallow steps back up to the verandah looked a mile high. Her knees felt like putty. All the horror and shock and fear of the last few minutes suddenly washed over her, and combined with the terror of the plane crash and the desperation of her futile efforts to make this man provide her with transport to the coast. Her senses reeled. She groped unseeingly for the wooden rail that ran beside the steps, and instead of the rail her fingers encountered a hand. A strong, hard hand, that took her own in a firm grip and steered her towards the steps, and up them, and did not loose her until she was sat down again on the chair she had vacated, was it a lifetime ago?

Her hand throbbed where he had held it. Instinctively she brought up her other hand to nurse it, but the sensation refused to go away. Her fingers tingled as if they had encountered a massive electric shock. Her arm felt numb, and yet strangely, wonderfully alive, with a life of its own that it had never felt before. It wanted to reach out and hold again, hold for ever, the hand of the tawny stranger. It even made a small, independent movement towards him, and Storm gripped it convulsively, pressing it down into her lap, afraid to let it go. Afraid of the sudden tumult that invaded her senses through the one brief grip of his hand, and set her mind reeling just when she most needed it to remain clear and cool.

'I must have had a bump on the head when the plane crashed,' she told herself shakily. Or else it was the jungle. She had heard that the jungle affected people strangely.

'I ought to be used to handsome men by now.' She grasped desperately at her self-control. As an actress rapidly approaching the zenith of her profession, she had

had enough experience of handsome men. She had been wooed by them, kissed by them. But always on stage. Off duty, for some reason she never tried to explain even to herself, she had kept herself aloof.

'Even so, I can cope with men, however handsome,' she assured herself staunchly, and tried without success to stifle the insistent voice inside her that questioned jeeringly,

'You can cope with men. Some men. But can you cope with this one? Can you cope with yourself?'

And gazing up at him with wide, dark, frightened eyes, meeting the hard green lack of welcome in his own, she dared not allow herself to think of what the true answer must be.

If only I could get away! she thought. If she could go now, instantly, whether it was by wheeled vehicle or canoe she no longer cared, then once out of sight of this man she would cope. But if she had to remain with him, under his roof, even for another twenty-four hours, she feared it would be too late.

'A few hours ago, I hadn't even met him,' she tried to defend herself against the voice.

'Hours ... days ... what does time matter?' it asked indifferently.

'I loathe him,' she quelled it, passionately. 'He's callous, indifferent. . . .'

'You may loathe him, but you can't ignore him,' the voice persisted remorselessly.

Steel could not ignore a magnet. It was like some invisible force, drawing her towards him, stirring into life emotions she had not even known she possessed. One touch of his hand was enough to set up a clamour inside her that took her normally unshakeable poise by storm, awakening feelings that not all the love scenes she had ever played out on stage had been able to evoke.

He disturbed her. He frightened her. And until the landslide was cleared, and the watercourse flowed normally again across the game reserve, it appeared he intended to virtually make a prisoner of her in this remote jungle village.

And she did not even know his name.

CHAPTER TWO

'I DON'T know your name.'

She voiced her thoughts. Some of them—not all of them. She was not prepared to voice all of them, not even to herself.

'Rann Moorcroft.' He described her a mocking bow, and his green eyes glinted at her. Storm flushed. Her words had sounded prim, as if she was some Victorian miss, insisting on a formal introduction. She almost replied, 'How do you do?' and stopped herself just in time as he added drily, 'Be my guest.'

'Here?' Immediately she wished that unsaid, too, but it was too late to stop it, and his look taunted her. It read all too clearly the doubt and uncertainty in her face, read the question that flashed through her mind,

'I wonder if I could get accommodation in the village huts?'

It interpreted the slight, instinctive shake of her head as she instantly rejected the idea. 'No, that's not possible.' But—stay here, in this bungalow, with Rann Moorcroft? She swallowed, and he spoke with insulting gravity.

'Have no fear, you'll be adequately chaperoned.'

Was he allaying her fears, she wondered confusedly, or letting her know clearly, and without words, that she need have none, because he was not interested? She stared at him, and her eyes dropped, knowing that he had read that question, too, and intended to leave her to work out the answer for herself, indifferent as to what her conclusion might be.

'Since we're name swapping,' he said casually, 'you'd better let me have yours, so that I can wireless the authorities at Kulu to tell them you're safe and in one piece.' He turned away from her as he spoke, and she leaned back in the chair, trembling, feeling as if she had embarked on another, longer, and far more dangerous journey than the one she had undertaken by plane. A journey that, so far as she was concerned, had crashed on take-off.

'Storm. Storm Sheridan,' she managed out loud.

'I mean your real name,' his eyes lost their glint and became hard, and impatient, 'not some fanciful stage name.'

'It *is* my real name,' she snapped back, stung to anger. It was not the first time the misunderstanding had occurred, and her irritation was not lessened by repetition. 'I don't suppose, being stuck out here in the back of beyond, you've ever heard of it,' she snapped disparagingly.

'I haven't.' He thrust her jibe back at her, neatly, promptly, and without preamble. He did not even attempt to be polite, to pretend he might have heard of it, as most people would have done, she thought furiously. He was as uncivilised as his surroundings.

'That scarcely matters.' Her shrug said it did not matter at all, to her, and she hoped hid the fact that, in spite of herself, it rankled. 'But the Crown Theatre will want to know my whereabouts, and so, presumably, will the Purser on the liner. If you can instruct the authorities at Kulu to telex them, no doubt they'll be reassured to know I'm in safe hands,' she said bitingly. 'And there must be someone who'll want to know if the pilot's safe, too,' she added as an afterthought, guiltily conscious that she had not noticed the latter's absence from the veranda until now, her mind had been totally preoccupied with arguing with her unwilling host.

'I doubt it,' Rann Moorcroft contradicted her drily, 'but I'll mention him to the authorities as well, just in case ... oh, there you are,' he broke off as the portly figure of the pilot shambled back on to the veranda from a room somewhere at the rear of the bungalow, as if in answer to her unspoken question. Rann might have tried to sound a little more welcoming, Storm thought critically, particularly as the other man had a plaster dressing across his forehead, which explained his disappearance. He had obviously made some attempt to tidy himself, but any lingering hope that remained in Storm's mind that the pilot might be able to canoe her as far as the coast

died as she looked at him. His red-veined face, and grossly
overweight frame, emphasised only too clearly the truth
of her host's words. The man was physically in no condition to take on the task. Which left her with no option
but to obey Rann Moorcroft's behest, to remain until the
river flowed across the game reserve once more.

The quick thrill of relief that flooded over her at the
thought left her shocked and bewildered. The magnetism
of this man was stronger than she had bargained for. She
shivered. Her reckoning that another twenty-four hours
under his roof would be too late was wildly out of date. It
was already too late. With a supreme effort she checked
her thoughts, and became aware that Rann was speaking
to her.

'You can have a room here in the bungalow. Le will
show you.' His eyes mocked her, daring her to question
his arrangement, but the mockery this time passed her
by. Her attention latched on to the name.

'Le?' Was this the chaperone he spoke of? Storm turned,
and stared.

The girl was stunningly beautiful. Her hair was brown,
and straight, and wound in a knot on top of her head.
Her eyes and her skin were of the same deep, warm
brown. She was like a perfect painting, come to life. A
brightly coloured skirt fell from her tiny waist to her feet,
and a white bolero-like jacket topped her loose blouse.
Beside her lissom grace, Storm felt suddenly stiff and
clumsy. She blinked, and somehow managed to return
the other girl's smile, while a dozen questions chased one
another through her bewildered mind.

'Why doesn't Rann introduce us properly?' she asked
herself desperately, and felt appalled by the depth of unexpected dread that squeezed her heart into an agonising
pain, in case he should introduce this lovely creature as
his wife. She knew that men whose work kept them for
long years under alien skies sometimes adopted the
country of their calling, binding themselves by marriage
to its people and its customs, and forsaking their homeland
to strike roots for the future with a people not their own.

Had that happened here? If this wild country had become Rann Moorcroft's kingdom, was this girl his queen?

Storm stole a glance at his face, and a hot rose tide of colour warmed the creamy pallor of her skin. He was watching her intently. His strange emerald eyes were fixed on her face, reading her thoughts, knowing the questions that teemed through her mind. Reading also—she caught her breath with quick apprehension—reading also her dread of what the answers might be. The rosy colour receded from her cheeks, and her eyes grew enormous, wide pools of blackness in her suddenly white face.

'Le's living here for the moment. . . .'

So he was . . . he had. . . . A tight band seemed to constrict Storm's chest, making it difficult for her to breathe, impossible for her to speak.

'. . . just while her husband is helping me to supervise the work of clearing the course of the river,' he finished casually.

'Her . . . husband?' The tight band round her chest vanished, and in its place came a wild, singing exhilaration, that had a silly effect on her head. It felt light and dizzy, and the room and Rann receded. His voice seemed to reach her from a vast distance, but her palpitating heart caught joyously at the words that her drumming ears found almost impossible to decipher.

'Krish is Warden in charge of the game reserve,' Rann offered. 'He's brought his entire staff along, to help us to clear the watercourse, and with Krish and his men withdrawn from the game reserve for what could be several weeks, Le couldn't stay in their bungalow on her own.'

His lips answered her unspoken questions, while his eyes mocked her for asking them. The gleam in them repudiated her right to ask, while telling her anyway, because it mattered nothing to him what she wondered, or what she knew. Le spoke, and Storm turned towards her blindly.

'You can have one of our rooms,' she said. 'Rann gave us two, but with Krish away at the work site all day we don't really need both of them.' She held out a tiny hand to Storm. 'Come and see,' she invited.

'And *you* come with *me*.' Rann spoke curtly to the pilot, and in his tone was something that brought Storm's attention back to the other man. She glanced at him, and grimaced her distaste. His eyes devoured Le, and in them was an expression. . . . Instinctively she turned and looked straight at Rann, and the stern set of his features sent a swift flood of relief through her. He, too, had seen, and his next words confirmed that he intended to take action.

'Until you leave here, you'll live in the men's compound,' he told the pilot curtly. 'Is that clear?' Without waiting for the latter's muttered reply he gave a quick jerk of his head that sent the airman sullenly shambling towards the veranda steps.

'I don't like that man.' Soft fingers grasped Storm's hand and drew her into a room at the back of the veranda. Le pushed the door to behind them, sat on the edge of the bed, and burst out laughing. 'Your face is a study!' she gurgled.

'I didn't know . . . I didn't expect. . . .' Storm stammered to an embarrassed halt.

'You didn't expect to hear me speak English,' the other girl finished for her, merrily. 'Krish and I both took it as our second language at school.' She tapped the bed beside her, and Storm sat down, grateful for her friendliness, unutterably grateful that they spoke a common language. Perhaps Le would help her to obtain transport, any kind of transport. Her need to get away was even more urgent now, and it had nothing to do with catching the vessel to England. Instead, her journey to the coast would be a panic flight, away from this village, away from Rann. She made herself listen to what Le was saying, to try to appear interested. She needed the other girl's co-operation as she had never needed anything in her life before.

'We found a knowledge of the language invaluable when we went to veterinary college in England. Oh yes, we both qualified there,' she answered Storm's questioning glance. 'Veterinary practice, zoology, the lot,' she grimaced. 'It was very hard work, but worth it, because it has got Krish what he wanted, the management of the game reserve here, and of course having more or less the same qualifications myself, it means that I can be of help to him as well. It's a career for both of us, in a way.' Her smile said it was a way of life, and she wanted no other.

'Unless I can get to the coast in time to catch the liner, my career will be ruined,' Storm burst out impulsively. 'Le, could you . . .?' She turned hopefully to the other girl.

'There's nothing I can do.' To Storm's dismay, Le shook her head. 'Believe me, I'd help you if I could. I heard you talking to Rann, so I know what it means to you. He would have helped you, if it was at all possible.' She either did not hear, or chose to ignore, Storm's disbelieving hiss, and went on persuasively, 'There are only the women left in the villages, and the very old men who're not capable of paddling a canoe any longer, and the able-bodied men really can't be spared from the work of clearing the watercourse. It is as Rann said.'

'I'd worked for just such a lead role for years!' Storm wailed despairingly, and knew that her career was only of secondary importance now in her need to flee this place.

'There'll be other parts for you to play,' Le consoled, happily unaware of the trend of her thoughts. 'The talent that gave you this part won't just go away. There'll be other productions, and other chances, for you.' She paused, and added deliberately, 'For the villagers, there'll be no second chance.' Her soft, husky voice begged Storm's understanding. 'Time means survival, for them,' she said simply.

'That's what Rann said.' Storm slumped back hopelessly.

'Why not treat it as an unexpected holiday?' the other girl coaxed. 'You won't be tied here indefinitely, and you can book in on the next ship back to England. Now the monsoon's ended, we're coming into a rather nice time of the year. Even the jungle has its attractions,' she smiled.

Did her words hold a subtle meaning? Storm eyed her suspiciously. If not, why should the mention of attractions conjure up an immediate picture of Rann Moorcroft in her mind? His leonine head, his deep, piercing eyes, and his air of leashed strength that reminded her of a tightly wound spring, that might at any moment explode into forceful action, and at once fascinated and frightened her.

Or was her fear not so much of Rann but of her own reaction to him? She poured scorn on the idea, trying to blow it out of her mind with a gale of self-derision, but it persisted like a nagging toothache, uneasy, probing.

'I ought to be impervious to handsome men by now,' she jeered at herself. But acting was different. However it was meant to portray reality, a stage play was not real. Stage heroes were not real, and neither were stage kisses. . . .

'I must be mad!' She thrust away the thought of what it would be like to be kissed by Rann Moorcroft. 'Stop it!' she commanded her mind desperately. Along that road lay disaster, and she had enough problems to contend with as it was. She grasped at the reality of the nearest one, to save herself.

'I haven't come equipped for a holiday,' she told Le ruefully. 'All my luggage was in the plane, and that burned itself out in a creek after we crashed. I've only got what I stand up in.' And that was crumpled, dirty, and sticky with perspiration from the humid, clinging heat.

'You can borrow some of mine,' Le offered immediately. 'We're about the same size,' she eyed Storm's slender figure appraisingly. 'I left my European clothes in the bungalow back on the game reserve, but you'll find a lungyi and a loose blouse a lot cooler here. I soon gave up wearing fitted dresses and slacks when I got back to the Province, they stick to you in the heat.'

'I've discovered that for myself.' Storm eased her jacket collar away from her neck with a wriggle.

'You can have a shower if you like, and then come and choose some clothes. I'll show you how to fix your lungyi so that it won't fall down,' Le promised mischievously.

'A shower?' It was about the last facility she would have expected in such basic accommodation as a jungle bungalow, Storm thought, amazed.

'We've got our own running water,' the other girl laughed at her surprise. 'There isn't a choice of hot and cold, I'm afraid, it's all just tepid, but at this time of the year, just after the monsoons, there's plenty of it. Come and see our plumbing,' she invited.

It was simple, but supremely effective. 'It looks like. . . .'

'Split bamboo,' Le confirmed her guess. 'It's split and

fixed like this at the back of all the huts in the village, in one long, continuous pipe. There's masses of bamboo growing wild everywhere round here, so there's no shortage of material. One end of the pipe is thrust underneath a waterfall farther up the hillside. While there's water coming down the fall, every hut in the village has a running supply. When you want some, simply block the pipe and let it overflow into your bowl until you've got enough, then unblock it again so that you don't deprive the next hut downhill for any longer than is necessary.'

'What a wonderful idea,' Storm enthused, 'is it one of Rann's?'

'Oh, no, the villagers have used it with various modifications for as long as anyone can remember,' Le took the local ingenuity for granted. 'Rann built the shower, though.' She led the way down a short flight of steps. 'It helps that the bungalow's built on stilts. The height of it means the bamboo guttering has to be high, too, so it was easy to build a shower hut on the ground underneath the pipe, and fill the tank for it by the same means.' Le demonstrated the working of it proudly. 'The used water simply drains into the ground and quickly dries up.'

'It works like a charm.'

Refreshed, and feeling a lot more human, Storm returned to her room to find Le brushing her hair in front of the mirror, and a scatter of clothes spread out for her inspection on the bed. The bright cottons brought a sparkle of appreciation to her eyes, and Le said,

'I brought lots of clothes with me, in case we had to stay for some time, so I've got plenty to spare,' she excused her generosity. 'I'll show you how to fix your lungyi.' She demonstrated with the ankle-length cotton skirt until she was sure that Storm was able to twist and tuck the top securely round her without danger of it descending round her feet.

'You always ought to wear your hair long, it looks lovely hanging down to your waist like that,' Storm told her, gazing at her companion appreciatively while she finished dressing.

'I let it down in the evenings.' A shy smile lit Le's eyes. 'I always let it down for when Krish comes home.' She broke a blossom from a flowering spray that she had dropped beside the mirror, and held it up against her hair. 'I just need to fix this—oh, I've left the clip in my room, I'll have to go back for it. I'll see you at dinner.' It sounded incongruous in the middle of the jungle, but Storm said nothing as she went on obligingly, 'Gurdip will ring the bell when he's ready for us to begin eating. The others will be here in about fifteen minutes.'

'How do you know?' Storm asked her curiously. She noticed Le did not wear a watch, but the conviction in her tone made it sound as if Rann and her husband were daily commuters, due at any moment now off the evening train.

'By the elephant bells,' Le smiled. 'The men use two or three of the elephants to bring them back to the village before they turn them loose for the night. You can hear the wooden bells coming for some time before they actually get here.'

She paused, and in the ensuing silence Storm caught the sound that Le's more accustomed ears had picked up some minutes before, a soft, musical clonking that for all its lack of resonance was strangely lovely, heralding the approach of the men of the village to their waiting families. Heralding the evening meal in company with Rann. . . .

'You've left one of your flowers behind.' She checked her thoughts abruptly, and held out the rest of the sweetly perfumed spray towards Le.

'The bloom I've got will be enough, I only need the open flower.'

'In that case, I'd like to wear the bud, if you don't mind?' Storm decided impulsively. The pale petals of the half opened bud would sit among her own short dark curls as effectively as the fully opened flower in Le's long hair. It was a pity, she reflected wistfully, that the custom of wearing flowers in the hair was not more widely indulged in by Western women; it was pleasant, and attractive, and utterly feminine.

'Well, of course . . . if you want to?'

The sudden doubt in Le's face took Storm by surprise. The other girl had been open-handedly generous with her

clothes. Was there some reason why she did not want to
share her flowers? She had picked them herself when she
took Storm outside to show her the shower hut, so it was
not as if they were a gift from her husband.

'Would you like the bud back?' she offered instantly,
but Le shook her head.

'No. No, you wear it.' Her smile returned, as if a
thought had suddenly struck her, and there was a hint of
merriment in her face that puzzled Storm. 'You wear it,'
she insisted, seeing Storm hesitate, 'it'll look lovely among
your curls,' and she disappeared in search of a clip with
which to fix her own.

Storm turned to the mirror, and her sense of unreality
grew as she regarded her reflection in the glass. The length
of bright acid green cotton fell crisply to her feet. She
buttoned up the loose pale yellow blouse, and pinned her
ivory brooch on to the white and oddly tailored-looking
jacket which made a perfect foil for her dark hair and
eyes. Except for the pallor of her skin, and the deep, soft
curls in her hair, it might be Le herself gazing back. But
there the resemblance ended, Storm thought bitterly. Le
was happy. Le was settled. Her career and her marriage
had united, and complemented one another. Le waited
with eager anticipation for her husband's return, while
she, Storm. . . . She bit her lip, picked up a comb, and
drew it savagely through her curls, as if to try to scrape
away the thoughts that turned her mind into a veritable
mill-race underneath them.

She dreaded meeting Rann again. In a few short hours
a man she had never set eyes on before in her life had
turned it upside down. It would have been bad enough,
she told herself despairingly, if she had been able to leave
straight away for the coast, and the liner, as she wanted
to, and seek escape in her work to repair the inroads he
had made into the defences which until now she had been
able to erect around her heart. But now. . . . She swallowed, with a dry throat. Now she would be forced to live
under Rann's roof for weeks, to see him every day.

'I still want my lead role in the musical,' she told herself
fiercely. 'I still want my career.' But if her mind was convinced by her fervour, her heart failed lamentably to re-

spond. That erstwhile impregnable organ, untouched by a succession of handsome and persuasive suitors from her own profession, cried like a child in the night that it wanted Rann . . . Rann . . . Rann. . . .

'I mustn't let him suspect.' With trembling fingers she thrust the flower into her curls, her blinded eyes unable to judge the results from her blurred image in the mirror. 'Whatever happens, he mustn't guess.' She blinked her eyes clear. 'It's just a temporary infatuation, that's all,' she assured herself. 'Love at first sight only happens on the stage, not in real life. You ought to know that.' The reminder of her profession brought her some small comfort. 'If I'm good enough to be chosen for the lead in a big musical, I ought to be able to act well enough to cover up my own feelings,' she rallied herself staunchly. 'I'll simply pretend it's a lead role in a play that's booked to run for several weeks.' She drew on her pride to aid her. If she herself was not fully convinced by her own arguments, that would not have to matter, so long as she succeeded in convincing Rann. She would have the whole of her life afterwards in which to try to convince herself. She patted the half opened creamy flower bud into place, and turned as a light tap sounded on her door.

'Le?' She stepped lightly across the room towards the opening door. 'How do I look?' she asked, brightly—and stopped.

'It isn't Le, it's me,' Rann said unnecessarily.

'I didn't expect . . . Le said dinner would be another fifteen minutes . . . she lent me some of her clothes. . . .' Storm stammered to a confused halt.

I'll have to do better than this, she told herself desperately. Where was her vaunted acting ability? Where was her voice control? Her self-control, that took her through first night nerves, and brought the plaudits of the audience to her feet? It was ridiculous that an audience of one should have the power to make her go to pieces like this, she berated herself scornfully.

'The costume suits you.' He made it sound as if it was stage costume, instead of everyday clothing. As if she was acting, she told herself indignantly. It was a common fallacy that stage people were incapable of being their real selves. She was acting, but not in the way he imagined.

'When in Rome,' she retorted tritely, and her smile was brittle as she lifted her face to him.

'Do you always adopt the customs of the country, as well as its costume, when you travel?' His voice was hard, and his eyes again held that look of contempt as they swept from her small, sandalled feet across the expanse of bitter green cotton, the contrasting delicacy of yellow and white, and came to rest on the flower tucked deep in the waves of her hair.

'If you mean my flower, I think it's a pity we don't adopt the same custom in the West.'

'So you approve of it?' His voice held something else besides a question, and she stared up at him, uncomprehending.

'Of course I approve of it. It's a wonderful idea,' she retorted defensively, though defending herself against what she had no notion. Why should she not approve? she asked herself bewilderedly. The flower was beautiful, much nicer than artificial adornments.

'In that case, it's a pity to disappoint you.'

He slammed the door to behind him with a swift, backwards kick of his heel. She heard the dull thud of wood against wood as if in a dream, at the same instant that his lips claimed her own. She had no time to retreat, no time to realise what he was about to do. In one devastating, all-illuminating second, she discovered what it was like to be kissed by Rann Moorcroft.

Many men had kissed her before in the course of her stage career, caresses as artificial as the plays they served. Many more men had wanted to kiss her, but she held herself aloof, refusing to unlock the door to her secret, inner self that she had saved, she realised now with despairing finality, for this moment of disenchantment. For a man who did not want her, who resented her presence, but who was demonstrably willing to take advantage of it while he could.

Rann Moorcroft's kisses were like lightning. Like thunder. Like storm. They were hard, and angry. They punished her, though for what reason she could not begin to guess. His hands on her shoulders held her against him, gripping her as if they would shake her rather than caress her. She flinched away, struggling to pull herself free, but he held her fast. Desperately she arched herself away from him, willing herself not to respond, but his lips demanded a response, drawing it from her against her will, like life-giving water from a well. Her breath deserted her, her head swam, and she felt herself go pliant in his arms.

'This is madness!' her terrified mind protested. 'Tropical madness.' It was like a fever in her blood, whose cause and remedy were the same. Her bemused mind grasped desperately at the last remnants of control, but the sheer, compelling magnetism of his kisses proved too strong. Every fibre of her being reached out to meet them, calling for more. If this was madness, it was a sweet insanity, like the compelling beat of jungle drums, intoxicating, hypnotic. Her lips clung to his, parting under their fierce pressure. She swayed, and closed her eyes. She did not need them to see his tawny head bent above her, his lean, tanned face, every feature of it was deeply etched on her inner vision until it dominated her whole mind, her whole world, blotting out everything else.

'Rann. . . .' She was breathless and panting when at last he let her go, and her eyes glowed, luminous with newly awakened joy.

'Now that you've given your flower a trial run, and satisfied yourself that it really works,' he thrust her from him abruptly, 'I'd advise you to take it off before you come in to dinner. The pilot's going to live in the men's compound while he's here, but we've got no option but to allow him to have his meals with us, and he's been in the Province for long enough now to know the significance of the flower you're wearing in your hair.'

'The significance . . .?' The harsh contempt in his tone lashed her, taking the glow from her eyes and the eager exhilaration from her face.

'Don't try to tell me Le didn't let you know what it means?' he sneered his disbelief. 'She's wearing a siri flower herself, as she's entitled to. It's a fully opened bloom, with which the married girls customarily welcome their husbands. Young maidens wear the tightly closed buds, and the half opened ones,' he paused significantly, and his strange green eyes pierced her like spears, 'the half opened ones, like the one you're wearing now, are used by the older, single girls who feel themselves ready for marriage, to let it be known that they're looking for suitors.'

'So that's why. . . .' Her hands rose to shelter her burning cheeks, and her eyes were wide with dismay on his rock hard face as he went on cuttingly,

'If you insist upon flaunting an open invitation, you've only got yourself to blame if it's accepted,' he flung at her contemptuously.

CHAPTER THREE

SHE longed to defy him. She longed to stalk out of the room with her head held high, and still bearing the siri bud. And then she remembered the pilot, and the look on his face when he first set eyes on Le, and her courage faded. If he really was aware of what the bud signified. . . . She raised a shaking hand and snatched it from her hair, and threw it on to the bed.

'It'll probably fade soon anyway, in this heat,' she snapped, and swept past Rann without a glance—and promptly found her legs entangled in the green, unyielding cotton of her lungyi.

'Girls wearing the local dress don't take long strides.'

He caught her as she tripped and staggered off balance, and put her safely on her feet again, and she hated him for the grin of derision on his face. 'If the ladies want to put on speed, they tuck up their lungyis into a loincloth, out of the way.' His eyes laughed at her embarrassment, daring her to try the same remedy, and her face flamed.

'I can learn to cope with it by myself,' she hissed at him furiously, acutely conscious of the interested stares of Le and the brown, slender, fine-looking man who stood beside her.

'Come and meet Krish.'

Storm could not blame the other girl for what had

happened. Le's eyes laughed a question as they met her own, but her smile was friendly, and completely without malice as she put out her hand to draw Storm forward, inviting her to become part of the small, intimate gathering. Making her welcome, Storm thought bitterly, even if Rann did not. Le could not know, and Storm hoped fervently she did not guess, what damage her innocent trick had done to her own heart. Before Rann had kissed her, she was confident she could cope. But not now.

'You sit here beside me, Mac, and Storm on my right.'

The pilot appeared, and Rann became the urbane host. He settled Storm in her chair, directed the pilot to his, and left Krish to attend to Le. It was deftly done. Without making it obvious, the two men sat one on each side of the Scot, effectively separating him from any close contact with the girls. He could not even see Le, Storm realised with quick amusement, unless he deliberately leaned right forward and looked round Krish, and glancing at the dark, strong face of the game warden, Storm doubted if the pilot would try. The latter, she realised uncomfortably, was sitting directly opposite to herself. Doubtless Rann did not consider that she needed the same protection as Le, and a sharp stab went through her at the silent inference. It would have been nice, she thought wistfully, to have felt cosseted as well. For Rann to want to cosset her.

'Before you go home, you must visit the game reserve,' Krish pressed her hospitably from the other side of the table. 'Already we're achieving more than I had believed possible in so short a time. We've introduced several endangered species, and they're beginning to establish themselves, and to breed.'

Storm's sense of unreality returned. The manservant, clad in a long white garment, moved silently around the table dispensing soup. Conversation flowed easily, intelligent, interesting. It only needed candles in tall silver sconces, she thought disbelievingly, for them to be dining in some elegant country home in England, instead of in a wooden bungalow on the edge of the jungle. The men both in tropical white; herself and Le in long skirts. It did not need much imagination to translate both into evening dress. The pilot struck the only discordant note. He remained silent, morose, making no effort to join in the flow of talk. Perhaps his head still hurt, despite the attention it had received, Storm thought sympathetically.

She tried to draw him into the conversation. If only the pilot would talk, it might help to alleviate the strain of Rann's presence at her side. She tried to concentrate on the conversation, but all the time she was feverishly aware of Rann's every movement, of the deep tones of his voice, replying to Krish, and Le. She dipped her spoon into the rich soup, and it might have been river water for all the taste it had for her. The curry that followed it scorched her tongue, but that passed unnoticed too, because the only awareness she seemed to be capable of was for Rann.

'The plane's a write-off,' she chatted desperately to Krish, aware that she was talking too much, and unable to stop, because silence would leave her at the mercy of her own thoughts. 'I hope it's adequately insured?' she babbled on.

'I wouldn't know,' the pilot shrugged heavily. 'But if it isn't, maybe it'll teach them as owns it to spend some money in keeping their property in decent repair,' he snarled vindictively. 'The crate was a flying disaster, anyway.' He sucked noisily at his soup.

So Rann's guess that the plane did not belong to the pilot had been correct. That at least relieved her conscience on that score, she thought thankfully. Instinctively she glanced up at Rann, but instead of the camaraderie of shared thoughts, there was a, 'What did I tell you?' gleam in his eyes, and she immediately looked away again, nettled by his attitude. He was impossible! she told herself angrily, and made herself smile sweetly across the table at the pilot.

'Does your head still hurt?' she asked him sympathetically. 'Was the cut very bad?'

'Bad enough,' he responded in a surly voice. 'You saw it for yourself.' And he lapsed into silence again.

'I didn't look too closely.' She had been too shocked to investigate, after the plane had belly-flopped into the clearing and slewed crazily across a scatter of bushes and boulders before coming to rest on the edge of a creek, tilting at a terrifying angle that threatened to deposit it at the bottom of the steeply shelving bank at any moment. It was the tilt that saved them. The acute angle forced the fuel flowing from the broken pipe down over the bank and away from the body of the plane for the few vital seconds that it took them to scramble clear and run for the shelter of a nearby boulder before the build-up of fuel ignited with a roar, and a mighty explosion that made the jungle rattle.

A piece of flying metal had struck the pilot a glancing blow on the head, and he had dropped like a log, temporarily stunned. Even now Storm could not remember from where she obtained the necessary strength to roll him over, search in his pockets for his handkerchief—her own small cambric and lace square was useless for such a purpose—then scramble down the creek bank to soak it, before hurrying back on legs that felt like the proverbial jelly. She pressed the sopping cloth against the welling cut on the pilot's head, staunching the bleeding and bringing him back to consciousness at the same time. Which was how their guides found them when they appeared from out of the gloom of the jungle. Storm could not remember when she felt so glad to see another human being. The men were an unprepossessing sight, but by now so was the pilot, and her own appearance could not have been far behind, she acknowledged, as she gratefully hailed the strangers with the weapons slung across their shoulders.

'They didn't wait for me to thank them,' she remembered now, regretfully. 'As soon as we were in sight of the bungalow they disappeared back into the jungle. It would have been nice to be able to thank them, even if they didn't understand a word I said.'

'Perhaps you'll meet up with them again while you're here,' Le consoled.

'The men could hardly be from among the villages hereabouts,' Krish put in, looking thoughtful. 'The old men don't carry weapons, and all the young ones are working like beavers to unstop the watercourse. I wonder. . . .' He broke off, and his face was reflective.

'They were fairly youngish men, and I should recognise

them again, I'm sure,' Storm said confidently. 'The one man, he seemed to be a sort of leader, had got the most awful scarring on the one side of his face. It was as if all the lower part of his jaw, and his shoulder, had been badly burned at some time, and not properly treated.'

'Maung Chi!'

Rann and Krish both spoke at once. It was evident that they recognised her description. It was equally evident that it was unwelcome news to both of them. As unwelcome as her own arrival, Storm thought wearily. She looked from one to the other, puzzled. It did not need her artist's sensitivity to feel the suddenly charged atmosphere at the dinner table. A ferocious scowl marred Krish's pleasant face, and Rann looked frighteningly grim. Even the pilot's indifference seemed to her to be assumed. He prodded at the food on his plate with studied interest, but his whole attitude had about it an air of tense listening, like a wild creature, wary of impending danger. Le just looked unhappy, Storm thought.

'Do you know him?' I appear to be the only one who doesn't, she realised, and it suddenly became important to her that she should share in their knowledge. Since she had to share in their lives for the next few weeks whether she wanted to or not, she might as well learn something of the area while she was here, she decided, illogically resenting the fact that she was in the dark as to the reason for their unexpected reaction. It made her feel shut out, superfluous. But it was not the lives of the others in which she wanted to share, it was in Rann's ... only Rann's. . . .

'I know him,' Rann confirmed tautly, speaking directly to her for the first time since the meal started.

'So do I,' Krish added with feeling from the other side of the table, 'but I didn't expect him to be this far up country, not yet.'

'You said you were afraid this might happen.' Le's eyes held a look of strain.

'It was bound to happen sooner or later,' Krish shrugged resignedly. 'As soon as the river stopped flowing through the reserve, it wouldn't take very long for Maung Chi to realise what the animals would do. He'd know

they'd make for the other arm of the river here, that was
still flowing. And where the elephants went, Maung Chi
and his men would surely follow,' he said resignedly.
'Particularly when it dawned on him that I'd withdrawn
my rangers from the reserve to help in the work here,
virtually giving him a clear field until we'd got the river
flowing again.'

'You can have your men back if you think it's best,
Krish.'

Storm stared at her host in disbelief. It can't be true,
she told herself incredulously. Rann Moorcroft, actually
deferring a decision to another person. How totally out of
character! she told herself sarcastically.

'It's decent of you, Rann,' Krish sent a look of quick
gratitude at the other man, 'but it's more important to
unblock the watercourse. That's the root cause of all the
trouble, and the longer it remains blocked, the more animals are likely to die. More even than Maung Chi could
take,' he added harshly. 'We'll press on, and catch up
with him later,' he decided and there was that in his voice
that said the decision hurt.

'Who is this Maung Chi?' Storm felt her temper rise. It
was like being a spectator at a football match, watching
the ball being kicked from one player to another, and not
knowing any of the rules of the game. 'Tell me?' she
demanded.

'Maung Chi's a notorious ivory poacher,' Rann told
her in a clipped, throwaway, 'what's it got to do with an
outsider?' kind of voice that roused her anger even further.
He made no pretence that her presence here was other
than a nuisance to him, she thought hotly, and yet without
her presence he would not have known that the poacher
was in the vicinity in the first place. That, at least, entitled
her to share in the knowledge of what was going on, she
defended herself stoutly.

'Maung Chi's a Burmese.' Did Krish sense her resentment at Rann's uncommunicative attitude? At any rate,
he filled in the background for her, she thought gratefully.
'When the police in his own country got too interested in
his activities, he disappeared, and turned up here, still
poaching,' he finished bitterly.

'Ivory poaching?' It sounded like something out of Rudyard Kipling, and she said so with open incredulity.

'On the contrary, it's a very real threat to the elephant herds on the reserve,' Rann joined in the conversation with impatient bluntness. 'The poachers have got no conscience about conservation, all they want is a quick profit, and they find a ready market in carved trinkets for the tourist trade on the coast,' he gave a glance of acute dislike at the small ivory elephant pinned to her jacket, and Storm flushed angrily.

'You can hardly blame the tourists for that,' she retorted spiritedly. 'The shops offer souvenirs, and the tourists buy them.'

'Without pausing to think what their purchases mean,' Rann interrupted her remorselessly, condemning her for not thinking, heaping on her a share of the blame for the erosion of the elephant herds. 'If there was no market, there wouldn't be the incentive to poach.'

'Then surely the thing to do is to catch the poachers, not to blame innocent holidaymakers for buying what's offered in the shops.' Storm repudiated his blame, laying it back on his own shoulders, even as she secretly vowed, I'll never wear the brooch again. I wish I hadn't bought it in the first place. She had loved it, regarding it as a typical souvenir of a country that boasted elephants, but now its very presence on her jacket seemed to be an offence. But to take it off now would be openly giving in to Rann's dictatorship, and that she was determined not to do. She lifted her chin defiantly, and left her brooch where it was.

'We intend to catch them,' Rann promised her grimly, 'in fact, by bringing you here to the bungalow, Maung Chi might have just made the one mistake that will give us the clue we've been looking for.' He turned away from her abruptly, and asked the pilot, 'Where was it exactly that you ditched the plane?' His manner was the reverse of conciliatory. His voice was an order, rather than a request, and for some unexplained reason Storm found herself holding her breath. His question did not seem to surprise the pilot, she noticed. Was this the danger the man had been tensed, and waiting for?

'Where?' Rann demanded, as the man remained silent, and the pilot began to bluster.

'Well . . . er . . . sou'-sou'-west of here, I reckon. I dunno, for sure. I got knocked out by this crack on the head. Ask her.' He jerked an uncouth thumb in Storm's direction. 'She'll tell you I was knocked out,' he muttered. 'I dunno for sure which direction we took.'

'You must have known. . . .'

'Of course he didn't know,' Storm interrupted Rann furiously. Really, he was nothing but an unfeeling bully! she told herself angrily, to harass a man when he had been in a plane crash, and been injured into the bargain. Surely his questions could wait, at least until the morning? A wave of tiredness washed over her, and she wished the dinner and the day was well over, but in spite of her weariness she felt obliged to defend the pilot. 'He was hardly in any condition to walk, let alone to know where he was going,' she protested vehemently. 'Why, he had a job to try and keep up with the men as it was. I tried to get them to slow down for his sake. For both our sakes,' she emphasised, 'but they didn't seem to understand what I was trying to tell them. They just kept on going, and pulled us along with them. I'd probably be more capable of finding my way back to the clearing than the pilot, at least I hadn't had a bang on the head to confuse me.'

'I'll bet they pulled you along real fast,' Krish interjected, and Storm looked across at him, surprised. She had not expected Krish to join in the bullying. He seemed much too nice, much too gentle.

'They were only trying to help us, to get us to a place where we could find help.' Her eyes accused Rann, condemning his unhelpfulness.

'Far from trying to get you *to* any place, Maung Chi must have been desperately anxious to get you *away* from that clearing.' Rann turned on her forcefully, and the look on his face silenced the protests in her throat. 'During the last six months he and his gang have operated commando-style raids on the elephants in the game reserve, and it doesn't take long for that kind of persistent whittling to decimate even a big herd. From the number they've already killed to our certain knowledge, they must have netted a large bag of ivory, and it must be cached somewhere, if they haven't already managed to get rid of some of it.'

'We've tried every way to check their activities,' Krish put in. 'There's been a spate of ivory poaching right across the country, which makes us suspect that there's a big organisation behind it, and, of course, a ready market for the tusks. But although we've caught some of the poachers, they wouldn't talk, though the men received heavy jail sentences. This makes us suspect that there's someone behind it who's willing to pay enough to buy the hunters' silence.'

'You told me money wasn't of any value in the jungle,' Storm reminded Rann sharply. He had told her, and now his words were proved to be a lie.

'Money isn't of any use to the ordinary families who live in the jungle villages,' he retorted promptly. 'The ivory poachers are a different category altogether. They're itinerants. They live off the jungle while they hunt, and haunt the gutters of the coast towns to squander their ill-gotten gains until they've got none left. When they're broke and sober again, they return to poaching, and it all starts over again.'

'If only we could find out how they get the tusks away!' Krish drove his fist on to the table top in a gesture of frustration.

'The clearing might give us the answer,' Rann said crisply, and four pairs of eyes fixed themselves on his face. Three pairs questioningly. The fourth. . . . Storm found herself watching the pilot, and wondering what he was thinking.

'The haste with which Maung Chi and his men brought you away from that clearing is suspicious in itself,' Rann said thoughtfully. 'The fact that they showed themselves to you at all is suspicious.'

'Surely it was just a gesture of common humanity,' Storm protested. Even Rann must acknowledge that there was a spark of decency in every human being. 'He could have simply left us there to cope on our own.'

'You'd probably have been missed, and he wouldn't want to risk that. It would have meant a search from the air, which might have revealed some things Maung Chi would prefer to be kept hidden. No, it was safer for him to bring you here, and leave you, in the hope that you'd resume your journey as soon as you'd rested, and leave it at that.'

'And you think . . .?' Krish pressed him.

'I think the plane must have crashed close to the poachers' cache of ivory.' Rann's glance pierced Storm, pressing home the fact that he knew he was correct in his assumption, 'and Maung Chi wanted you away from the place in as short a time as possible. He daren't risk you starting to wander round, searching for a way out of the jungle for yourselves, and probably stumbling on his cache by accident. He probably relied on the fact that you wouldn't be able to find your way back to the clearing again even if you tried—wouldn't want to, with the plane burned out, and your luggage gone, there'd be nothing to go back for. No, I reckon he thought he was fairly safe in bringing you here,' he followed up his reasoning, 'but it does point to the means by which they've been disposing of the tusks, and how they reckon to get rid of them,' he answered Krish. 'A helicopter could land in a clearing, and if they're using that sort of transport, their organisation is bigger than I thought. They've probably been making regular collections under cover of darkness for some time. That way, it'd save them any difficulty in getting rid of a large quantity of ivory at once, and remove any temptation for the poachers themselves to try and sell tusks for individual gain.'

'A helicopter—of course!' breathed the game warden. 'It's a lead, Rann, the first real one we've had.' His eyes lit up with excitement. 'We could wireless the other areas that are suffering in the same way, and warn them to keep an eye open for likely clearings, and search in the vicinity, on the offchance.'

'We'll have to search here as well,' Rann responded sombrely, 'and quickly, before they have time to remove any ivory they've got waiting.'

'We can't spare the time from clearing the watercourse.'

'We'll have to spare the time for this,' Rann answered

decidedly. 'If we don't, we risk losing the poachers and their ivory. We've been hunting them for too long to let this chance slip.'

'You can spare the time to go hunting ivory poachers, yet you couldn't spare a man to take me to the coast!' Storm burst out angrily, and Rann slanted her a cold glance.

'It would have taken two men four days to get you to the coast, and then return here. With luck, you and the pilot should be able to guide us to the clearing where you crashed, in the same number of hours. Which brings me to what I was saying when I was interrupted,' he added crushingly, and Storm flushed resentfully as he turned to the pilot and deliberately repeated his previous words.

'You must have known your flight path, so it follows you must have had some clear idea of your whereabouts when you crashed. Don't prevaricate, Mac. I mean to find out,' he told the pilot sternly as the other man began to haver again.

'Well now, let me think. . . .' Mac forked curried meat into his mouth in unwholesome amounts, and began to chew, his brow furrowed as if in serious thought.

He's stalling, Storm guessed. Why? What reason could the pilot have for not wanting to guide Rann back to the clearing? There was nothing there, the plane was a wreck, and by now the fire would not have left much even of that.

'Well?' Rann rapped impatiently, and the pilot gave a start, and swallowed convulsively.

'Ugh . . . this curry . . . hot as fire. . . .' He began to choke and splutter, and fumbled in his pocket for his handkerchief, and Storm jumped to her feet in alarm.

'Bang him on the back, quick,' she begged, but Rann remained unmoving. 'How can you just sit there?' she began furiously, as the pilot's paroxysms grew.

'Sit down.' Without taking his eyes off the airman's face, Rann reached out a hand and pressed her back on to her chair.

'Krish?' she begged urgently. If Rann was so indifferent as to let the pilot choke without raising a finger to help him. . . . And then her amazed eyes saw that the game

warden, too, sat quietly, not attempting to help the man
to regain his breath. Krish's dark eyes rested intently on
the pilot's face, and Storm followed his look, and her fright
subsided. The man was making a convincing display of
choking, but his face had not changed one iota from its
normal florid hue. By now, if his display was to be
believed, he should be going blue.

'That's enough!' Rann quelled him sharply, and the
man's antics ceased as if by magic.

He wiped his face with his handkerchief, and looked
warily across at his host. 'You ought to tell your cook to
go easy with the curry the next time,' he growled with an
unconvincing attempt at bonhomie, and started to stuff
his handkerchief back into his trouser pocket.

Storm thought interestedly, He's cornered. I wonder
how he'll answer now? when the pilot suddenly let out an
angry roar.

'My watch! My gold hunter! It's gone. . . .' He began
delving deep into his trouser pocket with a frantic hand,
feeling at the contents, his whole attention concentrated
on sifting them for the missing watch as if he had forgotten
all about ivory and ivory poachers. 'What have you done
with it?' he shouted at Storm.

'What have I done . . .?' She stared at him in bewilderment.

'Yes, you. I felt you take my handkerchief out of my
pocket after we crashed. You thought I'd flaked right out,
didn't you, and wouldn't know what you were up to?' he
snarled. 'You must have taken my watch then. I had it
before we crashed, and I haven't got it now. You're the
only one who could have taken it.'

'I took your handkerchief to try and stop the bleeding
from your cut,' Storm faltered, completely taken aback
by his unexpected attack. 'I went to the creek to wet it. I
didn't even see your watch.'

'That's a likely story,' the pilot sneered. 'No wonder
you offered to guide them back to the clearing. Was that
where you hid my watch, in the creek? I suppose you
thought you'd go back to collect it later, when all the hue
and cry had died down?' His face was ugly as he glared at
her across the table.

'I tell you, I didn't touch your watch,' Storm denied indignantly. 'What would I want with a man's watch anyway? I've got one of my own.' She thrust her wrist forward, with her own slender gold timepiece still intact.

'Gold hunters are valuable.'

'Money's of no use in the jungle,' she flashed back, and could have hit herself for repeating Rann's words. How he must be laughing, to hear her say them. She turned on him, at bay.

'I didn't even know the pilot had got a watch,' she insisted. 'I. . . .' Suddenly her voice broke. It should not matter to her what any of them thought, she berated herself furiously. But it did. It mattered what Rann thought. Without warning, the events of the longest day she had ever endured caught up with her. The colour drained from her face, and the fire from her eyes, to be replaced by a suspicious brightness. She gave a small, hopeless gesture and slumped back in her chair.

'I think. . . .' began Le tentatively.

'I think we'll resume this conversation in the morning,' Rann decided, and his eyes were fixed on Storm's face. Accusing her? Disbelieving what she said? He made no attempt to back her up. There was no reason why he should, she told herself bleakly. She was a stranger to him, more of a stranger, even, than the pilot, whom at least he knew by repute. 'First thing tomorrow morning, we'll make an attempt to find the clearing where the plane crashed,' he spoke impartially to both Storm and the pilot, his face expressionless, giving away nothing of his feelings, or his views on which of them he believed to be telling the truth. 'Since you're likely to find the trek through the jungle arduous, I suggest you both try to get a good night's sleep.' He gestured to the hovering manservant, and spoke quietly to him in the local dialect.

'Thakin!' The man nodded, and disappeared.

'I'll go and wireless round the other areas, and speak to the wardens, before I turn in,' Krish decided.

'I'll come with you.' Le slipped her arm through her husband's, and with a quiet goodnight they both went out.

You know where your room is,' Rann spoke to Storm,

and she nodded, numbly. 'I'll take Mac over to the men's compound. Goodnight.'

The pilot did not speak, and Rann did not wait to hear her answer, which was just as well, she decided wearily. Her throat seemed to close in and trap her words. They stuck there in a hard lump that hurt with a pain that matched the increasing brightness of her eyes. She stumbled through the door of her room, and blinked her eyes to clear them, searching for her safari suit and the handkerchief she remembered leaving in the jacket pocket. Her eyes needed the attention of the handkerchief, urgently.

Her bed had been turned down, and mosquito netting draped round it, since she was last in the room, but of the safari suit she had left lying across the bed there was no trace. Perhaps whoever turned down the bed had put it away. With dragging steps she crossed to the wardrobe.

It's empty. With a slight frown she turned away and opened the cupboard. The lungyis and blouses Le had lent her were neatly folded and stacked. The siri flower rested on top of the chest of drawers. But her safari suit had gone.

Why should anyone want to take my suit? she frowned—and felt her legs go weak as the only possible answer to her question presented itself.

Rann must have wanted the suit so that he could search the jacket pockets for the pilot's watch. He spoke to his servant, gave him an instruction, she remembered, just before they left the table. He must have relied on her being too weary to search for it that night, perhaps hoped she would not even miss it.

He believed the pilot, not me. She began to tremble. Rann believed I stole the watch!

CHAPTER FOUR

'COME in!'

Someone knocked softly on her bedroom door. Slowly she struggled to surface through clinging mists of sleep. It must be the floor maid, come with her early morning tea. Drowsily she turned over, waiting for the familiar, cheerful 'Good morning'. It did not come. The only sound was the energetic splashing of water, as if someone was taking a shower nearby.

Curiosity dissolved the mists, and Storm opened her eyes. What they saw jolted her into full wakefulness, and she sat up in bed abruptly, memory of the previous day flooding back. Gone was her comfortable hotel bedroom, with its window view of blue seas and golden beaches. In its place were the bare walls of Rann's wooden bungalow, the room unadorned, unless one could count the wilted siri flower, limp on top of the chest of drawers, its pristine loveliness expired in the breathless heat.

Like the hopes it professed, Storm thought with quick depression. Shiny and bright one minute, and faded beyond recall the next. With an effort she shook the treacherous thought away, and slid out of bed.

I wonder who . . .? Winding the bed sheet round her, she opened the door a crack and looked out, but her early morning caller had vanished. She was about to shut herself in again when her eyes fell on the offering left on the floor outside.

Tea? Oh, bless whoever brought it! Evidently Rann's servant had some consideration, even if his master had none. Gratefully Storm bent to lift the tray with its small aluminium pot and single cup and saucer—and nearly dropped it again as she espied the neatly folded pile placed next to it.

My safari suit. And my hanky. Swiftly she turned and placed the tray safely on the chair next to her bed, and returning to the door, scooped up her clothes. She glanced hurriedly from left to right of her door, but there was no sign of the servant, and no sign of Rann. The shower still tinkled cheerfully below her window. She closed the door softly, and returned to sit on the bed, and discovered she was trembling again.

A cup of tea—that'll cure it. Backstage, it was her dresser's panacea for first-night nerves, so it should serve her now. She reached for the pot with hands that shook. The metal pot clinked against the cup as she poured out, and she spooned sugar into the liquid with a liberal hand. The hot, sweet result steadied her, and as she sipped, her heartbeats slowly returned to normal.

Whoever took my suit away last night did a good job, she decided grudgingly, shaking it out flat to examine it. The jacket and slacks had been carefully washed and pressed, and repaired. The tear on the pocket corner, caused by her hasty exit from the plane, was now neatly, almost invisibly mended, and the smudges and stains had quite disappeared.

I'll have a shower, and put it on, she decided.

The splashing sounds had ceased, and a tuneful whistle proclaimed that the occupant of the shower hut was nearly ready to depart. Storm drew the bed sheet tighter round her, and crept to the window to peep out.

At that moment Rann looked up. Sun glinted on tawny hair, and narrowed his vivid eyes so that their expression was hidden from her. He ducked under the shower hut, and turned to look straight up at her window. Straight at her. She knew a moment's swift thankfulness for the sheet's friendly cover, and instinctively pulled it more tightly round her. Rann was dressed only in khaki bush shorts. His feet were thrust into open sandals, but he had not bothered to put on a shirt. He moved, casually slinging his towel across one tanned, muscular shoulder. It rippled with health, topping an athlete's frame that could not have borne a superfluous ounce, Storm guessed confusedly.

No cup of tea is proof against this, the thought crossed her panic-stricken mind. She wanted to run, but her wooden limbs refused to move. She wanted to tear her eyes away, but his slit green stare transfixed her.

If he'd only call, or wave, or say something, she thought

frantically. But he stood motionless, with his head tilted
back, watching her, his expression a closed book. Her
heart began to beat with slow, agonising thuds, and unconsciously her hand rose to her throat to ease the
throbbing pain.

'Thakin!'

The voice of his servant called him, breaking the spell.
Rann turned to answer him, and Storm felt as if shackles
had dropped from her shaking limbs. She leaned limply
back against the wooden wall of the room, and held on to
the window frame for support. Her breath hissed through
her teeth in shallow gasps, and in spite of the humid heat
she felt deathly cold.

'The shower's free. I'll give you ten minutes before I
come and grab it,' Le's gay voice called from just outside
her door.

'Coming!' Somehow Storm made her limbs carry her
across the room to her bed. Somehow she forced her
palsied hands to pick up soap and towel and her clothes,
and stumbled down the steps to the shower hut, dreading
that Rann might still be there, dreading that he might
not. Her mind spun round and round in a dizzy turmoil,
but when she reached the bottom step he was gone, and
she fled for the sanctuary of the shower hut and slammed
the door behind her.

The astringent douche of cool water worked even better
than the cup of tea, and she was able to reply to Le's
cheery chatter in a more or less normal voice when she
eventually emerged from her room to the summons of the
breakfast bell.

'Won't you be hot, in slacks?' the other girl questioned,
glancing at the freshly immaculate suit.

'I haven't got used to walking in a lungyi yet,' Storm
excused herself. 'I'll change after breakfast and have another practice. I can walk as far as the village huts and
back, to try to get used to it.' She did not add that she felt
more confident to face Rann when she was dressed in her
own clothes.

'You'd do better to keep on your slacks,' Rann strolled
up the veranda steps beside Krish, and joined them where
the table was already laid for the meal. 'You'll find it

easier walking on the jungle tracks in your suit, and the slacks will be some measure of protection for your legs. From what you told me yesterday I imagine the clearing where the plane crashed is some way from here.' He reached in his shirt pocket and brought out a map, and proceeded to flatten it across the end of the table.

'We roughly sketched a map of the area when we first prospected here for hardwoods,' he commented to Krish. 'From what I can gather, the clearing where the plane ditched should be round about here. This is the only size-able creek in the vicinity,' he traced the line of it across the printed page with a lean brown finger, 'so it must be somewhere along its length, within walking distance from where we are now. I'll get the pilot to confirm his flight route, which should give us an intersecting line with the creek, and more or less pinpoint the spot for us.'

'That shouldn't be too far for you to walk, now you're feeling rested,' Krish smiled across at Storm reassuringly.

'Since I shan't be going anyway, the distance doesn't concern me,' she retorted. Rann's easy assumption that she would fall in with his plans without protest nettled her. The arrogance of the man! she thought furiously, to take it for granted that if he wanted to go off on a will-o'-the-wisp ivory hunting expedition, everyone else would automatically follow suit. 'I'm not going,' she stated her own position quite clearly.

'You'll be in the bungalow on your own,' Le began concernedly. 'I'm going with Krish to the work site today.'

'I'll be glad to sit around and rest,' Storm lied promptly. She did not need to rest. Perfect health, and a mere twenty-five years, ensured a swift recovery from the trials and frights of the previous day, and she had never felt better in her life. At least physically. Mentally, she was not so sure. She did not trust the strength of her own defences if she remained in Rann's company for long. Particularly if Le and Krish were not coming with them. Her mind took fright at the knowledge that she and Rann would be on their own, and strengthened her resolve not to go with him.

'Mac can guide you back to the creek. If he's willing

to, that is,' she emphasised through tight lips, stressing that the pilot, too, was entitled to make up his own mind. Simply because they had the misfortune to drop, literally, on Rann's doorstep, and circumstances—and Rann— were obliging them to remain there, it did not mean that they were also obliged to comply with his orders, she told herself defiantly.

'You said last night that you'd be better able to find your way back to the clearing than the pilot,' Rann turned on her, and her resolve nearly melted. His set face held an icy determination that said she would go with him whether she wanted to or not.

'Since you weren't disposed to help me to reach the coast, I see no reason why I should put myself out to help you,' Storm retorted, and marvelled at her own calm. It took every ounce of her acting ability to produce, but she managed it. It was a pity she did not have a more appreciative audience, because it was the best performance she had ever given, she told herself triumphantly. So why should she suddenly want to cry?

It's delayed action shock, she bolstered her courage, nothing else. Nothing else that she was prepared to admit to, even to herself. Aloud she said indifferently,

'If you care to ask the pilot, *he* might be willing to go along with you.' Repeating, without words, that she was not.

'Thakin! Thakin!'

Rann's manservant hurried up the veranda steps with agitation written clear across his countenance.

'What is it?'

'The man with the cut head has gone. Gone.' His gesture into thin air was eloquent.

'I told him to remain in the men's compound,' Rann began sharply.

'He must have crept out, Thakin, while the others slept. They were weary from their work of moving rocks,' he excused his fellows.

'I don't blame them,' Rann immediately put his mind at rest. 'The pilot will return. He'll have to, when he gets hungry.'

'He has a gun, Thakin. The godown's been broken

into.' The man faltered to a halt with a hopeless gesture.

'The godown?'

'A gun?'

Rann and Krish both spoke at once. Ran recovered first, and rapped,

'Has anything else been taken?'

'I didn't stop to check, Thakin. I ran straight here, to tell you.'

'Come on Krish, quick! Let's go and find out.'

The two men took the veranda steps at a run, and Storm turned to Le.

'What's a godown?' she asked perplexedly.

'A store hut,' Le replied briefly. 'The one they're talking about holds food supplies for the work force at the river in the one half, and materials for the site in the other. I know it contains some explosives, as well as a rack of rifles and clips of ammunition,' she said worriedly.

'There's one rifle missing, a belt of ammunition, and half a dozen sticks of dynamite are gone,' Krish announced a few minutes later. 'Oh, and some packets of dehydrated iron rations.'

'But why?' Le cried. 'Surely the pilot won't try to reach the coast on his own? He'll never get there, not on foot, through the jungle?' she said worriedly. 'There's all those miles of swamp lower down the mountains, and it's obvious he's in no condition to stand the journey without help.'

'It's my guess he hasn't gone very far away,' Rann butted in grimly.

'You reckon?' From Krish's expression, his mind was running along similar lines.

'I reckon Mac thought over what we said last night about the ivory poachers, and decided to try to make it back to their cache and join them if he could,' Rann confirmed. 'He'd not be welcome with the poachers unless he brought along his own supplies. It was a masterly touch, taking the dehydrated food along with him. It would ensure his ready acceptance by Maung Chi's men, they'd no doubt find a change of diet very welcome,' he guessed drily.

'You think the pilot knew the ivory poachers? He

showed no signs of recognising the men who came to us
when the plane crashed.' Storm stared from one to the
other in bewilderment. The whole thing was bizarre, and
more unreal than any play she had ever acted in.

'I doubt if he actually knew the poachers,' Rann replied
in a clipped voice, 'but I was watching his face while we
talked at dinner last night. There was no doubt his interest
was aroused, even then.' Storm had been watching the
pilot, too, and wondered what he was thinking, but she
had never dreamed of this. She listened in a daze as Rann
continued,

'With the plane, and therefore his immediate living
gone, Mac knew he'd have to turn to something else
anyway, and this must have offered a readymade solution.
Cash, and a lot of it, without too much hard work.'

'But it's illegal.'

'That wouldn't bother a man like the pilot.' Rann
turned on her a look of silent derision that added, 'don't
be naïve,' and she flushed hotly. 'Now I suggest we eat,
and go our separate ways.' He gestured the others to their
seats, and signalled his servant to start serving the food.
'It's imperative I find that ivory cache before the pilot
does. Take your walkie-talkie set with you, Krish, and if
we have any luck I'll come through to you on the air, and
let you know.'

'If you find the cache, sit tight,' Krish suggested. 'As
soon as you come on the air I'll send an oozie with one of
the pack elephants, and we can relieve Maung Chi of his
ill-gotten gains, and store them in the godown here. We'll
have to spare a couple of men to stand day and night
guard over it in any case, now the pilot knows that it
contains rifles and ammunition. What were the guns like,
that Maung Chi and his men carried when they were
with you?' he quizzed Storm interestedly.

'I don't know much about guns,' she answered doubtfully. 'I know they weren't rifles, I should recognise a
rifle, I think. The ones the men carried were bigger, the
barrels looked huge.'

'Old-fashioned elephant guns,' Krish hazarded a guess.
'So their weapons heaven't changed, even if their method
of transporting the ivory has. It was a worn-out elephant

gun that scarred Maung Chi in the first place, and made
him so easy to recognise,' he told Storm. 'The barrel was
thin, the charge was too strong, and it exploded in his
face. He was lucky it didn't blow his head off.' His expression said he almost wished it had, and Storm shivered.
This was a different side to Krish, a hardness that betrayed
the depth of his dedication to the game reserve, and the
wildlife it contained.

'Once Maung Chi and his men have seen the rifle the
pilot stole, they'll want the same,' Rann predicted.
'There's an even chance they'll try to raid the godown.
We could have done without this complication,' he
frowned, 'it's going to hold up the work on site.' His inference was obvious, and Storm went scarlet, and then
white. If Rann regarded herself and the pilot as the complication, then he himself had compounded the difficulty
by his own lack of co-operation, she thought angrily.

'It wasn't my fault that the plane crashed,' she flared.
'I didn't come here by choice, and I didn't want to
remain.' She thrust the blame for herself and the pilot
remaining, squarely back on to Rann's shoulders, but if
she expected a softening of his attitude towards her she
was doomed to disappointment. He said curtly,

'Unfortunately you did come here.'

'If we hadn't you wouldn't have known ivory poachers were in the area in the first place.'

'And the pilot wouldn't have had a new career presented to him on a plate,' Rann thrust back at her harshly.
'Neither would he have raided the godown to equip himself for his work before he set out to find Maung Chi and
his men, and incidentally advertise to them that there are
modern rifles and ammunition available here if they can
manage to steal them, and get away with it. Now, it means
we'll have to withdraw two men from the work on the site
in order to stand day and night guard over the stores.
The least you can do in return is to help repair the damage
your presence here has caused.'

'It would have taken less time if you'd lent me a couple
of men and a canoe to get to the coast in the first place,'
Storm reminded him bitterly. 'At least then they'd only
have taken four days. Now, you'll have to spare two men

indefinitely to guard your store hut.'

'Not if we can round up Maung Chi and his gang first,' Rann retorted. 'Which is where you come in, to help locate the clearing where you crashed.'

'Which is where I don't come in,' Storm declared forthrightly. 'I've already told you, I'm not coming.'

She faced his grim-visaged stare defiantly. He can find the clearing for himself, she decided mutinously, and wished suddenly that he would switch off his stare and look the other way. It seemed to go on and on. It was like trying to fend off a master fencer with a walking stick. His eyes seemed to slice straight through her defiance, putting it aside as if it was too flimsy to be considered seriously. An aeon of time passed before Rann spoke.

'You can't remain in the bungalow all day, completely on your own,' he said decisively.

'I shan't be on my own. Your servant will be here.' She did her best to appear indifferent.

'He'll be at the work site, where he goes every day to prepare food for the men.'

Storm hesitated, nonplussed. The idea of remaining on her own in the bungalow was not attractive. She was not normally of a nervous disposition, but. . . .

'You can't stay here alone, Storm,' Le cut across her thoughts in a worried voice. 'It isn't as if the bungalow is near to the village huts. They're a full hundred yards away. What if the pilot comes back? Or one of Maung Chi's men?'

Or the leopard that took the pi-dog. . . . Storm's own thoughts took up the cudgels against her, and she bit her lip, undecided. What if. . .? Her mind baulked.

'Storm will come with me,' Rann answered Le flatly. As if she did not have any say in the matter, she fumed silently, and tried to stifle a sneaking feeling of relief as he went on, 'From now on, while Mac and Maung Chi and his men are on the loose, Le must remain with Krish, and you,' he directed a look at Storm that seemed to bore straight through her, 'you will remain with me.' His expression evinced no pleasure at the prospect of her company, and a pang went through her that was joined by a stab of fear as he added, 'Either of you would make an ideal hostage so far as Maung Chi is concerned, and I've no intention of being put in a position where I have to decide between you and a godown full of rifles and ammunition.'

CHAPTER FIVE

IF it came to the crunch, I wonder which Rann would put first? Me, or his wretched rifles? Storm asked herself sourly. Looking at the uncompromising set of his shoulders under the austere khaki bush shirt, as he swung along the dim green track ahead of her, she did not doubt that his preference would be for the rifles. He himself carried one, slung across his shoulder. She wondered nervously if it was loaded.

'You'll have to slow down,' she called out to him angrily. 'I can't possibly keep up with you, if you insist on taking strides like a giant.' It was all very well for Rann, she thought resentfully. His only problem was ducking his six feet plus frame under overhanging branches. He stepped easily over tree roots, creepers, and all sorts of unidentifiable objects that barred her own path along the narrow jungle track, and through which she picked her way with shuddering aversion, unsure which was creeper and which might be the motionless form of a snake.

'Don't use delaying tactics with me,' he snapped back at her impatiently, but he stood still nevertheless, and waited for her to catch up with him.

'I'm not using delaying tactics,' she panted, 'I'm simply trying to keep you in sight.' That, at least, was true. The possibility of losing sight of Rann, and being stranded on her own in this dim green vegetable world, filled her with unnamed horror. It was stiflingly hot. She brushed a hand across her face, and it came away wet. Her freshly laundered suit was already limp with perspiration, and her slacks clung to her legs with a clammy embrace that made her long for a shower and a change of clothes.

'For goodness' sake, stand still for a minute or two,

and let me get my breath back,' she gasped. 'It's like being in a Turkish bath here!' She flapped irritably at the cloud of flies that hovered over her head, all seemingly intent on begging a ride on her flushed face.

'I'll have another look at the map while you rest.'

He did not seem to notice the heat. 'He's inhuman,' Storm told herself resentfully. His shirt showed dark patches of damp, but he opened his map and studied it as intently as if he was at ease in his own study.

'How long do you estimate it took you to get from the clearing to within sight of my bungalow?' he asked her without looking up.

'I don't know.' His face tightened, and she went on hastily, 'I really don't. After just enduring a crash landing, seeing the plane explode and go up in flames, and attending to a half unconscious man with a bump on his head the size of an egg, I was hardly in any condition to notice the passing of time. Besides,' she added vindictively, 'the men who were with us were as inconsiderate as you are. They raced us along at a speed that took every ounce of strength I had left to keep up with them.'

'Do you recognise any landmarks along the track?' To her chagrin he ignored her sally, and persisted with his questioning.

'No,' Storm answered him shortly, then taking a glance at his expression, deemed it politic to add, 'The only thing I remember was some trees with red bark. The sun caught them, and they seemed to glow. They stood at a bend in the track,' she recalled.

'Then we're on the right route.' He snapped the map closed, and returned it to his pocket.

'How can you tell?' She did not want to know, she was not interested, but her whole body cried out for just a few more minutes of rest.

'Because I know the stand of hardwoods you're talking about,' he answered her crisply. 'We came across them when we first reconnoitred the area around here for timber. They're valuable wood, and we hoped there might be a good stand of them, but there are only about half a dozen or so trees, not worth the effort of felling and dragging them out,' he said indifferently. His eyes held a curious gleam as he spoke, and Storm stared at him suspiciously.

He was just testing me, to see if I'd deliberately misled him, she realised furiously. And she had walked straight into his trap, responding automatically, like a child being asked a question in class.

'If you imagine I'm trying to lead you astray, you're very much mistaken,' she shouted at him angrily. 'The quicker we reach the clearing the quicker we can go back, so far as I'm concerned. I can think of dozens of things I'd rather be doing at this moment than charging about in the steaming heat of the jungle, looking for a probably non-existent hoard of ivory!' She felt she hated ivory. She certainly hated the jungle. She tried to make herself believe that she hated Rann. She stared from the dark, shadowed mystery of the trees to Rann's face, with open aversion to both. Incredibly, he was laughing—laughing at her. Her colour rose to resemble her temperature. 'I can't see anything to laugh about,' she cried heatedly.

'No?' he enquired silkily, without making any attempt to hide his amusement. He laughed straight down into her face, and Storm itched to smack him. 'Surely,' he murmured, 'if anyone's going to be led astray, it should be *I* leading *you*?' His green eyes narrowed with laughter, and Storm's temper snapped. Without stopping to think, she raised her hand.

'Don't.' The amusement fled, and his eyes became twin chips of green ice. She did not see him move, but without being aware of how they got there, she discovered his fingers round her wrist. Steel fingers, that held her arm motionless, unable to move. Their fellows gripped her other hand, and in a second both her wrists were behind her back, his arms encircling her.

'That was very unwise of you,' he chided her with deceptive gentleness, and icy fingers tingled along her spine at the underlying steel in his tone.

I wish I'd remained behind in the bungalow, she thought, panic-stricken. Desperately she tried to twist her face away, but his one hand transferred to both her wrists, holding her with ease, while he cupped the fingers of the other hand round her chin and tipped her face up to his.

He took his time—a long, long time. It went on for ever, until it blotted out the jungle, and the heat, and the flies, and time stood still. With helpless dismay Storm felt herself respond. She did not want to, she was determined not to, but she could not help herself. This was what she had been afraid of, if she found herself alone with Rann. Her resentment and anger were not proof against the heady intoxication of his kiss, just as her puny strength was no defence against the steel-hard grip of his arms.

His lips explored hers with a deadly expertise, demanding her response, and then, when he felt the eager seeking of her lips move under his own, he laughed again triumphantly, and let her go, and his eyes challenged her, daring her to try again to strike him now that her hands were free.

'You beast!' Storm hissed. She did not dare. His look warned her what might happen if she did, and she could not trust herself if he kissed her again. She was more afraid of herself than she was of Rann.

Instead, she wiped an insulting palm across her lips, as if to try to wipe out the feel of his kiss. She knew even as she tried that it was useless. Her lips burned with an insatiable fire that longed to be fed, and the pain of them yearned for only one balm.

'You beast!' She faced him bravely, with flashing eyes, acting as she had never acted in her life before, as if her life depended upon it, when she knew, despairingly, that her heart's life from now on depended only upon Rann.

'The jungle's full of them,' he taunted, 'which is why,' his demeanour changed, and became stern, and watchful, and he reached down a hard hand and gripped her round the waist, 'which is why you must keep up with me. We must be very close to the clearing by now, which means close to Maung Chi, and his ivory cache.'

If he had not slackened his pace to accommodate her, she could not have hoped to keep up with him. She trembled so much that when they started to walk on again, she stumbled and would have fallen had he not gripped her tightly and held her up. Surely he must feel her trembling? She despised herself for her lack of will-power, for allowing herself to remain within the circle of his arms, instead of flinging herself free and walking independently, proudly, on her own. But her independence seemed to have vanished along with her pride, and she walked crouched against him, and told herself that she clung to him only because she feared the pilot, or Maung Chi, or the myriad watching eyes that must be following their progress from the dark, silent depths of the trees. And she knew that it was none of these things that made her cling to him, but something that was stronger than herself, stronger than her willpower or her pride, that had insidiously crept in and taken over both since the moment she first set eyes on Rann.

'There are the trees with the red bark,' she gasped. She pointed, and he dropped his arm from round her waist, and she felt bereft. She watched him in numb silence as he consulted his map again. After a moment or two he nodded as if he was satisfied, replaced the sheet in his pocket, and said to her quietly,

'Walk behind me, and don't talk.' With the ease of long practice he shrugged the bandolier of the rifle from off his shoulder and walked on ahead of her along the track, slowly, with an alert caution, the weapon balanced lightly in his hand. A thrill ran through Storm as she followed him. His lithe, silent gait, his watchfulness, reminded her irresistibly of the magnificent creature of the wild that the colour of his hair so closely resembled.

'We're here!' He stopped, and she bumped into him, and forgot his injunction to remain silent, in her excitement at recognising the clearing. 'We're here,' she repeated eagerly, 'that's where the plane burned out. Look, you can see the tip of one of the wing spars. And that's the rock we sheltered under, when the fuel exploded.'

'I thought this might be it,' he answered her calmly, and a flash of irritation surged through her at his sureness.

'If you were so certain of where the clearing lay, why did you drag me all this way with you?' she cried indignantly. She felt hot, and limp, and mentally and physically exhausted, drained not so much by the effort of struggling through the oppressive heat along the rough jungle track as simply by being with Rann.

And this is only the second day with him. What of all the weeks that lie ahead? she asked herself bleakly. Krish had told her the work on the blocked river course was only a third completed, and they had been slaving at it for three weeks now. That left at least another six.

'I'll never find the strength,' she whispered despairingly.

'You'll be fine when you've had a rest,' Rann answered her briskly, and she started. She had not realised she had spoken out loud. She would have to be careful, he must not suspect. . . .

'Come and sit in the shadow of the rock, where you were before,' Rann urged, and Storm glanced up at him, cheered by his unexpected consideration.

'This is exactly where I was before.' She sank gratefully to the ground. 'The pilot collapsed over there,' she indicated a flat patch of ground in front of her, and Rann dropped down on to it on one knee.

'Now tell me, from which direction did Maung Chi and his men approach you?' he asked, and his eyes were intent on her face.

So it had not been consideration for herself that had moved him to suggest she sit in the shade. Her cheerfulness vanished. I might have known, she told herself bitterly, but she answered him nevertheless, too weary to resist.

'Over there, where the vegetation's thinned out a bit.'

'It looks like a game track, similar to the one we've been following.' Rann stared at it with narrowed eyes, assessing his surroundings. 'They're the tracks the wild animals use when they come to the creek to drink,' he answered her enquiring look. 'The poachers would use them, too, when they wanted game for the pot.'

Storm felt beyond caring about the poachers, or what they ate. Her head throbbed like a jungle drum, and she leaned back limply against the rock.

'You can do whatever you like, I don't intend to move another step,' she told him exhaustedly.

'I'm not going far along the track. . . .'

'You must go on your own, I'm staying here.' If Rann wanted to chase around in the heat, let him, she thought

uncaringly. At least in the shadow of the boulder she was
out of the direct rays of the sun, which beat remorselessly
upon the rest of the clearing until it resembled nothing so
much as an oven.

'If you promise to remain where you are, and not stray
away from the boulder?' Rann demanded, and Storm
snapped,

'I'm unlikely to want to roam around in this heat, even
if you do.' She closed her eyes, and wriggled herself into a
more comfortable position against the warm rock.

'In that case, I won't be long,' Rann promised.

Storm kept her eyes closed, and did not bother to reply.
She did not care if he took forever, she told herself rebelli-
ously. She heard his footsteps recede across the sunbaked
ground, and then there was nothing, except heat, and
silence. She began to relax.

'Oh, go away!' Her peace was shortlived. The cloud of
flies that accompanied her along the track through the
trees decided to follow her into the shade. They settled
with infuriating persistence upon her face and neck and
arms, until she could bear their irritation no longer.

'I'll break myself off a switch,' she decided, 'that'll at
least keep the pests at bay.' There was ample greenery
around to provide her with plenty of choice, and she reluctantly heaved herself to her feet and made towards a
mixed clump of bamboo and twiggy bushes that grew at
the edge of the clearing nearest to where she had sat. A
slender wand of green waved at shoulder height among
the bamboo clump.

'This will do nicely.' She thrust her arm into the clump
to snap it off. It proved to be tougher than she had bargained for, and her struggles to snap the pithy green stem
raised a veritable storm of tiny insects.

'Ugh!' She brushed them off her arm with a shiver of
revulsion, and backed away hurriedly with her newly
acquired switch clutched in her hand. 'That's better.' She
waved it to good effect, and revelled in the cooling
draught that it produced as an extra bonus for her efforts.
Freed from the nuisance of the flies, and cooled by the
draught, she felt her interest in her surroundings revive.

The clearing was silent. I always thought jungles were

noisy places, with parrots and things screeching, she thought. She eyed the solid wall of green with uneasy eyes. She wished now that she had kept her eyes open when Rann left her. She did not know in which direction he had disappeared. He might, or might not, have gone along the path she indicated. The silence was oppressive. It seemed to close in on her, as solid as the jungle wall that edged the clearing, eerie, and somehow threatening.

Don't be silly, she scolded herself. She was not normally prone to nerves. Rann can't be far away. He's around, somewhere. So, too, might Mac be, she realised unhappily. Or Maung Chi and his men. What was it Rann had said?

'Either of you would make an ideal hostage.'

I'll go and have a look at what's left of the plane. She took refuge from her thoughts in action, and fanning herself vigorously to counteract the roasting heat, she made her way towards the creek, resisting an urge to look over her shoulder as she went.

'What a mess!' she muttered.

The charred skeleton of her erstwhile transport rested forlornly across the steeply sloping bank of the creek, held suspended by the weight of its engine across the lip of an overhanging shale shelf, that jutted out half way down the bank. Another couple of feet to the one side, Storm judged, and the wreck would have descended unhindered right into the bottom of the creek bed. Exactly as her suitcase had done.

'I don't believe it!' She stared incredulously at her suitcase. The end of it jutted out at the very edge of the water, every line of it begging her to collect it before the level of the creek rose, and irretrievably drowned it. Eagerly she slid down the bank, heedless now of the heat and the silence. Le's lungyis and blouses were lovely, but the prospect of having the use of her own clothes was even better.

Maybe Le and I can do a swap, she promised herself happily. She said she'd left her dresses and slacks behind on the game reserve. Storm leaned down and grasped her case, and pulled with both hands. The hinge was split, the case itself was badly scorched, but it was intact, she

saw with relief. She heaved it out on to the shingle jub-
ilantly, and gasped as what had appeared to be a non-
descript mud patch on the creek bank exploded in a cloud
of brilliantly coloured wings, disturbed by her sudden
movement.

'Butterflies! How lovely!' she exclaimed.

At rest on the mud patch, with their wings closely
folded to hide the brilliant scales, they so resembled the
colour of their resting place that she had not noticed they
were there. She watched, fascinated, as the insects fluttered towards the safety of the undergrowth on the edge
of the clearing. One of them flapped lazily to settle on the
wing of the plane.

My case won't hurt here for a while, I'll leave it for the
sun to dry out, she decided. The butterfly was too lovely
to be missed. Storm turned to scramble along the bank
towards it, eager for a closer look. Her feet slipped on the
loose shingle, and she was breathless when she halted just
below the plane's wing, as close to the wreckage as she
deemed it safe to venture.

What . . .? Her eyes lit on something much more solid
than the faery insect. It lay below the level of the burned
out wing on which the butterfly rested. She stared, frown-
ing, unable to make out the shape in the shadow of the
wreck, and then her eyes adjusted from the brilliant sunlight to the shade underneath the shale overhang, and she
realised with a startled gasp that she was looking at,

'Tusks!' she gasped aloud.

One edge of the plane's wing had caught at the earth
of the bank immediately under the shale overhang, rip-
ping it aside, and exposing——

Ivory. It must be Maung Chi's ivory cache. . . .

Storm crept closer, with one eye cocked warily on the
unstable wreckage, fearful that any sudden movement of
hers might cause it to slide, fearful that what she saw was
merely a trick of the light, an optical illusion fermented
by wishful thinking, and the intense heat of the sun.

'It can't be a natural thing,' she muttered as she went.
'The proverbial elephants' graveyard!' Elephants were not
in the habit of conveniently wrapping their tusks in sacking before they gave up the ghost, and the torn hessian

that hung limply, ripped away from the tusks by the intrusion of the plane's wing into their hiding place, was no optical illusion.

'I've discovered the poachers' cache,' she whispered, still unable to believe her good fortune. '*I've* discovered it, not Rann!' She did a little dance of sheer delight. 'He can't call me an unwanted complication now,' she told the butterfly triumphantly, feeling slightly light headed by her unexpected good fortune. 'Wait until I tell him!' she crowed happily, but the butterfly was uninterested in human triumphs, it took fright at her sudden movement, and rose and fluttered after its fellows.

I'll follow it, and come back for my suitcase later, Storm decided. The enclosed creek bed was, if anything, hotter than the clearing, and might account in some measure for her feeling of lightheadedness. Cautiously she climbed back over the lip of the bank again, and soon spotted the butterfly, already half way across the clearing, and fluttering towards the entrance to the game trail along which she presumed Rann had disappeared.

The insect was easy enough to follow, its wing span must have been at least five inches across, and its brilliant colouring resembled a fragment of animated rainbow, impossible to miss against the sombre green.

'. . . the bright elusive butterfly of love. . . .' She sang the words of the song unthinkingly, and without warning the brightness of the sunshine darkened, the spring left her step, and desolation swept over her as she dragged to a halt at the entrance to the game trail, and watched with dull eyes as her quarry vanished into the gloom of the trees. Symbolic, she thought bleakly, of her own wayward heart, that seemed to have disappeared from her own keeping, and fluttered helplessly, hopelessly, in the wake of,

'Rann!' Suddenly he was there. She had not heard him coming. She had not seen him. And now he walked towards her along the game trail, out of the half light of the trees, and back into the sunshine beside her. It glinted on the rich colouring of his hair, and made the clearing bright again. 'Thank goodness you're back!' She came to life again, the butterfly forgotten. 'I've got something to show you,' she began eagerly.

'It's a good job I *have* come back,' he gritted furiously. 'Have you taken leave of your senses?' he shouted at her angrily.

'Why . . .? What . . .?' She stammered to a halt, completely taken aback by his unexpected attack.

'I told you to stay in the shade of the boulder,' he thundered, 'and I come back to find you charging about in the full glare of the sun. Do you want to give yourself sunstroke, to add to my problems?' he questioned her furiously. 'Your face is like a beetroot!'

Of all the dictatorial, unflattering, chauvinistic . . .! Storm's thoughts ran out of adjectives. It was not herself getting sunstroke that bothered Rann, but his own possible inconvenience, she realised angrily. Indignation brought her voice back with a rush, and she shouted right back at him defiantly,

'I'm not obliged to remain in the shade of the boulder, simply because you told me to!'

'Common sense should have made you remain out of the sun.'

'I was following a butterfly. . . .'

'What butterfly?' The glance he flicked round the empty clearing dismissed her explanation as sheer fabrication, and her cheeks took on an even deeper hue. 'If you'd come along with me, following the game trail, at least you'd have been away from the direct heat of the sun.'

'If I'd come with you along the game trail, I shouldn't have collected my suit case, and I shouldn't have found Maung Chi's cache of ivory, either,' her words came out in a garbled rush, and his frown deepened.

'You *have* caught the sun.' Instead of reacting with delighted surprise at her news as she expected, he grasped her by the arm and hurried her back towards the shade of the boulder, and bade her curtly, 'Sit down.' He pressed her down into the shade, and his palm slid enquiringly over her forehead. 'Your head's like fire,' he rasped in exasperation.

And so was her temper, Storm decided furiously. What with the heat, and the flies, and Rann's disbelieving, high-handed attitude, she felt in imminent danger of coming to the boil.

'I'm not lightheaded, if that's what you're suggesting,' she snapped irritably, and flung off his hand with a toss of her head. The touch of his fingers was causing more havoc than the sun, and not just to her head. If he had only shown one iota of human concern for herself, instead of for his own convenience, she might have been tempted to give way to her feelings and cry, she thought despairingly. Perhaps it was a good thing that he shouted.

'If you don't believe I've found the ivory, come to the creek and have a look for yourself!' She sprang to her feet, frustration and fury combining to give her a surge of strength. 'I'll come along too, and pick up my switch.' She flapped a hand at the freshly gathering flies.

'What switch?' He continued to look at her doubtfully, as if he was still only half convinced that she was rational. 'The one I broke off from the bush, to keep away the flies. That's where I took it from,' she pointed impatiently towards the clump of bamboo, where the ragged bottom end of her switch was already turned brown in the heat. 'If you're not coming to the creek, I'll go on my own.' And without waiting to see if he would follow her, she went.

For some reason, the creek bank seemed to be twice as steep as it had done before. The bleached shale wavered in the pitiless glare, and the heat seemed to double in intensity as she slid down the bank, striking back from the stony sides with relentless vigour. Without giving herself time to think, Storm made straight for where she had left her suitcase, and the now wilted switch which she had dropped beside it when she ran after the butterfly. She bent to pick up the switch, and heard a slither of gravel from behind her.

So Rann had followed her, after all. She gave a small grin of triumph. 'Now you can see the suitcase is real, perhaps you'll believe me about the ivory as well.' Her eyes clashed with his in a measured stare that had about it the ring of foils.

'I'll send an oozie for your case, some time,' he answered indifferently, and fished in his pocket for a small battery-operated walkie-talkie set. 'If the ivory *is* real,' the glint in his eyes still doubted her, and she compressed her lips angrily, 'if the ivory *is* real, I'll need to alert Krish.'

'I'm not going to leave my clothes behind,' she declared stubbornly. 'Now I've recovered them, I'm going to take them back with me.' Who knew what might happen to them, before Rann condescended to send an oozie?

'You can't possibly haul a great heavy suitcase all the way back to the bungalow,' he growled impatiently, and put down his hand to take it from her.

'It's not all that heavy.' It was, but she would die rather than admit it.

'It's like lead,' he contradicted her shortly, and curled his fingers round the handle to test the weight.

'I can manage.' She refused to let go, and the unexpected resistance to his hold spilled the walkie-talkie set from out of Rann's fingers and on to the sunbaked shale.

'Carry it yourself, then, if you want to. You'll give up soon enough,' he retorted impatiently, and loosing the full weight of the case back into her hold, he bent to pick up the handset. 'Now show me where you say you found the ivory cache, so we can get out of this furnace, and back under the shade of the trees.'

'Look under the wreckage of the plane, below the shale shelf,' she directed him shortly. The case seemed to weigh a ton, but she struggled valiantly alongside him towards the remains of the plane. 'The wing's sliced the soil away and exposed some of the tusks.'

'Don't get too close, in case the wreckage slides.' Rann grasped her by the shoulder and pulled her to a halt.

'I'm not that silly,' she retorted scornfully, hiding her gratitude for the temporary halt. It enabled her to rest the case on the ground for a while. Bending to put it down caused her head to swim. Rann was correct, the creek bed *was* a veritable furnace. Perhaps she could just take a few of her clothes, and leave the rest to be collected later, she compromised. She would find some way to do it without losing face. To give herself time to think of a way, she made an energetic display of directing Rann's attention to her discovery. 'The ivory's just to the right of that blackened spar, you can see where the sacking's been torn from around the tusks.'

'Phew!' His awestruck whistle made full compensation for his earlier disbelief, and it was so like her own initial reaction that Storm almost laughed. Except that her sense of humour seemed to have deserted her. The wrecked plane, and the creek bed, and the ivory, began to waver in the most disconcerting manner in front of her eyes.

'It's only heat shimmer,' she tried to convince herself desperately. 'As soon as we're back among the trees, I'll be all right.' Vaguely she heard Rann start to speak.

'Krish. Come in, Krish.' A series of metallic clicks, and he shook the receiving set with a muttered imprecation.

'It probably broke something when you dropped it,' she hazarded without interest.

'If you hadn't jerked it out of my hand it wouldn't have happened,' Rann blamed her furiously. 'If I can't get it to work, I won't be able to contact Krish until we return to the bungalow, and I can use the main set there.'

'It doesn't matter. No one can get to the ivory, the plane's settled right across it. It'll need an elephant to move that great heavy engine.'

'Or a small charge of dynamite,' Rann reminded her grimly. 'Which is exactly what the pilot stole from the godown.'

The pilot. Storm wrinkled her forehead perplexedly. For the life of her, she could not remember what the pilot looked like. Suddenly it seemed important that she should recall what he looked like. She exerted herself to try and concentrate, but the heat would not let her. It beat down upon her swimming head with an almost solid force. It sapped her energy, and picked the thoughts out of her mind the second they formed, leaving it empty except for a peculiar buzzing sensation that seemed to start in her ears, and take over her whole head, leaving room only for the dismayed conviction that——

'I think I'm going to pass out,' she muttered faintly. And remembered nothing more.

CHAPTER SIX

SHE must have managed to catch the liner, after all. It rolled. She could feel it rolling, backwards and forwards, and from side to side. It made her feel queasy, which was strange, because she did not normally suffer from sea-sickness. She eased herself into a more comfortable position in the not very comfortable bunk, and tried to ignore the rolling. The liner must be riding out a storm.

It rumbled, as well as rolled, she discovered. Liners had no right to rumble, particularly first class passenger liners. It sounded as if it had got a bad attack of wind, and a giggle burbled up inside her at the vision of a large ocean liner getting wind. What remedy was there? she wondered hilariously. A liner was much too large to lift out of the water and pat on the back.

At least the ship's bell had got a pleasant tone. It was ringing six bells. She counted. No, it was eight. But the notes of the bell did not stop at eight, either, they continued on, and on. . . . It can't be, there are only twenty-four hours in a day. Perhaps it was a warning bell for something. She concentrated on the possibilities. There was fire, or shipwreck, or. . . . Her eyes flew open, and she stared.

Hide? It was grey, and tough, and she watched it bewilderdly. It moved, with the movement of mighty muscles underneath, and from somewhere underneath the muscles the rumble came again. This time, it sounded oddly familiar.

'It's an elephant. I'm on the back of an elephant.' Or, to be more precise, she realised with alarm, she was somewhere alongside the animal, suspended in what appeared to be a wicker pannier. And the elephant's stomach rumbled, as she had heard them rumble when the animals came together in a bunch from their day's work on the site, an orchestration of inner elephant that seemed a permanent accompaniment to the wooden bells that hung

about their necks. The soft musical clonking kept pace
with the animal's plodding steps, and Storm reached out
a cautious hand and grasped the top of the pannier that
held her. It seemed firm enough, and warily she pulled
herself to a sitting position, and immediately wished she
had remained where she was. The ground looked miles
away, and the pannier a frail network of interlacing twigs
that looked as if it might give way at any moment.

'Oh, my goodness!'

The oozie perched nonchalantly on the animal's head
turned round at her dismayed exclamation, and gave a
reassuring grin, showing teeth and lips stained red with
constant betel chewing. He spat with practised accuracy,
sending a stream of red juice over the top of the elephant's
ears and into the foliage at the side of the track. Bemusedly
Storm recognised the red trunks of the hardwoods they
had passed on the outward journey.

'Rann?'

The last she had seen of Rann was beside the cache of
ivory. With horrid clarity his words returned to haunt
her.

'Either of you would make an ideal hostage.'

Was the oozie on the elephant one of Rann's men? Or
one of Maung Chi's? She had no means of telling. Had
his grin been reassuring, as she thought, or—she paled at
the possibility—triumphant, because she was now his
captive? And where was Rann?

'Rann?' She called his name again, on a shrill note of
fear. The man sitting on the elephant's head looked round,
and said something to her in the soft singsong language
she had heard the women of the village using, but she
could not reply because she did not understand it.

'Rann?'

'I'm here.' His voice seemed to come from somewhere
just below her. She turned swiftly and looked down, and
had to grab at the sides of the pannier as it tilted alarm-
ingly at her sudden movement, but the wave of relief that
washed over her at the sight of Rann, walking beside the
elephant and slightly in front of her pannier, with his rifle
slung easily over his shoulder, effectively submerged her
fright caused by her high perch.

'How do you feel now?' He slowed his steps until he walked beside her, and tilting his head back he looked up full into her face. Her heart lurched as she met his keenly searching look, and began to hammer so wildly that she pressed her hand to her side to quieten it, convinced that he must hear.

'Demoralised!' would have been a truthful answer, and it was not occasioned by the sun, or by the alarming distance from the ground. Neither could match the devastating effect of his cool, green stare, but Storm felt disinclined to be that truthful, either to Rann or to herself. With an effort she pulled her scattered wits together. 'Where's your pride?' she berated herself, and before her heart could give her the answer she feared, 'Gone, along with the ambition to act,' she blurted out hastily,

'Relieved to see you.' It was a compromise, but it was the nearest thing to the truth she was prepared to give. 'I thought . . . I wondered. . . .' She ground to a halt, unwilling to let Rann know exactly how frightened she had been.

'You wondered if Maung Chi had captured you?' he queried, with disconcerting accuracy, and Storm felt a tide of warmth rise across her cheeks, that grew deeper as he continued deliberately,

'You'll be glad to know that Maung Chi hasn't kidnapped you,' and added with a grin, 'I have.'

Presumably he expected her to be glad about that as well. The indignant flush seemed to spread right over her, even down to her toes. The conceit of the man! she fumed. He had detained her against her will; inhospitably done his best to make her feel an unwelcome burden; he had effectively wrecked her career, and now—she swallowed hard—and now he actually expected her to be glad about it! She glared down at him furiously, and his eyes laughed up at her, noting the flags of temper flying at full mast in her cheeks, and challenging her to answer the absolutely unanswerable.

'I . . . you. . . .' She choked into silence.

'Thakin!'

By some mysterious signal the oozie halted his elephant, and held up his hand, warning them to silence. Storm could hear nothing, but from the rigid stance of both Rann and the oozie, it was obvious that the men sensed something that was hidden from her. For some reason she could not account for, Storm found herself holding her breath. A movement caught her eye and she looked down. Cautiously, without a sound, Rann slid the rifle sling from his shoulder until he had the weapon balanced lightly in his hand, and she felt herself go cold. Nothing stirred. Nothing called. The jungle seemed to be holding its breath as well, and waiting. For what? She strained her ears and her eyes, to no avail.

Crack!

It was faint. The sound was dulled by the weight of the surrounding foliage, but it was unmistakably a rifle shot. Storm glanced down quickly to Rann, but he did not heed her. He remained motionless, listening, with the total immobility of a wild creature straining with every sense alert to locate the source of the sound. Her heart began to behave in a curious fashion. He looked like the carved, bronze figure of a young god. . . .

Crack! Crack!

Two more shots came, so close together as to be almost indistinguishable. And then silence. It flooded round them like an invisible fog, closing them in. Storm felt an urgent desire to shout out loud, to destroy the silence. She even opened her mouth to call out, and instantly Rann moved. He turned to look up at her, and put a warning finger against his lips, as if he sensed her need and acted to stop it before it was too late. And then, with a signal to the oozie to follow him, he stepped out in front of the elephant with the lithe, silent, distance-consuming stride that so reminded Storm of the grace of the big jungle cats. Even the elephant seemed to heed his command for silence. She had not appreciated before how quietly such a huge creature could move. With the oozie alert on its head, it plodded after Rann like a big grey ghost.

Never had a journey seemed to take so long. Storm ached with tension, and her eyes ached with staring into the jungle on either side of the track, searching for she knew not what, so that it was with a sense of sheer anti-climax that they reached first the village and then the front of Rann's bungalow, and he unlashed the pannier and lifted her down on to the ground, holding her to make sure she was steady on her feet and not still dizzy, and commented in a matter-of-fact voice,

'I brought your suitcase in the other pannier. I'll have it taken into your room.'

It was like the proprietor welcoming her into a hotel on the first day of a seaside holiday. Laughter bubbled up inside her—hysterical laughter. She thrust it down ruthlessly, for on its back rode an urgent desire to cry. Desperately she clutched at Rann's arm, more to steady her nerves than her legs.

'Do you still feel giddy?'

'No. No, I'm fine,' she gasped. The tension of the last hour had made her almost forget about the effects of the sun. Her head still ached, but the agonised throbbing was subdued. Her skin was more painful than her head. 'I'll peel,' she prophesied ruefully.

'It's your own fault, you should have kept out of the sun,' he retorted unsympathetically, and added with unflattering impatience to be rid of her, 'If you can manage on your own, I need to contact Krish urgently.'

'I can manage perfectly well.' She loosed his arm, and her chin came up proudly. 'But since Krish must have sent the elephant and the oozie, I assumed you'd already managed to get in touch with him?'

'How could I, with a broken walkie-talkie?' His hard look blamed her for the damage, almost accused her of knocking it out of his hand deliberately, she thought indignantly. 'Krish sent the oozie on the offchance that we might need him, which is why he got there almost immediately after you fainted, otherwise we'd have had to wait until sundown, and get back somehow under our own steam,' he reminded her grimly.

Storm felt deeply grateful to Krish, not least for sparing her the journey back alone with Rann. He put out a hand to help her as they reached the bungalow steps, and she shrugged it off crossly. Her arm felt too sore to be gripped, and pride forced her shaking legs to support her until Rann turned away in the direction of his office, and the radio she knew was housed there, and without vouchsafing another word he left her to her own devices.

He might have told me what he thought the rifle shots were about, she bridled resentfully. She had a right to know. It was she who had discovered the ivory cache, not Rann. That, if nothing else, gave her the right to be included. His uncommunicative attitude shut her out, denying her right.

Oh, forget Rann! she told herself. Fervently, she wished she could. He seemed to intrude into her every thought and action. The sight of her suitcase resting on the chair beside her bed helped a little. Almost fiercely she prised open the lid and tipped her clothes on to the covers.

Thank goodness I packed them in plastic bags, she thought. When she filled her case at the hotel, she could not possibly have foreseen the unexpected bonus her careful packing afforded her now. Creek water had seeped into her case, but the dresses were untouched. She shook them out thankfully.

I'll have a shower, and come back and change, she decided. Rann would probably be some time before he returned from speaking to Krish. If she was quick, she could beat him to the shower.

'Ouch!' she exclaimed. The cool water was a benediction, except on her right arm. From her shoulder to her wrist, it seemed to be on fire. I'll have to find some cream or something to put on it, she decided. She patted it dry gingerly, and squirmed as it began to itch furiously. 'I can't stand this for long!' she muttered. The itching grew to a torment, and she rubbed it frantically, but the friction only made it worse. She inspected it worriedly. Her left arm was sunburned, but it showed a uniform red. The right one, for some reason, was not only red, but the colouring appeared to be more in the nature of a rash.

I'll put on a dress, and go and find Rann's servant, she decided. He'll probably be back from the site by now. She shied away from the thought of asking Rann himself for a balm. His blame was harsh—for being in the sun, for making him drop his walkie-talkie set, and his harshness rankled. He'll only say, 'I told you so', she decided, and hastily rummaged among the pile of clothes on the bed. This would do nicely. The white sundress could have

been made for the purpose, she thought with satisfaction.
Its perfectly fitted bodice disposed of the need of straps,
leaving her shoulders bare. The thought of clothes touching her arm was not to be borne.

'Perhaps, just while I go and ask Rann's man. . . .' He
might have different views on bare shoulders, and she was
unwilling to offend him. Besides, she needed an antidote
to whatever it was urgently. The itching by now had
assumed unbearable proportions. It was all she could do
to steel herself not to scratch. She reached for the scarlet
and white striped bolero that went with the dress, and
immediately dropped it again with a scream.

'Rann! Rann!'

She stumbled backwards away from the bed, tripping
over the bedside chair in her haste. She grabbed at it for
support, and the chair and the suitcase resting on the seat
descended to the floor with a resounding crash.

'What the . . .?' The door hit the wall with an even
louder crash, and Rann burst into the room with a brow
like thunder.

'What on earth's going on?' he demanded angrily. He
reached out and held her upright as she staggered away
from the chair, and she gave a sharp cry of pain as his
fingers gripped her sore arm.

'Ooh, my arm!' she cried shrilly. 'Do be more careful!'
Did he have to grab her as if she was made of cast iron?
she asked herself furiously.

'What's the matter with your arm?' He released it instantly, and bent to look at it. 'Did you fall? I heard a
crash. Was that why you screamed?'

'No . . . yes . . . no. . . .' Why couldn't he ask her one
question at a time? Storm wondered raggedly. 'I screamed
because of . . . th-that. . . .' She pointed behind her with a
shaking finger. 'On the b-bed,' she stammered, and with
a shudder buried her face against his shoulder.

'There's nothing . . . ah!' There was a slight pause, and
then she felt him begin to shake. She looked up into his
face, startled, and met the white glint of teeth, and emerald eyes brimming over with laughter.

'It's not funny!' She glanced behind her fearfully. 'I
hate spiders!' The one sitting comfortably in the middle

of her bed cover was easily the size of a tennis ball. She half expected it to bounce. It was a muddy grey colour, with eight woolly legs. 'It's moving . . .!' Her voice rose hysterically as it began to amble across the cover.

'It won't hurt you. They're harmless.' Rann picked her up bodily as she made a convulsive movement to back away, and she clung to him, shivering. If one spider was on the bed, she dreaded to think what might be on the floor. 'Lie down and rest for a while, you're shaking all over.'

'Don't put me on the bed. Don't . . .!' Her voice rose to a shriek, and without preamble he shook her roughly into silence.

'Don't be hysterical,' he commanded her sternly. 'I'm not going to put you next to the spider, what do you take me for?' he demanded. Storm did not care. At the moment all she cared about was the intruder on her bed. 'Gurdip?' He raised his voice and called, and his servant appeared soft-footed at the door. Rann said something to the man that raised an amused grin on the brown face, and to Storm's horror he bent and cupped his hands round the spider, and with not the slightest sign of repulsion he carried it carefully outside. 'Now lie down.' Rann lowered her gently on to the bed.

'There might be another.' She strained to stay in his arms.

'There won't be another. If one of those spiders meets another of its kind, it eats it,' he said confidently. 'In any case, Gurdip probably brought it into your room in the first place. Those spiders usually prefer the trees outside.'

'He brought it in here, deliberately?' She raised herself up angrily. 'If he thinks that sort of thing is a joke——' she started indignantly.

'It's no joke, I assure you.' She could not have agreed more, which was the first time since she had met him that she and Rann had agreed on anything, she thought unforgivingly. 'The local people catch the spiders and bring them into their houses to mop up any insects they find there. They prefer them to flies and cockroaches,' he went on casually, 'and the fact that he brought one into your room means that he was doing you a favour. Those spiders are highly prized for their usefulness by the local people.'

'That's one favour I'd rather not have!' Storm rejected the intended kindness with a shudder.

'I'll make sure in future that you don't,' Rann promised with a grin that resembled the one on the face of his servant as Gurdip departed with the cause of her terror. Men were all alike, Storm thought resentfully, they simply never grew up. They both thought her fright was highly amusing. She rubbed her itching arm with an irritable hand, and glared at Rann fiercely.

'What's the matter with your arm?' Her movement brought his attention back to his earlier question.

'It itches,' she answered him shortly. She did not want to admit it to Rann. She did not want to let him see just how sore it had become.

'That's obvious,' he retorted, 'and if you keep on scratching it in that manner, it'll very soon be raw.' He sat down on the side of the bed and picked up her arm by the wrist, careful not to let his fingers touch the soreness. 'Let me see.'

'It's only sunburn.' She tried to pull away. 'A dab of cream will cure it.'

'It'll need more than a dab of cream to cure this.' He inspected her arm with a frown. 'When you were in the clearing, which hand did you use to break off your switch from the bush?' he asked, apropos of nothing.

'My right one, of course. I'm right-handed.' Why did he have to ask such silly questions? she wondered crossly.

'And you don't itch anywhere else?' He asked another one.

'No, of course not.' Wasn't one itching arm enough? Her temper spilled over, the combination of heat and elation, fright and exhaustion, all rolled together in one hectic day, snapped her sorely tried control. 'I've told you, a dab of cream. . . .'

'Bamboo ticks probably thrive on dabs of cream,' he remarked laconically.

'Bamboo . . . what?' Her voice rose in a horrified squeak.

'Bamboo ticks,' he repeated remorselessly. 'You must have disturbed a nest of them when you broke off your switch, and they've made a meal of your arm. If you'd remained in the shade of the boulder, as I told you to——' he added critically.

'I'd have been eaten alive by flies by now,' she snapped. 'For goodness' sake, can't you do something about my arm? The itching's driving me mad!'

'So will the cure,' he promised ominously, and proceeded to demonstrate the truth of his prediction five minutes later, when he busied himself with cotton wool and a bottle of something that smelled almost as badly as it hurt.

'Ooh, it stings!' Storm protested, screwing up her face in anguish as the fiery liquid seared her skin like acid. 'What on earth is it?'

'Spirits of turpentine,' he retorted, without slackening his ministrations. 'It's an old-fashioned cure, but it's effective, so sit still and don't wriggle.' It was easier said than done, and his assurance was small comfort as he soaked her arm from fingertips to shoulder with remorseless thoroughness, until her entire limb felt as if it was on fire.

'You brute!' she whimpered, unable to keep back an involuntary gasp of agony.

'It's your own fault,' he gave her no sympathy. 'Perhaps it'll serve to remind you to treat your surroundings with more respect in future. When you know more about the jungle, you'll. . . .'

'I shan't be here long enough to learn about the jungle,' she snapped back. 'What on earth anyone wants to live here for anyway is beyond my comprehension, what with the awful heat, and the insects, to say nothing of poachers, and pilots, and. . . .'

'It isn't all bad,' he answered her quietly, and something in his voice made her look up at him questioningly. 'It's got butterflies too, remember?' There was an odd expression on his face, a lurking something deep in his eyes that for some reason stilled the spate of angry words that tumbled from her tongue.

'Lie down and try to sleep until Le comes back,' he bade her when he had finished. 'The turpentine will work the trick on your arm. It'll be sore for a day or two, but so will the sunburn—they'll both go, in time.' He bent

down, and with unexpected gentleness tucked the mosquito netting securely round the bed. The net made a
thin mist between them, hiding his expression, cutting her
off from him. Suddenly Storm wished the net was not
between them. She strained her eyes to see through it, to
try to read the thoughts that lay behind his casual words,
but the effort of trying to pierce the flimsy netting made
her eyes smart. Or maybe it was his unexpected reminder
about the butterflies. She blinked hastily, and not very
successfully.

The bright, elusive butterfly of love. . . .

She did not want to think about butterflies. She gave
up trying to read his expression, which was gone now,
anyway, as elusive as the butterfly. Perhaps she had only
imagined both? The stinging in her eyes grew worse, until
they began to rival her arm, and she turned on her side,
away from Rann so that he should not see the tear that
escaped and rolled down her cheek, unhindered because
she did not want to bring up her hand to brush it away
and bring her weakness to his attention. He might think
she was crying because of the hurt of her arm, but her
heart hurt even more, and no amount of spirits of turpentine could cure that.

She closed her eyes and lay still, and after an endless
minute she heard his footsteps leave the side of her bed
and go towards the door. It opened and closed, softly,
and she relaxed, lying limply still, but before more than
half a dozen tears had time to follow the first, the thoughts
of butterflies, and ivory, and mysterious shots that Rann
still had not explained to her, became jumbled together
in her dazed mind, as exhaustion claimed her, and she
slept.

CHAPTER SEVEN

'MY arm's better,' Storm lied defensively, before Rann had time to speak.

'It looks better than it was,' he contradicted her coolly. He looked up from the map he was reading, spread out across the breakfast table the next morning, and his eyes flicked across her arms, noting that the inflammation had subsided, noting that the one was still, nevertheless, very sore. 'I told you it would be,' he added casually, and returned to studying his map.

Storm scowled at his bent head. He was so sure of himself, she thought bitterly, and longed to do something to dent that complete sureness. It irritated her. It infuriated her. It made her feel as if she was helplessly battering against a steel door, that only hurt her own fists, and made absolutely no impression upon Rann. He was so calmly convinced that, because he himself had treated her arm, it had no other choice *but* to get better, she thought resentfully.

'Eat a good breakfast,' he spoke without looking up, 'it's going to be a long day.'

'I don't want anything to eat.' She immediately rejected the idea of breakfast. 'I'll just have a cup of coffee.'

'Please yourself,' he returned indifferently. 'You'll be the hollow one before we get back to the bungalow tonight.'

'I don't care, I . . . oh, Gurdip, thank you for my suit.' She grasped eagerly at the diversion as the servant appeared. It was too hot for a battle of wills with Rann, she told herself limply, and tried not to think that it was a battle she would inevitably lose, as she had lost all the others she had with him. 'And thank you for these, too,' she indicated the ingenious fly swat-cum-fan, and the wide-brimmed coolie type hat, both made of rushes, which she had discovered placed on top of her freshly washed and pressed trouser suit, nestling beside her tea tray when

79

she awoke. 'It was kind of you,' she thanked the elderly man gratefully. At least Gurdip was friendly, he spared no effort to make her feel at home, even if one of his efforts in the shape of the spider had so badly misfired. Different from Rann, who seemed to spare no effort to make her realise what a nuisance her presence was to him.

'Gurdip cut the rushes, and wove them up specially for you last night, after he saw what a state your arms were in,' Rann commented, and added deliberately as he reached for the marmalade, 'just as he made the chapattis freshly for you this morning.'

It was blackmail. Rann knew it, and Storm knew it. His eyes bored into hers, challenging her across the table. Daring her to refuse the chapattis. Daring her to wipe away Gurdip's happy smile as he waited to watch her enjoyment of his thoughtful offering. Between the two of them, Storm felt as if she was caught in a pincer movement from which there was no escape, trapped between the twin pressures of Rann's challenge and Gurdip's happy expectancy. She was not equal to the pressure. She could not refuse. Rann knew that, too. She gave him a hostile glance, and forced her hand to reach out and accept the food, forced her lips to smile gratefully at its kind provider, the while she hated Rann with a fierce hatred for once more, and so easily, bending her to his will.

'They're lovely, Gurdip. I've never tasted any so good as the ones you make.' They tasted of nothing except the sourness of defeat, and it took all Storm's acting ability to look as if she appreciated food that bade fair to choke her as she chewed. To convince her benefactor of the success of his efforts, she took another, and spread it with the thin wild honey she found such a delicious combination, and tried unsuccessfully to ignore the quick uptilting of the corners of Rann's well shaped lips that mocked her capitulation, turned the chapatti into straw in her mouth, and made her take a hasty gulp of coffee to help it down, when she would much rather have hurled the cup and its contents, as well as the chapatti, straight at his tawny head.

'Thakin?' The oozie she had seen the previous day

beckoned to Rann from the bottom of the veranda steps, and he rose instantly. A brief exchange followed, then the oozie went back towards the village, and Rann folded up his map and turned to Storm.

'If you've finished your breakfast, you'd better tag along with me.'

He might at least try to show a bit of enthusiasm for my company, she thought abrasively, but curiosity got the better of her resentment, and she asked instead,

'What did the oozie come for?'

'One of the other men sent him to fetch me. It saves time if I go to them,' he commented, noting her raised eyebrows. 'They've got their elephants to wash preparatory to the day's work.'

'There's no need to be sarcastic,' she snapped, bright flags of temper staining her cheeks. Even if she was a newcomer to the jungle and its ways, there was no need for him to be quite so patronising.

'Come and see,' was all he answered, and set off in the wake of the oozie towards the village.

It was still early, and she supposed cool by local standards, but the sun was nevertheless strong. She settled her coolie hat on her curls, and hesitated. It would have been nice to have tucked a flower in the band. She thought longingly of the sweet-scented siri bud. It would have been nice to defy Rann. . . .

Better not, she decided with a shrug. Particularly as we're going to the village. She picked up her fly swat instead, and followed Rann. The village was already awake and busy. Women busily trod boards to prepare rice for the day's meals. A pi-dog scratched itself and gave a wide yawn at the new day. Children played in the shallows where the river widened into a large, open pool, at which all the village ablutions seemed to take place. Storm had seen the women there scrubbing their washing and their children with happy impartiality.

This morning, the pool was the scene of busy activity. At least half a dozen elephants lay, sat, or otherwise reclined in the water, like stout matrons in a beauty parlour, Storm thought amusedly. Their oozies joined them, their lungyis tucked up out of the water into loincloths,

while they energetically soaped and swilled their huge
charges, all the while keeping up a cheerful flow of exhor-
tion and banter as lather and water flew freely.

'Do you believe me now?' Rann slanted her a glance
that brought the ready colour back to her cheeks, and
made her glad of the kindly shelter provided by the wide
brim of her hat.

'You must have to import a lot of soap if this is a daily
ritual,' she ignored his jibe, and concentrated on prac-
ticalities to cover her confusion. She refused to apologise
for her blatant mistrust.

'They don't need manufactured soap here, like they
don't need money,' Rann rubbed in the local independence of man-made goods. 'They gather the soapy bark of
a tree to serve their needs, and they use sand from the
river banks to polish the animals' tusks.'

'They certainly gleam,' she acknowledged, startled out
of her black mood at the unexpected display.

'Like ivory?' he grinned, and added, not without a certain pride in his voice, 'it's a matter of pride that each
oozie keeps his own animal in tip-top condition, they vie
with one another who shall have the best looking beast.'

'Like our own men at home, with their horses and their
cars,' she laughed, enjoying the simile. Enjoying his
answering laughter, that formed an unexpected warm link
between them.

'It isn't all bad. There are butterflies, too. . . .'

The scene before them was on the credit side of the
jungle ledger, like the butterflies, she realised, stealing him
a swift upward glance. His face held the merry, unguarded
enjoyment of a boy as he watched the antics of the elephants, each one trying to prolong its daily bath, like small
children begging for just one more splash before it was
over, and her heart contracted with an almost unbearable
pain. This was the other side of the coin, of Rann, as well
as of the jungle. The side that laughed, and loved, and
played. Not the stern, harsh side, that was the only glimpse
either had vouchsafed to her so far. The bleakness of that
other side unfroze a little as she watched beside Rann,
and her lips curved into a smile to match his own. She
did not see him glance down at her. The brim of her hat

hid her eyes from him, and just as effectively hid his face from her eyes unless she turned to look up full at him, and she was too absorbed in the novel scene in front of her to look away, or to notice the strange expression that flitted across his face as she smiled, and when he spoke, and she looked up at the sound of his voice, the expression was gone, and she remained unaware as he said,

'Come farther back, the oozies are bringing them out now.' One by one the riders chivvied their reluctant charges out of the water, and lined them up dripping on the bank. Only one man did not join in the work. He held a spear in one hand, a deadly-looking weapon that glinted in the sun, and he remained silent and watchful, constantly beside the one oozie and his animal, a huge creature with great curving tusks. Storm shot an apprehensive look towards Rann as the three made their cumbersome way to the bank.

'The spearman's there to protect the oozie,' he answered her unspoken question quietly. 'That particular tusker is dangerous. It's got an uncertain temper, and the oozie can't be on guard the whole of the time. Now and then his attention has to be elsewhere, and he's vulnerable to •ttack, so the spearman keeps watch. The elephant knows that while the spearman's there, it pays to behave.'

It was as if a chill wind blew across the pool, and Storm shivered. Without warning the coin had flipped back again, revealing once more the side of the jungle she knew best, the cruel, harsh side, that filled her with fear and dread, and a longing to flee this awful place, that tore her in two, because at one and the same time she longed to remain so that she could be with Rann.

'Why does the oozie ride such an animal?' The description of 'red in tooth and claw' was never more apt, she decided with a shudder, only now she could add tusks to the list as well.

'It's a matter of pride, with the men, to boast that they ride a rogue,' Rann answered her casually.

'Oh, men's pride . . .!' Storm exploded wrathfully. As if pride mattered.

'Only the most experienced oozie is capable of handling a dangerous elephant,' Rann pointed out reasonably.

'It's got a metal bell.' The sharp sound stood out against the softer, musical clonking of the carved wooden bells worn by the other animals.

'The dangerous elephants all wear metal bells,' Rann answered calmly, 'it enables them to be picked out easily from the others.'

'It's a pity the idea isn't extended, to include human beings,' she retorted sharply, unable to resist the thrust.

'Base metal bells for the men, and silver ones for the ladies?' he suggested softly, with one deft stroke turning her barb neatly back on her, pricking her with the sharpness of it, and then before she could draw breath for the retort that came rushing to her tongue he went on evenly, 'It serves as a warning when the men have to track down their animals in the jungle each morning. With the bell round their necks, they're unable to take their riders by surprise.'

'I thought working elephants were tame animals?' It was Storm's turn to be surprised now.

'So they are, but they're not kept in stables, like horses,' he answered. 'After they've finished work for the day they're hobbled and turned loose into the jungle to graze. The oozies know the tracks of their own animals, though sometimes they have to follow them for several miles before they catch up with them, and even then they don't always come meekly. They're not unlike horses in that respect,' he smiled, 'they know that once they're caught there's a day's work ahead of them, and they have to be coaxed. Which is why we're here now.' His tone became brisk, workmanlike, shutting her off from him. Folding up the brief, happy interlude, and putting it away. Never to be looked at again? She would always remember it, Storm thought wistfully, even when, if ever, enough years had passed between then and now, so that the memory of Rann no longer hurt. She would remember. But would he? Drearily she admitted he would not. He would remember the oozies, and the elephants, because they were important to him, but he would not remember her.

'Why *are* we here?' she answered him automatically with her voice, while her heart asked, 'Why am *I* here? Why, oh, why did I come?'

'Because while one of the oozies was tracking his elephant this morning, he came across some more tracks which he wants to tell me about.'

He did not explain what the tracks might be. He might not know himself until the oozie spoke to him, but it did not prevent resentment boiling up again inside Storm at his deliberate lack of communication. It was as if she was so insignificant in his scheme of things that she did not even begin to count when it came to passing on information. She fumed in silence as the oozie with the dangerous tusker left his animal in charge of the spearman, and stepped forward to speak to Rann.

Storm waited with growing unease while they talked. The elephant stood quietly enough, but her eyes were drawn as if by a magnet to the huge, curving tusks, and the long, sinuous trunk, that before today she had always regarded as one of Nature's practical jokes. Watching it move, constantly reaching out, now here, now there, she saw it in a different light. The strong, muscular length of it was like a huge whip thong, that could easily fell a man beneath those enormous, trampling feet.

If only Rann would stop talking! Her mind screamed with tension, and she had to make a conscious effort to unlock her clenched fists, and found when she did that her palms were wet. She rubbed them against her slacks legs to dry them off, and turned towards Rann.

'Rann?' For a heart-stopping moment she missed him, and her heart hammered a tattoo of relief as she lowered her eyes to where he squatted on the ground opposite to the oozie, both men intent on the map the elephant rider drew in the dust with his finger.

'Let's go back to the bungalow, I want to radio Krish, to warn him.' At last Rann stood up. He took Storm by the arm, spoke briefly to the other oozies, then turned and strode back towards the bungalow, drawing her with him.

'Warn Krish about what?' She had to trot to keep up with him, but he made no attempt to slacken his pace, and she was unable to slow down even if she wanted to, the pressure of his hold kept her beside him. She was breathless, but she had no desire to be left behind. Again, she had the irresistible urge to look back over her shoulder. She could not forget the almost stealthy silence of the animal that had carried her in its panniers. The urge became too much, and she shot a quick glance over her shoulder, and promptly stumbled against Rann.

'What are you looking behind for?' He urged her on, impatiently. 'If you've left your fly switch, you can go back for it later.'

'I haven't, I've got it here,' she swung it up for him to see. Anything rather than admit the reason she looked behind her. To prevent him from questioning her, she rushed on hastily, 'Anyway, what's the hurry? Whatever the oozie said, it can't be all that important that we have to run in this heat.' She felt hot, and cross, and for some unknown reason frightened, and her temper responded in kind.

'This is a lot more important than you feeling hot,' he retorted unsympathetically. 'The oozies found the spoor of a wounded elephant when they were tracking their own animals at first light. They followed it up, and caught a sight of the beast on the other side of a ravine. Even from that distance, as soon as it saw them, it charged. It was a good job the ravine was between them,' he said significantly, and added in a hard tone, 'Mac is a fool, as well as a rotten shot.'

'Mac?' Storm creased her forehead. 'How do you know it was Mac who wounded the animal?' It was just like Rann to blame the airman, she thought critically. Just because he did not like the man.

'It had to be Mac. Those shots we heard yesterday came from a rifle. Maung Chi and his men use the old-fashioned elephant guns, and ivory poachers have more respect for their own lives than to leave a wounded elephant at large. An one of them would have followed it up and finished what they set out to do. And besides, there were three shots in all.'

'What has the number of shots got to do with it?' she asked bewilderedly. His explanations were getting more and more unclear, and she had as much difficulty in keeping up with his words as she had with his strides.

'They have this to do with it,' he answered her crisply,

and forced her up the veranda steps without slackening his pace. 'With his first shot, Mac must have either missed altogether, or winged the beast. My guess is that he hit it. Elephants are difficult to miss,' he added, and there was a wealth of compassion in his voice that was not matched by the granite set of his face as he continued, 'A wounded elephant can be deadly. When the first shot hit it, but failed to kill, the beast probably charged Mac, which would account for the next two shots being so close together. The man would fire again in desperation, and then again. Then he probably dropped his rifle and ran for it, because if his magazine was empty, he wouldn't have time to reload.'

'He might still be somewhere in the jungle, wounded!' Storm exclaimed in horror. 'You must send out a search party. Now, before it's too late.'

'It's a waste of time,' Rann rejected her plea out of hand. 'If the elephant caught up with Mac, it's already too late. And if not, then he escaped with a whole skin,' he deduced practically, and Storm stared at him in stunned disbelief.

'How can you be so callous?' She had accused him of being made of teak. She maligned the teak trees, she decided caustically. They, at least, were living, feeling things. 'Have you got no feeling?' she hammered at him wildly.

'My feeling is for Krish, and Le, and the men working on the site.' Rann rounded on her savagely, and she backed away, frightened by the sudden fire in his eyes. 'My feeling is for a magnificent animal, shot out of hand by a man avaricious for quick profit, and callous enough to leave the creature wounded, and a menace to other people's lives. It's seen a human being as the cause of its agony, and it's hardly likely to differentiate between one person and another. It'll attack on sight, which is why I need to warn Krish so that he can put the men on their guard.' He flung open the door of the wireless room with a force indicative of his feelings, and flicked a switch on the set with a practised hand.

'Krish. Come in, Krish.' He flicked the switch the other way, and the game warden's disembodied voice answered immediately,

'Krish here. What's wrong?'

'This.' Curtly Rann outlined the events of the morning.

'Thanks for the warning, I'll pass the word around,' Krish answered laconically, and even through her own anger Storm marvelled at the calm control of these men, the unemotional acceptance of danger that she herself found too hideous to contemplate.

'Now we're free to go.' Rann silenced the radio, and turned towards the door.

'We?' Storm stared at him. 'Where to?' More than ever, she wished she could remain in the bungalow. She stared out from the veranda at the encroaching jungle that seemed alive with silent menace.

'We're going to collect the ivory, of course.' He seemed surprised that she should question what he was about to do. 'Every hour that goes by increases the risk that Maung Chi will use the dynamite the pilot stole to move the wreckage of the plane from off the cache, and remove his spoils to another hiding place.'

'Surely if the pilot had managed to contact him, he'd have used the dynamite for that purpose before now?'

'Not necessarily,' Rann retorted. 'Maung Chi is hardly likely to take the pilot on trust the moment he appears, and wants to join the poachers. He may suspect a trap, which would account for Mac trying to shoot that elephant. The tusks would act as credentials of his sincerity.'

'Are *you* going to use dynamite?' Storm asked him nervously. She had not given any consideration as to the means Rann might use to recover the ivory.

'And advertise what I'm doing to the whole jungle?' he jeered. 'No, the oozie will get his elephant to push the wreckage of the plane over the lip of the shale overhang. Once it's off balance, its own weight will take it into the creek bed, and we can recover the ivory without any risk of it descending on top of us. You can ride in one of the elephant's panniers on the way to the clearing,' he added offhandedly.

'I'll do no such thing!' Visions of the tusker and the spearman rose terrifyingly before her mind's eye. 'I won't go near that animal,' she mutinied.

'We're not going to use the tusker for this job.' He read her thoughts with humiliating ease. 'We're using the same animal that Krish sent out to us yesterday. Here it comes now,' he gestured to where the elephant plodded towards the bungalow, stepping behind its rider and following at heel as meekly as a well trained dog. 'The elephant's a young female.' Rann paused as he started to descend the veranda steps to speak to the oozie, and threw back over his shoulder with a grin, 'The females are *usually* more docile than the males.'

Which means I'm not, Storm inferred grittily. I'll show him just how docile I'm prepared to be! She set her lips in an obstinate line, and picking up her fly swat like a banner, she settled her hat firmly on her head and followed him down the steps. She was not prepared to take rebellion to the point of remaining in the bungalow on her own. I'll walk to the clearing on my own two feet, if I melt in the attempt!

'*Hmit!*' The oozie halted at the bottom of the bungalow steps, and called an order to his elephant. Storm watched fascinated as the cumbersome animal dropped on to its haunches, and then stretched out on the ground with all four legs extended like a huge, soft toy, and waited quietly for its rider to mount.

'You're next.' Before she realised what he was about to do, Rann moved swiftly, and scooped her up high in his arms.

'Loose me!' she hissed at him furiously, acutely conscious of the oozie's interested stare. 'Put me down!' She tried to hit at him with her fly switch, but his arms tightened round her, circumventing her move.

'I told you, you're going to ride to the clearing today,' he said calmly, and lifted her bodily into the pannier hanging from the side of the elephant.

'And I said I'd walk!' Her hat dropped from her head, and she grabbed at it ineffectually as it rolled on to the ground. 'Let me out of this thing, I want my hat,' she demanded angrily.

'Certainly.' Rann bent swiftly and recovered the escapee headgear. 'No lady should go out in the sun without

her hat,' he said with infuriating gravity, and dropped it
haphazardly on to her head. It slid over her eyes, temporarily cutting off her vision, and even as she pushed at
it to free her face, his voice rang out a sharp order.

'*Htah!*'

The pannier gave a wild lurch as the elephant obediently rose to its feet, and Storm loosed her hat and
grabbed at the wicker sides instead, then the lurching
stopped and an even rolling sensation told her the animal
was already in motion.

'You. . . .' She felt strongly tempted to hurl her hat at
Rann. And then she thought better of it. It would be just
her luck if it landed under the feet of the elephant and
got trampled to bits. She sat up, and looked cautiously
over the side of the pannier.

'If you try to jump, you'll probably rick your ankle,' he
observed, then added something casually that chilled her
to the core, 'In any case, you're safer off the ground than
if you were walking.' He balanced his rifle easily in one
experienced hand, and strode forward in front of the elephant, and Storm had to press her fingers against her
mouth to stop herself from calling out to him,

'Rann! Rann, come back!' If the wild elephant was
anywhere in the vicinity, it would see Rann first. Her
heart misgave her as the full import of his words hit her
like a physical blow. It was unlikely that the wild elephant
would charge another of its own kind, but it would attack
on sight. That was why he insisted I should ride in the
pannier, she realised. Remorse choked her. She and the
oozie were comparatively safe, but Rann. ... Tears
blinded her, so that she could only just make out his figure,
swinging along with the lithe, flat-hipped stride she had
got to know so well, yards out in front of them along the
narrow jungle track. Much farther in front of them than
he had been when they returned from the clearing.
Offering himself as a target?

'I'll walk with you, going back.' She swung herself out
of the pannier and hurried to his side the moment the
elephant lowered itself to the ground and allowed her and
its rider to dismount in the clearing.

'You might have to,' Rann answered her casually, 'it

depends on how much ivory we remove from the cache. We might need both the panniers to carry it in.'

It was like a slap in the face. Her safety mattered only so long as it did not affect the recovery of the ivory. Storm went scarlet, and then white, and her feeling of remorse vanished.

'Whatever happens, you must keep the ivory safe,' she bit sarcastically.

'I don't want it damaged if I can help it,' Rann agreed equably. 'Damaged tusks don't command such a good market value.'

'So you think it's all right for you to sell the ivory, but not for other people to do so?' she questioned him hotly. 'If it's wrong for Maung Chi, it must be wrong for you as well.' It was sheer arrogance on Rann's part, to assume that he had the sole right, she told herself angrily.

'No one has the right to shoot game in the Kheval Province, except the game wardens themselves,' he contradicted her harshly. 'And the wardens only do so under licence, to control the population of the herds. And there's a genuine market for the ivory of the animals that are culled, which is where these other tusks will go, and the proceeds will benefit the game reserve instead of the money going to line the pockets of the poachers.'

There were twelve tusks in all. Six elephants. Storm felt a thrill of pure compassion run through her at the wanton waste of precious wildlife, as she watched their own pack animal obediently put its weight to the wreckage of the plane and push it over the shale overhang. It performed its task to the accompaniment of a mighty bellow that made Storm jump almost out of her skin with fright at the sheer unexpectedness of it.

'The elephants often do that, when they're working,' Rann laughed outright at her discomfiture. 'If you'd been to the work site, you'd be used to it.'

'I haven't, and I'm not,' Storm snapped angrily, incensed by his open amusement, but curiosity got the better of her annoyance when the two men began to work with small shovels they had brought for the purpose, carefully easing away the soil of the bank to expose two large crates thrust back deep into a natural cave under the shale overhang, and covered with soil in a manner that, but for the plane's wing slicing into it and disturbing the covering, would have guarded it for ever against casual detection.

Their busy activity disturbed a cloud of butterflies that was settled on the same mud patch as before, and as they rose into the air and fluttered away Rann straightened up from his task for a moment and wiped his forehead with his handkerchief, and his eyes followed the brightly coloured cloud. And then, without warning, they left the insects and locked with Storm's, and something intangible flew for a moment between them. Then, just as suddenly, whatever it was folded its wings and disappeared like the butterflies, and Rann turned once again to his task, and there was only her own wildly beating heart to tell Storm that it had been there at all, and the bleak, empty space to prove that it had gone.

'The tusks must be worth a fortune,' she remarked. One by one the men loaded them into the waiting panniers. Their own elephant stood docilely enough, snatching now and then at a clump of nearby wild bamboo, and chewing contentedly, like a child licking a lollipop while its mother collected the groceries, Storm thought amusedly.

'It'll help to finance one or two of the projects Krish has in mind for the Game Reserve,' Rann agreed.

'It's filled both the panniers.' Storm felt an illogical resentment rise in her that the tusks had taken up both the panniers. She had not wanted to ride here. Now she most urgently wanted to ride back.

'The elephant needs a balanced load,' Rann observed, and added, 'I'll help you on the way back. You rode out, so you won't be too tired to make the return journey on foot.'

He had it all planned, Storm told herself furiously. He'd got it all worked out beforehand. But with his hand holding her own to guide her; with his arm round her to lift her over the rougher stretches of the track, no matter how hard she tried to hold on to her anger, it would not last, and without it she had no armour against him, and her feet tripped lightly in tune with her treacherous heart, that wished the journey back to the bungalow might go on and on, for ever.

'I think we've earned a long, cool drink don't you?' The ivory was locked away in the godown, and a slim, brown, competent-looking man sat crosslegged and watchful in the shade of the store hut, nursing a rifle on his lap with an ease of manner that spoke volumes for his familiarity with the weapon. The oozie had disappeared with his elephant, and there was just Rann and herself, and no one else in the bungalow, because Le and Krish had not yet returned from the work site.

'Spoon some more honey into it, if it isn't sweet enough.' He poured from a large stone jug, and handed her a tall glass, and she sipped gratefully. The drink was cool and sweet, with an underlying sharpness, but it was not capable of quenching the sudden fire than ran through her veins at the accidental touch of his hand as she took the glass from him, at the cool green stare of his eyes as they met her own above the rim.

'It's sweet enough.' The sharpness of it screwed up her face, while the sweetness tempted her to drink again, risking the bite of it on her tongue. It was like her relationship with Rann, sweet and bitter at one and the same time, tempting her to touch, and knowing that to touch was to be hurt.

'More?' he asked.

'No, thank you.' Storm shook her head. It was not more to drink that she craved. Her heart yearned for refreshment that food and drink could never give. 'Save the rest for when Le and Krish come back,' she suggested.

'Le and Krish won't be back for some time yet,' he replied with quiet certainty, and taking her glass from her suddenly nerveless fingers, he put it on the table alongside his own, and reaching out a long arm he encircled her waist and drew her towards him.

'Krish might be back early today. They might come back because of the ivory.' Panic made her babble as he bent his head above her.

'The elephant bells will warn us in good time.' His lips silenced her protests. They pressed firmly down upon her own, savouring the tender fullness of her mouth, touching her blue-veined lids, and discovering the frantically beat-

ing pulse spot deep in the hollow of her throat. A low
murmur that was no longer a protest broke from her
parted lips, and she lifted her face to his, seeking his mouth
with her own, its magic touch rendering her ears deaf to
the approach of elephant bells, and capable of listening
only to the wild, sweet peal of joy that rang in her heart,
unheeding the insistent alarm that clamoured in her mind,
warning of the underlying sharpness, and the pain.

CHAPTER EIGHT

'I THOUGHT you might have an encounter with Maung
Chi and his men, once they discovered you'd removed
their cache of ivory.' Krish poured himself a drink from
the jug, and slaked his thirst with relish. 'We came back
early in case you might need reinforcements.'

He did not seem to notice her flushed cheeks and
tousled hair, Storm thought with relief. She drew sharply
apart from Rann as the game warden and his wife saun-
tered towards the bungalow from the direction of the village, and straightened her curls with hurried hands. Her
head still reeled from the feel of Rann's fingers combing
through her hair, playing with the springy, clinging soft-
ness of it, and it was with an effort she managed to quieten
her panting breath as the two ascended the bungalow
steps hand in hand.

'Le suspects,' she realised confusedly. The other girl's
eyes were more discerning, and she gave Storm a mischievous smile, but to the latter's relief Le said nothing,
and contented herself with sipping her drink, and listening
as the two men conversed.

'We saw nothing of the poachers,' Rann replied, and
added soberly, 'At a guess I'd say they were busy trying
to track down that wounded elephant. They're unlikely
to feel easy about their own safety on that score, and
they've no reason to suspect that we're aware of where
their ivory hoard is hidden. *Was* hidden,' he corrected
himself with satisfaction. 'Did you see any sign of the

elephant, on your way back from the site?' he questioned Krish.

'None.' The game warden shook his head. 'We kept a sharp lookout, but there was nothing.'

'What do you think the animal might do? Assuming that it's still on its feet, that is?' Rann deferred to the game warden's superior knowledge.

'It'll make for water,' Krish replied with certainty, 'particularly if its wounds induce a fever.'

'That means the river. Our arm of the river,' Le realised, her eyes wide with concern. 'The other arm isn't flowing yet.'

'I know,' Krish nodded seriously. 'But at least it'll be on the other side of the river from here. It'll probably hide out in the kaing grass. It grows by water,' he explained kindly to Storm. 'It's tall, anything up to twelve feet high, and sufficient to provide cover as well as fodder for the animal. Luckily there's none on this side of the river for a considerable distance on either side of the village. The people have cleared the land for their crops.'

'The elephant might come across, to raid the crops for food.' Le looked apprehensive.

'I doubt it,' Krish shook his head reassuringly. 'Remember, the creature's been wounded. How badly, we don't know, but it's bound to be weakened, and in that condition it's most likely to seek cover and easy grazing, and the kaing grass will provide both, as well as being close to water. Fortunately the banks of the river are fairly steep, so they should act as a deterrent to its trying to cross. With its immediate needs provided for, there'll be nothing to drive it across the water, so anyone on this side of the river should be safe enough,' he asserted confidently. 'The danger lies in meeting the animal in the jungle on the other side of the river, going to and from the worksite, but all my rangers are armed and on the lookout. The problem on this side of the water will arise from Maung Chi and his men wanting their ivory back,' he deduced shrewdly.

'The poachers won't have any scruples about trying to recover it,' Rann agreed, 'and once they discover their hoard's missing, they won't be long in working out who's responsible, and where it's likely to be held. Mac can tell them where the godown is, in relation to the layout of the village.'

'From there, it'll be a short step to them putting their heads together and planning how to get it back,' Krish predicted. 'They're almost certain to try,' he added worriedly. 'I just wish I knew how they intended to go about it.'

'We'll double the guard on the godown during the hours of darkness,' Rann decided. 'You and I can take turn about to keep the guard company during the night, and one of us must always be on hand here during each day until we can get a police helicopter to collect the whole load of tusks and take them into safe keeping.'

'I could usefully use another day on site,' Krish began doubtfully.

'In that case, I'll remain here tomorrow, and you take the next turn of duty.' Rann settled the rota decisively, his whole attention taken up with what he was planning with Krish. Forgetting the sweet moments that had passed between them as if they had never happened. Anger burned in Storm at his easy forgetfulness. She stared at him with brooding eyes. He was as impenetrable as the jungle itself, shutting her out as surely as the dark wall of green on the other side of the river hid its secrets from her eyes.

, They're both alike, her thoughts ran miserably. Cruel, heartless. I hate them both, she told herself passionately, and back came the refrain that for a few bright, transient moments she had almost forgotten, If only I could get away! She stirred restlessly, and flicked at a persistent fly with an irritable hand. The cooling effect of her drink had worn off, and the heat seemed more oppressive than ever.

'I'm tired of ivory, and poachers, and landslips too.' Le sent her a keen glance. 'I want to wash my hair, and try on some pretty dresses, for a change,' she hinted.

'Come and try on the ones in my suitcase.' Storm jumped up eagerly, but although she was sitting next to Rann, he did not turn round. 'He won't even notice I've gone,' she thought drearily, and with an immense effort made her voice bright and interested for Le. 'You said you regretted not bringing a trouser suit with you, from the reserve.'

'I should have brought at least one,' Le acknowledged. 'Slacks are hot, but they're more convenient to wear on site than a lungyi.'

'I've got two trouser suits in my case, you can have one of them if they fit.'

'I'll be glad to,' Le responded gratefully. 'Slacks really are better than skirts when you want to take long strides. I find a lungyi a hindrance when I want to climb over rocks and debris on the site.'

'I haven't mastered the art of walking in a lungyi yet.' What was the point? Storm wondered drearily, but she had to keep up the pretence in front of Le. 'I forget, and stride out, and trip myself up.'

'You'll have plenty of time to practise tomorrow,' Le consoled. 'Rann's staying here to be near the godown, so you'll have all day. If you can learn to wear a lungyi and be comfortable in it, you'll have the perfect excuse to buy a new one when the market comes upriver,' she smiled.

'A market? Coming here? I thought Rann said there was no wheeled transport capable of coming this far inland?' Storm's brow darkened. If Rann had deceived her about the transport, she would never forgive him, she told herself fiercely. If he had loaned her the transport she asked him for, to get her to the coast, she would still be heartwhole, and the heartache and the misery, and the longing and the loathing that tore her in two, need never have been.

'The market comes up the river, literally,' Le explained. 'The traders bring their wares by canoe, and set up shop along the banks. It's a once-a-year treat, when the monsoon spate has gone from the waterways, and before the dry season renders the level of the river too low for it to be navigable.' The other girl's eyes sparkled in anticipation and Storm regarded her curiously. Le was highly educated, professional, with a string of letters after her name that could command her a well paid post anywhere in the world, and yet she was still able to take a child's delight in a simple village market. Suddenly, Storm felt envious of her wholehearted enjoyment of her environment, her dedicated acceptance of her way of life that, so long as she was with Krish, needed nothing but the barest essentials to make her happy.

'What do the traders usually bring with them?' Storm was not interested, but anything was better than the silence that gave free rein to her thoughts.

'Anything the jungle can't provide,' Le said simply. 'Rolls of cotton, anything made of metal, like cooking utensils, and bangles and so on, and combs for the women's hair. There's fruit and vegetables that can't be grown in this particular area, and of course dried sea fish.'

'But what can they possibly take in return?' For the life of her, Storm could not see what the village could provide that the coast could not.

'Why, woven baskets and pottery ware, of course,' Le looked surprised. 'You've seen for yourself some of the things the people weave from the rushes, and the mud from the river banks hereabouts makes wonderful pots. But of course, human nature being what it is, the women like the metal cooking pots best,' she laughed. 'You'll see, the canoes will be here at any time now that the river level's reasonable,' she promised.

'Would the traders take me back to the coast with them, when they return?' Storm asked impulsively. 'If they've sold their produce, there's bound to be space left in the canoes.'

She should have felt elation at the prospect of getting away, from the jungle and from Rann, but the pang that twisted her heart as she waited for Le's reply hurt almost as badly as the pain that was already lodged there. She listened with bated breath as Le spoke.

'The traders don't sell for money,' the other girl reiterated patiently. 'They barter their goods with the local people for clay pots and woven baskets. The canoes have to return fully laden to make their journey worthwhile. They won't have room for a passenger,' she said sympathetically.

Storm winced at her innocent choice of words. Rann hadn't room for a passenger, either, she thought bitterly.

Her coming had disrupted his work, causing men to be taken from the work site. It had also netted him a large haul of ivory which would bring ultimate benefit to the game reserve, but the thought was small consolation to her later as she tossed wide-eyed and restless in the darkness of her room, and tried in vain to find a cool spot on the sheets on which to rest her fevered body in the breathless heat.

She pressed desperate hands against her ears, striving to shut out the incessant pattering of dew on the bungalow roof, that hammered like tiny drumbeats throughout each night, accompanying the wider orchestra of night sounds from the jungle outside, a constant chorus of coughs and grunts, chirps and croaks, made all the more sinister to her straining ears because she could not guess what their origin might be, nor what they might portend. It was as if her whole surroundings combined in concert to try and drive her away, and she responded listlessly the next morning to Le's suggestion,

'When I went to the pool with Krish this morning, the women were already busy weaving and making pots ready for when the market canoes come. Why don't you stroll along there and take a look?' she suggested brightly. 'It'll give you a bit of practice walking in your lungyi, and you might find it interesting to watch them at work.'

Anything was better than remaining in the bungalow with Rann. He did not appear at breakfast, and neither did Krish.

'They've gone to sort out a rota of men to guard the godown,' Le explained, and drained her cup of coffee with every appearance of haste. 'Krish wants to be early on site this morning because he won't be going tomorrow. Have a nice day,' she wished Storm cheerfully, and with a quick wave of her hand she was gone.

'I'll go, too, before Rann comes back,' Storm decided. She rejected the idea of breakfast. She would eat later if she felt like it. She gave a swift look over the veranda rail, but there was no one in sight, and with a sigh of relief she picked up her hat and her fly switch and made her way down the veranda steps, keeping cautious eyes on her feet in case they tangled with the long cotton of her skirt.

'Where are you going?'

She almost fell off the bottom step when he spoke. One moment the area in the vicinity of the bungalow was deserted, and the next moment, there was Rann. Too late she realised that when she looked out across the veranda rail, he might even then have been walking below it, out of sight.

'I'm going to the village,' she blurted out, angrily conscious of her rising colour. 'Le said the women would be preparing for the market.' In her confusion the fly switch fell from her hand, and she bent quickly to pick it up, thankful for the temporary respite to hide her burning face.

'The dress becomes you.' She had put on a different one this morning, a poem of delicate yellow that made a vivid contrast to her own black eyes and curls, but his eyes looked not at her dress, but raked her face, and hair.

'I'm not wearing a siri bud, if that's what you're looking for.' Her cheeks flamed as it dawned upon her what he was looking for, and she pulled her hat over her curls with an angry tug. From where she stood on the bottom step, her face was nearly on a level with his own, and she glared hotly into his eyes, and wondered how she could dismount from the step and get round him, and go on her way without an undignified tussle to oblige him to allow her to pass. The added height of the step was an advantage, in that it brought her nearer to his own height, but he was standing directly in front of her with one hand resting lightly on the rail, and to get past him she would have to give ground and walk right round him. Pride demanded that Rann should be the one to move. Her chin lifted, and her stony look did battle with his own.

'Please let me pass.' She heard her own voice with detached disbelief. It was like the heroine of a play, demanding of the villain, 'Unhand me!' Only this was not a play. This was real life, and there was no neatly contrived ending. If Rann refused to move, she had no idea what to do next.

'Certainly.' She looked up quickly, instantly suspicious of his unexpected capitulation, but unprepared when he reached out and grasped her round the waist, and lifted her off the step and put her down in front of him, on the ground. The brim of her hat caught against his shoulder and tilted her headgear back away from her face, in imminent danger of falling off. With a quick hand he put spread fingers across the back of her head, holding it on, and by accident or design deftly tipped her face up to meet his. With a swift movement he stooped and planted a kiss on her parted lips, laughing into her startled face as he swung up the veranda steps with the mocking injunction,

'Mind you don't trip over your skirts this time!'

He made it impossible for her to walk away and *not* trip over her skirt. She was burningly conscious of him watching her, observing her every step. She did not need to turn round to know that he was leaning lazily over the rail of the veranda, his eyes keeping pace with her every move as she tugged her hat back into place, thankfully hiding her scarlet cheeks under its friendly brim, and cooling them with jerky, nervous fans of her fly switch.

The distance between the bungalow and the village huts seemed to stretch for ever. In vain Storm tried to tell herself that it was no worse than walking across a stage under the critical eye of a casting director. In vain, she drew on her acting ability to force her steps to a slow, careless stroll. The long cotton skirt caught at her toes, making her progress clumsy and uncertain, betraying her own uncertainty to Rann. Every instinct screamed at her to lift up her skirt and run, to flee to shelter from the cool green stare that, even when her back was turned and her eyes could not see him, pierced her like a knife, making her rawly aware of him as if he was walking beside her. It seemed a lifetime before she reached the perimeter of the village huts and stumbled breathless and trembling into their shelter, diving among the cluster of thatched homes to cut herself off from Rann's stare, and only then did she turn round and go limp with relief that the huts hid the bungalow from her sight, and hid herself from his.

'Oops-a-daisy!' It must be a universal language, Storm decided with quick amusement, and smiled back at the tottering baby who staggered towards her out of the nearest hut, and confidently clutched at her hand and her skirt as being the nearest support for uncertain legs. The baby's weight on the thin cotton bade fair to unsettle her inexpertly fixed lungyi, and Storm held the toddler upright with one hand, and grabbed at her threatened skirt with the other, the while her eyes mutely begged for help from the mother, who emerged from the hut in search of her tiny offspring. Speech was unnecessary, Storm realised thankfully. Brown eyes laughed into black. Competent arms scooped the baby on to an accustomed hip, while skilful brown fingers fixed her lungyi securely back into her waist. Friendship established, the mother put the toddler back on to his own small feet, picked up a pile of rushes, and holding one baby hand each the two women strolled together companionably towards the river bank, to join others already grouped there in an impromptu working party, chattering happily as they wove intricate basketware ready for the advent of the market canoes.

The gathering was universal, too, Storm thought wistfully, watching them. It reminded her achingly of the Women's Fellowship working parties in her own village at home, busily forgathered on tasks to benefit the community, and amply repaid for their efforts by the close-knit companionship of shared lives, and shared interests, and warm friendships built up over the slow passing years. She had not realised before how much she missed it, nor how high had been the price her profession exacted, with its demand for constant change, playing for a few weeks here, a season there, and then, inexorably, travelling on again. Always seeking an elusive something on the other side of the hill, only to find it was never there, but perhaps, the next time, over the next hill. . . .

She sighed as she looked back over the road she had travelled so far, and her eyes became bleak as they viewed the road that still lay ahead. It looked empty and cold. She would return to her profession when she returned to England. Not to the lead part she had lost because of Rann, but as Le pointed out, there would be other parts for her to play. But she knew, despairingly, that the added sparkle that enlivened her performances in the past would be missing from any she might play in the future. The extra zest that lifted her work above that of other, mundane performers, because her heart was wholly dedicated to acting would be gone. In future, her performances would lack that extra zest, and fail because of it, because her heart could not belong in two places at the same time, and she had given her heart to Rann.

And he did not want it.

She hugged the toddler to her, seeking comfort from the small, warm body, and envying the soft-eyed, smiling mother with an envy that was like a spear through her heart, because all the while she held the other woman's child her arms ached to hold one that belonged to herself, and to Rann.

As if it sensed the bleakness of her thoughts, the baby began to whimper, and its mother leaned forward and coaxed it into smiles again with the soft rustle of a hand full of rushes, and with a gurgle of delight the baby slipped from Storm's arms and tottered across the sun-warmed earth, and plonked itself down amid the rushes to play. Tears stung Storm's eyes at the little one's defection, illogical, childish tears, that shamed her for her unaccustomed lack of control, and to hide them she pretended an interest she did not feel for the basket weaving going on around her.

The local women reacted with disarming friendliness. They made room for her among their circle. They showed her how to weave, giving her a ready-started basket and a supply of rushes, taking her to their hearts with a warmth that bid fair to make her tears overflow. If only Rann would do the same. . . . She blinked hard, and forced her trembling fingers to weave, and to her surprise soon found herself becoming absorbed in the task with genuine interest.

It only needs someone now to make a cup of tea, and it would be just like the working parties at home, she thought with an inward smile, and nearly laughed out loud as one of the women brought out some strange-looking fruit, and what appeared to be roots of some kind, and offered them round as refreshment to her companions. She held them out to Storm, who smiled her gratitude but took only fruit. She had not bothered with breakfast, and the emptiness inside her could have something to do with lack of food, she thought hopefully. She bit into the fruit. It had a peculiar taste, but it was pleasant enough, but she shook her head at the offer of the root. To her Western eyes it looked unpalatable, and she was unwilling to offend her companions by taking food that she did not want to eat. The donor pressed her earnestly, pushing the root towards her, patently concerned that she did not want it, and Storm hesitated. Perhaps she should just take a little, and maybe forget to eat it without making it too obvious. She was about to stretch out her hand and accept some, when the baby sneezed.

'Bless you!' she responded automatically, and swallowed her fruit just as her own nose began to tickle. Her sneeze seemed to set off a veritable epidemic among her companions, and she burst out laughing. Then she stopped, because she realised that the other women, far from laughing, had gone deathly quiet, and their faces were serious, and watchful. It was then that Storm smelled smoke.

. 'Surely it can't be one of the cooking fires?' It was too early in the day for the women to be cooking. She had not seen a single fire alight when she came among the village huts.

'It's coming from the other side of the river,' she realised with relief, as a thin haze came drifting towards them from across the water. For a horrid moment she had feared that one of the cooking fires had got out of hand. Reassured, she relaxed, and picked up a piece of prettily striped reed and held it out towards the baby, hoping to attract its attention, but even as she turned the mother snatched the child into her arms, and a babble of chatter broke out among the women. A shrill cry from one of them brought the older children from playing in the shallows of the pool. Storm noticed their instant obedience with approval, and within minutes the mothers had gathered up their basket work, and shepherding their young ones before them, disappeared into their respective huts, and shut themselves in. The baby's mother made urgent gestures for Storm to follow her.

Surely the smoke isn't all that bad? Storm felt puzzled

by their seeming panic. Perhaps it's just that I don't understand their language. It might not be panic at all, but merely the women giving vent to their feelings about the smoke disturbing their pleasant working party, she decided, conscious of her own ignorance of their mode of speech. Nevertheless, she followed her new-found friend. She had no desire to get her delicately coloured skirt smudged by sooty smoke, and it would be interesting to see inside one of the small thatched homes. She was almost up to the doorway when she remembered her half-finished basket.

It only needed a spark to destroy it. She had worked hard on her basket. If she took it back to the bungalow with her, Le would show her how to finish it off, and having something to occupy her hands would help her to get through the evening. Her mind shied away from the evening, the long hours when, somehow, she would have to force her tongue to make polite conversation; force her bruised mind to concentrate on something, anything else, besides, 'Rann, oh, Rann. . . .' Suddenly the basket became necessary to carry her through the evening ahead. The smoke was a lot thicker now, and getting worse by the second. She could hear the sinister crackle of fire from the high wall of light, waving grasses on the other side of the river.

Thank goodness the waterway's good and wide, she thought. It should stop the fire easily. The huts were situated by the pool, which was much shallower than the river proper, and a lot wider, with long, sloping banks, and there was little to catch fire on this side of the water except for light scrub, which was growing well away from the huts themselves.

Ugh! It's as bad as garden bonfires at home. Storm pressed her handkerchief over her nose and mouth, and bent to pick up her basket. I'll get back to the bungalow, never mind going into one of the huts. The doors were all tightly shut against the smoke now, anyway. She straightened up with the basket safely in her hand, and froze where she stood.

The elephant saw her, at the same moment that she saw the elephant. It was an enormous tusker. Its long, gleaming ivories made a fearful sight as it emerged through the smoke at a lumbering run. As if in a nightmare, she heard Krish's voice saying,

'It'll seek cover, and easy grazing, and the kaing grass will provide both. There'll be nothing to drive it across the water.'

The fire was driving it across the water now. She stared at it with horrified eyes, heard again Rann's warning, 'It'll attack on sight,' and knew that it was about to do just that.

'Rann! Rann!'

The elephant's enraged bellow drowned her scream. Its huge ears flapped like warning flags, and it curled its trunk into its mouth like a coiled spring and charged towards her through the pool, scattering water in waves on either side.

Even as she turned to run, Storm knew she had no chance. Its wounds had done nothing to curtail the animal's speed, and it came at her through the water three times as fast as she could possibly run. She grabbed up her skirt and ran just the same. Her breath sobbed in her throat, and her heart pounded in an almost unbearable stitch of pain in her side. She could feel the vibration of the huge beast's pounding feet beating into her through the hard, hot earth. The huts loomed up as if in a mist, and she spun towards them, instinct making her take the one desperate chance for her life. If she could dodge among the huts, out of the animal's sight. . . . The sharp turn was her undoing. At the sight of the huts she forgot her skirt. Her nerveless fingers loosed it to hold her aching side, and the cotton dropped round her feet in a tangling drape that caught at her toes and sent her sprawling on to her face.

She hit the ground with a force that knocked the breath from her body, and cowered where she lay, her hands over her head, in an extremity of terror such as she had never experienced before, helpless to move, and too frightened even to think.

CHAPTER NINE

'Rann! Rann!'

Desperately Storm pressed herself against the inhospitable earth, and her lips formed his name in a wordless cry, over and over again. She had all the time in the world to cry his name. All the time in the world, and none.

If only. . . . Bitter regret washed over her at the useless waste of it all. It did not occur to her until much later that the regret was only for Rann, for what might have been between them, and achingly, was not. She did not regret her lost career, the lure of fame and wealth that would inevitably have been hers; the tinsel glitter and the excitement of constant change in what could have been a dazzling career. In the last few seconds she had left to her, before the elephant exacted its ultimate revenge for someone else's crime, her thoughts had room only for one thing.

'Rann . . . Rann. . . .' she moaned faintly.

Her terror-numbed mind did not register the shot at first. The thundering vibration bearing down upon her rocked the earth, coming closer . . . closer. . . .

Crack!

The thundering vibration stopped, and a skidding, slithering sound replaced it. A pause, and then a slow, heavy thump shook the earth. Then silence. Blessed, heavenly silence, that left her fainting body supported on the hard ground, and left her mind unhindered to think its thoughts of Rann. From what seemed to be a long way away, she heard footsteps racing towards her, light, human footsteps, that did not vibrate through the earth. Rann's footsteps. Even as she recognised them, they stopped beside her.

'Storm?'

He slid to his knees beside her and lifted her up, cradling her close in his arms. She opened her eyes, and his face swam into her line of vision, blurred and indistinct,

and out of focus. She resented it being out of focus. It was
the one thing in the world that she wanted to see clearly,
while she still had time. She blinked to try to clear her
eyes. She felt his fingers stroke back her hair from her face,
lightly tossing aside the soft black curls, and knew a pang
of regret that they did not stay to play with them, as they
had done on the veranda. Perhaps they, too, knew that
there was not time. . . .

'Storm?'

The urgency in Rann's voice penetrated the daze that
clouded her mind, and she blinked again, more successfully this time, because his face came into focus, clear,
and strained, and oddly white under its mahogany tan. It
hovered over her, blotting out the rest of the world,
wrapping her in a small, safe cocoon in which there was
only herself and Rann.

'Can you stand up?'

Why should she want to stand up? she wondered
vaguely. All that she wanted, all that she would ever want,
was to remain where she was now, cradled in Rann's
arms, caught to him in a close embrace, except, perhaps,
that she wanted to put her own arms round him, to hold
him even closer. She gave a small sigh and stirred, and
lifted her arms to put them round him.

'Try to stand up,' he urged her. He did not seem to
understand that she wanted to remain where she was for
ever. She tried to tell him, but for some reason her voice
refused to work, and he lifted her up and stood her on her
feet, but even though he supported her against him, with
his one arm still round her, it was not the same. The
world came back, tearing aside her precious cocoon. The
baby's mother ran from her hut and came towards them,
talking rapidly to Rann. She saw his face harden, and he
replied in words that Storm could not understand, but
which clearly satisfied the woman, because she went back
into her hut again, leaving them alone, but the precious
moments were gone, damaged beyond repair. Resentment
at the unwanted intrusion burned in Storm, even as
delayed shock caught up with her and she began to tremble violently in his arms.

'The elephant crossed the river.' The trembling turned

into long, convulsive shudders, that shook her slight frame like a mighty wind among aspen leaves. Urgently she tried to stop them, but the shock was too strong, the terror too recent, and she clung to Rann with shaking hands and let the tears flow, washing away the fear and the shock. 'I was so afraid.' But not for herself, only afraid that she would never see Rann again. She raised drenched eyes to his, willing him to understand.

'You should have gone with the other women, into the huts. You'd have been safe enough if you'd gone with them. The woman who came up to us just now said she tried to make you go with her.' His tone criticised her for not going, for placing herself in danger unnecessarily. Storm stared up at him, stunned, unable to believe his criticism. Surely he must know that she did not understand, when the women tried to make her go with them? She had been about to follow them into the huts, but because of the language barrier she had not understood the dire urgency, the need to go with them right away. She had thought they were merely fleeing the choking effects of the smoke from the burning kaing grass. Suddenly it became important that she should make Rann realise she had not understood. In a high, shrill voice, she defended herself.

'I *was* going with the women. I was going with the baby's mother into her hut, but I went back to fetch my basket. They gave me a basket that had been started, and a supply of rushes, and showed me how to weave.' She stammered to a halt, appalled at the green fire in his eyes.

'You—did—what?' He ground out the words like bullets, through furiously gritted teeth. 'You actually risked your life, to go back for a rush basket? You risked being trampled to death, for the sake of a paltry basket?' he shouted incredulously. His voice, his lips, were tight with anger against her.

Put like that, her action was indefensible. But it was not like that at all. Anger rose in Storm to match his own, at the injustice of his criticism, at his obtuseness in not understanding her lack of comprehension of the danger, the urgency. Her anger dried her tears, and thrust aside the shock, and she shouted back at him in fiery justification.

'How was I to know what would happen? I thought the women were running to get away from the smoke. I wasn't to know that the elephant would come charging out at me like that!'

'Krish told us it would seek shelter in the kaing grass,' Rann retorted harshly, 'you were there when he said it, so you must have heard.'

But again, she had not understood. 'I didn't even know it *was* kaing grass growing on the other bank,' she flung back at him wrathfully. 'I'm not an expert on the flora and fauna of the Kheval Province. Besides, Krish said the animal wouldn't cross the river.' If Rann could use Krish's remarks as a weapon against her, so could she against Rann, Storm decided hotly. It was unfair to blame the game warden, when the real danger lay in her own ignorance of the local conditions, but the only alternative was to accept Rann's blame, and that she refused to do.

'If you'd gone with the other women, it wouldn't have happened.'

'If you'd lent me the transport to get to the coast in the first place, when I asked you to, none of it would have happened,' she thrust back at him spiritedly. 'It isn't my fault I came here, but it's your fault I've remained.' She hated the place, she told herself passionately, she loathed the whole wide Province, where danger lurked at every step, almost as much as she hated Rann.

'Thakin?' The baby's mother approached them again, and in her hands—Storm's eyes widened—she held a long, thin-bladed knife. Instinctively Storm shrank back against Rann, but he only nodded to the woman, and spoke, and with a cheerful smile she hurried off again. Storm turned to watch her go, and for the first time since she fell, she saw the elephant, around which the women from the village were already starting to gather, chattering and gesticulating.

What a waste! Suddenly the anger and the shock and the fear died within her, and left only an immense pity. 'What a waste,' she whispered brokenly. What a short time before had been vital, pulsing life now lay in a pathetic, crumpled heap beside the pool. Even now the animal looked enormous, and Storm shivered again, and tried

not to think what might have happened if it had not been
for Rann.

'It isn't all waste.' His voice was crisply practical. 'The
animal will provide the village with meat for a long while
to come, and the tusks can go to join the others in the
godown—they'll eventually benefit the game reserve.'

'Elephant meat?' Storm had not regarded elephants as
being edible before.

'The women cut it up and dry it. It lasts well if it's
preserved properly.'

'Ugh!' The thought of performing such a grisly task
sent fresh shudders through Storm, this time of revulsion.
'Can't the women wait until the men come home from
the site, and leave them to do it?'

'They daren't wait, because of the heat,' Rann responded. 'They have to do it right away, while the meat's
still fresh. I shouldn't stay to watch, if I were you,' he
advised her sagely as more women hurried past, with
knives, and baskets similar to those which they had been
weaving on the river bank. 'They'll start right away, and
be busy at it for the rest of the day. Come back to the
bungalow, where it's cool.'

And where she would be out of the way? She went with
him, just the same. She had no wish to see the erstwhile
working party engaged on their present task. Perhaps it
was the thought of that, or maybe the aftermath of shock,
that made her feel so sick. Urgently she longed to stretch
out on one of the long cane chairs on the veranda, and
close her eyes and forget everything, particularly Rann.
The fire left her, and she clung to his arm and stumbled
beside him with dragging steps, the cane chair acting as a
magnet on the journey back that seemed to be twice as
long as when she started out. She swayed to a halt at the
bottom of the veranda steps, and measured their height
with dismayed eyes.

I'll never get up them without help, she told herself
with conviction, and said aloud, faintly, 'I don't think I
can manage.'

'Thakin! Thakin!'

A wild outburst of shouting came from by the godown.
Vaguely Storm thought she detected the uncouth tones of

Mac's voice. Vaguely the thought crossed her mind that he must have escaped unhurt after all, after he had shot at the elephant.

'Thakin. . . .'

. 'Hold on, I'm coming!' Rann reacted with quicksilver speed. He gave no sign that he had even heard her own plea for help, Storm thought resentfully. With a quick injunction to, 'Help yourself to a drink, there's a supply of cooled fruit juice in the kitchen,' he left her to her own devices and ran towards the mêlée erupting outside the door of the godown. Dimly the realisation penetrated the fog in Storm's mind that there was some sort of raid going on. Men were trying to get into the godown, and the guard was battling to prevent them. Rann was going to the man's rescue and leaving her to mount the veranda steps as best she could, alone.

'The ivory's more important to him than I am,' she muttered.

Anger at Rann's desertion gave her the necessary strength to force her failing legs to mount the veranda steps, one painful step at a time, clinging on to the rail beside them with both hands, in order to hold herself upright. After what seemed a lifetime of effort she reached the top, and a wave of faintness engulfed her and nearly sent her down again to the bottom. With an immense effort of will she rallied her failing senses and stumbled the other way, towards the long cane chair. She collapsed into it, and lay back and closed her eyes, and gave herself up to the welcome darkness that blotted out the noise from the godown, and Rann, and the gripping nausea that threatened to overwhelm her.

She could not have been in a faint for very long. Not nearly long enough, she decided with a grimace as a stab of agony shot through her and brought her back to harsh reality with a painful jolt. She sat up with a groan, and clutched her middle. It felt as if a whole herd of elephants, not just one, was running all over it.

'I told you to help yourself to a drink. There's plenty in the kitchen.'

Rann was back. He held a big stone jug in one hand, and a couple of glasses in the other, and liquid made cool pouring sounds as he charged the two.

'Have a drink of this.' He offered her one of the glasses, and she shook her head. 'It'll cool you down,' he insisted, still proffering the glass.

'I couldn't touch it,' she gasped, and doubled up as a specially severe pang pierced right through her.

'Hey, what's the matter?' He put down the jug and the glasses and bent over her, his face registering concern. It was a bit late for him to start feeling concern, Storm thought waspishly, but she felt in no condition to tell him so. 'Did you hurt yourself when you fell?'

'No,' she answered him shortly, too overwhelmed by the pain to attempt to enlarge.

'Which side does it hurt?' He pulled up the back of the cane chair to make an easy rest for her. She would much rather he let her rest in his arms, the pain might have felt better if he did, she thought wistfully. Her heart mourned the bleakness of having to rest on the chair back, instead of in his arms, but her middle gave her no rest at all, it carried on hurting with a fierceness that began to frighten her.

'If you're worried about appendicitis, forget it,' she told him baldly. 'I had my appendix out years ago.' That was some comfort, but the pain left an open question to which she had not got an answer.

'If you didn't hurt yourself when you fell down, and it isn't appendicitis, then it must be something you've eaten,' Rann used the process of elimination in a confident voice.

'It can't be anything I've eaten.' She felt a perverse satisfaction at being able to undermine his confidence. The last thing he could accuse her of was greed, she told herself thankfully. 'I've had nothing except a piece of fruit since dinner last night.'

'What sort of fruit? Was it something Gurdip gave to you?'

What did it matter what sort of fruit it was? she asked herself crossly. It was only a couple of mouthfuls anyway, so it could not be that.

'Tell me,' he insisted, and rather than argue she gave in, and told him.

'It was . . . ooh . . .!' Between groans she gave as good a

description as she could remember of what the fruit was like. 'Gurdip didn't give it to me. The women were all eating it, by the river bank, and they gave me some. It didn't upset them, so it couldn't have been that.'

'Did they give you anything else to eat with it?'

What did he have to keep on about the fruit for? Storm wondered crossly, and snapped,

'If you must know, they offered me what looked like a root of some kind. It looked horrid.'

'And you didn't eat any of it?' he guessed shrewdly.

'No, it looked revolting—I told you.' How he guessed she had no idea, but it was no concern of Rann's what she ate and what she did not, she told herself angrily. He would be telling her how to breathe in and out, next. . . .

'That's your trouble,' he diagnosed crisply.

'What is?' She gazed up at him in bleary puzzlement, relieved and resentful at his easy confidence at one and the same time. She could never imagine a time when Rann did not feel supremely confident in his own decisions, she thought crossly, but she felt too ill to challenge his diagnosis, she only hoped he would be equally confident about prescribing something to relieve her agony.

'The fruit's delicious, all the local people are very partial to it.' She could have told him that, the women had eaten of it freely. 'But it contains a powerful irritant, for which the root they offered you holds an antidote. To eat the one without the other is courting disaster.' And she had eaten one without the other, and disaster had struck. She looked up into his face, and hated him for the glint of laughter that lit his eyes at her predicament.

'It isn't funny,' she groaned bitterly.

'Not to you,' he agreed blithely, and she could have slapped him, but she did not have the strength. 'I'll get you something to cure your collywobbles,' he promised with maddening cheerfulness, and disappeared kitchenwards, whistling under his breath. 'I'll mix it with your drink, then it won't taste quite so awful.' He returned and poured a finely ground powder into her glass, and stirred it briskly, while Storm watched him with deepening suspicion. The powder had the exact colouring of the root that the local women had offered to her.

'It's the same root,' he confirmed, reading her look accurately, 'only it's ground up finely. Now drink it. All of it,' he insisted, and held the glass against her lips with his one hand and the back of her head with the other.

'Don't drown me in it!' she gurgled, and tried to wriggle free from his hold.

'I'm making sure you drink all of it,' he insisted as she tried to shudder away from the half empty glass. The root was finely ground, but the drink did nothing to disguise its awful taste, she discovered. 'Take another couple of swallows, and finish it up.' He held the glass to her lips remorselessly. 'I don't want my sleep disturbed by your groans in the night.'

'It tastes awful!'

'The taste will make you remember in future to do whatever the local people do. That's your only protection, until you're used to the do's and don'ts of life in the jungle,' he told her practically.

'I shan't be staying here long enough to need to find out the do's and the don'ts,' she assured herself grimly. The inexorable flow of the antidote drink into her mouth prevented her from saying so out loud. Rann was only concerned about himself, about the possibility of his own sleep being disturbed, not about her wellbeing, and he did not try to hide the fact, she told herself resentfully. If it had been the other way round, with Rann feeling ill and herself doing the nursing, she would not have cared about losing sleep.

'Lie back and rest,' he advised her briskly when she had swallowed the last of the evil-tasting concoction to his satisfaction. 'You should begin to feel normal in half an hour or so, the root works quickly when it takes hold. I'll be in the radio room if you want me.'

She would always want him, but pride forbade that she should tell him so. She wiped her lips with an angry rub of her hand, then lay back and closed her eyes, feigning indifference. He might have stayed with me, if only for a few minutes, she thought miserably, but his footsteps receded in the direction of the radio room, she heard the door open and the atmospherics crackle as he snapped the set into action, and began to speak.

'Moorcroft here. . . .'

Then his voice became muffled and indistinct, and she knew he had closed the door, shutting her off from him, so that she should not hear what he was about to say.

'I don't want to listen to his conversation,' she muttered to herself crossly. She only wanted to listen to the sound of his voice, not to the words he spoke, because they were not meant for her, so they did not interest her. They were not the words she longed to hear, would never hear, from Rann. . . .

A slow tear forced its way beneath the long curling lashes that made sooty crescents on her cheeks. Other tears threatened to follow the first one, and to hold them back she forced her mind to think of something else, anything else besides Rann.

What had happened at the godown? She concentrated desperately on the godown. She had meant to ask Rann what the uproar there had meant, but the pain inside her drove everything else out of her mind. The shouting and the sounds of strife had died away, just as the strife inside her, mercifully, was beginning to disappear. Already the worst of the pain had subsided, allowing her to lie back on the long cane chair and relax, and ponder idly on what the noise by the godown had been about. The root must be a powerful antidote to whatever it was, she decided drowsily, and gratefully allowed her weary body, and even wearier mind, to slip into healing sleep.

CHAPTER TEN

'To think, the last thing I said to you before I went off with Krish to the work site this morning was, "Have a nice day"!' Le laughed.

She perched on the edge of the table and watched amusedly as Storm struggled up in the cane chair, rubbing her eyes and yawning, and trying not very successfully to shrug off the clinging shrouds of sleep.

'I must say, being chased by an elephant, raided by

ivory poachers, and poisoned by eating fruit, isn't my idea of having a nice day,' she twinkled.

'Nor mine, either,' Storm retorted ruefully. 'What brings you back so early?' she asked curiously. She did not want to think about the day so far. Having Le to talk to would effectively protect her from her own thoughts. She cast a quick look round the veranda, but Rann was nowhere in sight, and she heaved a small sigh of relief and asked, 'Is anything wrong at the site?'

'We're not early, it's knocking off time,' Le retorted. 'Krish dropped me off here to save me the walk back from the pool.' She made it sound as prosaic as a bus stop, Storm thought with quick amusement as the other girl went on, 'He's gone with the oozies to the village to see the elephant. Or what's left of it, by now,' she added.

'I didn't hear the elephant bells coming.' Storm did not want to think about that other elephant, nor about the task on which the women of the village had been engaged for the greater part of the day. 'I must have been asleep for a long time,' she realised with surprise.

'It's small wonder you slept, after the adventures you packed into the morning,' Le teased, and added half seriously, 'Perhaps it's as well, because you won't get a lot of sleep tonight if the village celebrates in its usual manner.'

'Celebrates what?' So far as she herself was concerned, there was nothing in the day to celebrate. Storm looked back on the dreadful hours behind her with a shiver.

'Having all that meat dropped almost literally on their laps,' Le enlightened her. 'The village always celebrates a successful hunt, and having meat without the need to catch it themselves is a bonus at the moment, when the men have been too busy at the work site to spare time for their usual hunting. They'll hold a feast with some of the fresh meat, and that which they've dried will last them until the job's finished on the water course, and they're free to take up their own lives again.'

I wonder if they'll want to take up their own lives again, if they'll be glad to go back to their everyday, mundane tasks? Storm asked herself drearily. And hard on the heels of the question came the frightening conviction, I won't.

I don't want to return to the stage. The thought of returning to her work filled her with dread. Her inability to sustain her self-imposed role in front of Rann eroded her confidence in her own undoubted talent, and she viewed the years ahead with haunted eyes, seeing herself experience what she had seen other, less talented artists experience before her. The soon-lost bloom of youth. The changing taste of fashion, as fickle in the theatrical world as anywhere else, and the desperate search for ever more scarce parts to fit a face and a personality that was no longer 'in'. The long, dragging weeks of what her profession euphemistically called 'resting', and the parts that were left being given to other, younger actresses, leaving only the bright tinsel of souvenirs to tarnish slowly along with the memories of the too-brief hours that gave them birth. She sighed, and swung her legs off the long cane chair.

'I'm hungry,' she discovered with surprise.

'So you should be, you haven't eaten since last night,' Le scolded.

'How did you know?'

'Rann told us when he wirelessed us about the raid on the godown,' Le said knowledgeably. 'He was on the air for quite a time, telling us about your day.'

'He didn't tell me it was a raid on the godown.' A flash of pure jealousy shot through Storm like a knife. Rann had not remained with her for a moment longer than he was absolutely obliged to, to make sure she was on the road to recovery from her malaise. He did not even wait until she was fully recovered, she remembered bitterly. He found time to talk to Le and Krish, but not to her. Resentment smouldered in her like a slow fire as she sat beside him at the dinner table a short time later, and listened to him talking freely over the events of the day with the game warden and his wife.

'There's no doubt the poachers set fire to the kaing grass deliberately, to drive the elephant into the village,' he said to Krish in a clipped voice.

'Surely not?' Storm came to the table determined not to listen if Rann did discuss the day's events. If he would not talk to her about them beforehand, she would not show any interest now, she vowed, but in spite of her resolution to hold herself aloof she could not contain her gasp of horror at his words. 'What a terrible thing to do!' She blanched as she remembered the number of children who had been splashing in the shallows of the pool, playing about the banks while their mothers worked on their baskets in the sunshine. The poachers must have known the elephant would cross the river at the point where the banks were not so steep. 'They must have known?' She raised huge eyes to Krish, appalled by the trend of her own thoughts.

'They mean to get the ivory back,' the warden confirmed them. 'No doubt they hoped to use the elephant as a diversion that would send everyone running for cover, including the guard at the godown, and use the confusion to break into the store. They reckoned without Rann being here,' he finished with satisfaction.

'They took to their heels quickly enough when I arrived on the scene,' Rann grinned, and Storm swivelled a look of dislike in his direction.

The conceit of the man! she thought disparagingly, to assume that it was only he who had put the miscreants to flight. The guard at the godown was doing very well before he arrived, to judge from the uproar she had heard.

'What if the poachers come back?' Le looked nervous.

'I doubt if they'll make another raid right away,' Rann answered her confidently. 'They received a severe lesson at their first attempt, and they'll be in no great haste to report their failure to Maung Chi, I imagine. And besides,' he added casually, 'the men of the village will all be around for the next two days, which should effectively deter them from trying another break-in. The locals have no cause to love the poachers.'

'Won't the men be going to the work site?' Storm bit her lip vexedly. She had not meant to ask him, but it slipped out before she could stop it.

'We're giving the men and the animals a couple of days' rest.'

'Two days?' That was the length of time it would have taken a man to canoe her as far as the coast. 'You told me every minute was vital,' she flared angrily.

'Even elephants need to rest.' His green glance taunted her with the knowledge that he could stop the work on site whenever he chose, and he had not chosen to do so in order to meet her needs.

'Surely, two whole days. . . .' she criticised.

'Tomorrow the oozies won't be in any condition to work anyway,' Krish accepted events philosophically. 'The celebrations in the village will go on all night, and tomorrow the entire population will be sleeping off the effects,' he predicted. 'The next day the market canoes will be here. Everyone stops work for the market canoes, no matter how important the job is, so we might as well give in with a good grace and make the holiday official,' he grinned.

'How can you be so sure the market canoes will be here the day after next?' Perhaps that was something else Rann had heard on the radio, and not bothered to tell her about.

'Bush telegraph,' Krish enlightened her. 'Rumour flies in the jungle just as quickly as it does in a town, and it's never let us down yet,' he averred confidently. 'Oh, by the way, the village elders have invited us all to their feast tonight. Now's your opportunity to get your own back on the elephant for the fright it gave you,' he teased Storm.

'Surely they won't expect us to eat . . . no, I couldn't,' she shuddered.

'Of course they won't.' Le frowned at her husband. 'But the celebrations are worth joining, just the same,' she went on persuasively. 'There'll be mime, and dancing, and music. It'll be something to tell your people about when you go back home,' she coaxed.

She could not know how her remark hurt. Quick tears started in Storm's eyes, and she hurriedly used the pilot's excuse of a crumb gone down the wrong way, and took a hasty swallow at her glass to save herself from the necessity of having to reply.

'What shall we wear?' she asked, when she could control her voice sufficiently to make it sound normal, and could have laughed out loud at the incongruity of such a question. Nevertheless it remained. What did one wear to attend a celebration feast in the jungle? A trouser suit seemed wildly out of place, and might displease her hosts, whose womenfolk, in spite of their spartan way of life, yet remained essentially feminine. And she did not feel equal to struggling with another of Le's lungyis.

'Why not put on that burnt orange taffeta skirt you showed me?' Le suggested. 'It'd look gorgeous with that sleeveless black top, and the skirt's only calf length, so you won't trip up,' she added wickedly.

'What colour will you wear?' Clothes were a nice safe topic that held no snares, and Storm pursued it with a kind of desperation, all the while achingly conscious of Rann sitting silent beside her. Listening to her? Or bored, and wishing he was free to get on with the only thing that seemed to interest him, the job on the site. She stole a glance at his face, but he was looking down into his coffee cup with an inscrutable expression that gave her no clue as to where his thoughts might lie. Probably at the work site, she surmised drearily, and replied automatically to Le,

'The burnt orange skirt's a good idea.' She knew she looked good in it, and she wanted to look good tonight. She wanted to look especially good, for Rann, even though he would not notice what it was she wore.

'I'll wear pink,' Le decided, 'I've got a new blouse. Come and see,' she invited, 'the men will be ages drinking their coffee.'

'We'll give you exactly half an hour, and no more,' Krish called after them firmly, but glancing back Storm saw that Rann was already on his feet, his coffee cup pushed aside, and making his way with swift strides towards the veranda steps, as if he was impatient to be gone, and could hardly wait until she had left the table to release him to something more important, in his eyes.

Perhaps he would make some excuse, and stay away from the celebrations. He would want to be with the village people, she knew. There was a reciprocated liking and respect she had noticed between them, that she felt sure under any other circumstances would have made his absence impossible, but tonight Le and Krish would be together, and inevitably it would leave herself to be escorted by Rann.

'If he doesn't want to be with me, I'd much rather he stayed away,' she lied to herself stoutly, and swallowed back the ready tears that seemed always to lurk beneath the surface whenever she thought of Rann. With forced interest she inspected Le's new blouse, and the delicate silk lungyi which she held up for Storm's inspection.

'You only need a flower for your hair.' An open siri flower, the mark of a young married woman. Storm thought longingly of the sweetly scented siri bud, and resolutely thrust the thought aside, along with the swift regret that such wiles were not for her.

'Krish will bring me a flower to wear,' Le said confidently. 'It's customary,' she added casually, and Storm looked across at her enviously. She was so sure, so safe in her sureness, she compared wistfully.

'It's time we got dressed.' Le cocked her head to one side, listening. 'The drums are beginning already.' Her excitement was infectious, and in spite of her dark mood Storm felt anticipation well up inside her as she made her way to her own room and reached out her skirt and top. With quick fingers she pulled them over her head, smoothed down the clinging jet blouse that made a perfect foil for her creamy skin, and buttoned the richly coloured skirt that swirled in rustling folds over her slender hips. A pair of patent slippers to match her blouse, a quick comb through her hair, and then she was ready. It framed her face in soft dark curls, vying with the colour of her eyes which, if they were missing their usual sparkle, disguised it with quick waves of brightness that she could not quite blink away, and might serve as a disguise, she thought hopefully, to any casual observer.

'Come in, I'm ready.' She responded with surface cheerfulness to the light knock on her door. She was as ready as she would ever be to face Rann. Her mirror boosted her morale, and she turned away from her dressing table with new confidence. 'How does your blouse . . . oh!'

Rann appeared in response to her call, not Le. At the first sight of him, Storm's new-found confidence faltered, and fled. Coward. She tried to call it back, but it was not equal to the look of him standing watching her from just inside her door, tall and straight and bronzed, and dressed in fresh whites. And heart-stoppingly handsome. Her own vulnerable organ turned a painful somersault, and deserted her in the same craven manner as her courage. Without its support, a wave of giddiness assailed her, and she groped behind her and held on to the edge of the dressing table, and thought dizzily,

My skirt almost matches his hair. It was not an exact match. She concentrated on the colour with the keenness of desperation, holding on to it as an anchor for her swimming senses, lest the sight of him should make them finally desert her, and she should slip to the floor at his feet in a faint. 'My skirt's darker than his hair.' But the taffeta did not boast the crisp, touch-enticing waves of Rann's tawny mane. She had touched it once, on the veranda. A shiver spread from her fingertips down the length of her spine as she remembered the crisp feel of the waves against her hand.

'This matches your skirt,' he said, and held out something towards her.

'Matches my . . .?' She stared at it unseeingly. It wavered in front of her vision, and for a wild, hysterical moment she thought he was offering her a lock of his hair. She closed her eyes, then opened them again and saw— an orchid.

'An orchid?'

The deep orange beauty of it glowed like fire in his fingers. Like the fire that consumed her at the sight of him, burning away her courage and her heart, and leaving her to get along as best she might with the blackened ruins that were left.

'It's customary,' he said gravely.

That was what Le had said. His eyes watched her, probing her face. Waiting, as if he expected some particular response from her.

'It's lovely.' What other response did he expect? Perhaps there was some customary response, that she did not know about? Contrary to what Rann believed, Le had not initiated her into the local customs, and she stared back at him, at a loss.

'It's lovely.' That would have to suffice, because she did not know what else to say except, 'Thank you, it was kind.'

Still he waited, and the silence between them seemed to Storm's strained senses to stretch for ever. She could hear her own breathing, and the wild, uneven thumping of the pulse in her ears as her heart returned to its work and tried to make up for lost time by racing along at a pace so fast it left her dizzy again, and breathless.

'I'll pin it on for you.' He had a pin ready. He took it from his pocket, and stepped towards her. He had taken it for granted, she thought, that she would accept his gift. Rebellion stirred in her that he should take it for granted, but it was not strong enough to combat the living fire that he pinned to her blouse with fingers that seemed to scorch her shoulder with their touch through the delicate material, so that she felt convinced it must show marks of the burning. She flinched away, and he glanced up from attending to the flower, and looked at her and said,

'Did the pin touch you? I'll tuck my finger underneath, until it's fastened.' He slid his finger under the sleeveless shoulder piece of her blouse, and made the pain worse, not better, and Storm bit her lip so that she should not cry out at the hurt of it, and the even worse hurt that he had brought her the flower simply because it was customary, and had not brought it specially for her alone. To mask the hurt she spoke, breathlessly flinging words like confetti aimlessly into the silence.

'I've never seen an orchid like this one before, not even in London.' In the city it would have been wrapped in a cellophane box, perhaps with a ribbon, and sold for a fantastic price, but here. . . . She fingered the flower gently, turning away from Rann, pretending to look at it in the mirror because she could not see it closely now that it lay against her shoulder. Its glowing beauty made an exquisite corsage, fit for the most glittering assembly. Fit for a jungle celebration feast.

'They grow wild in the jungle,' Rann answered, and she looked up, startled, and met his eyes in the mirror, watching her. Still waiting for a response she did not know how to give? His words were ordinary enough on the surface, telling her the flowers grew wild close by. Trying to tell her something else? She gazed up at him, bewildered. Trying to tell her—what?

'There are butterflies too, remember?' he reminded her softly. His hands on her shoulders turned her round to face him, drawing her close against him, holding her there while his head bent above her. Her lips parted, trying to form an answer, but no sound came, and she looked back at him wordlessly. Was this what he was trying to tell her? Was he trying to defend his beloved jungle, letting her know that beauty existed, as well as fear? That fragile loveliness grew, in spite of the conflict. Love flourished, as well as evil?

What was the point of him trying to tell her all this, she asked herself bitterly, when she would never be a part of it? Soon she would be gone, and as far as Rann was concerned, forgotten. All this would be just another memory for her, another souvenir to tarnish along with the rest. Let him try to justify his love for the jungle if he could, she knew it was not love for herself. The knowledge gave her the strength to twist away from him, even as his lips pressed down upon her own, claiming the thanks for his gift that no doubt he considered his due. Their touch was torture, and wrung from her lips an anguished cry,

'No!'

With frantic hands she reached up and pushed him away from her with the strength of desperation.

'You'll crush my flower.'

It was as good an excuse as any. It was the only one her bemused mind could think of, so it would have to serve. She dared not meet his kiss. Another touch from his lips was enough to unlock a surge of longing that shook her like a mighty storm. Her will failed beneath the devastating force of it, and she pleaded with him,

'Don't crush my flower,' when what she really meant was, 'Don't crush my heart.'

'If you two don't soon come, the celebrations will be over before we get there!' Le's laughing warning floated through the door.

'Coming!' Storm called back instantly, and took advantage of Rann's momentary inattention to slip from under his hold. His hands dropped to his sides, but instead of turning away from her towards the door, as she expected him to, he stood, and for an endless moment he looked down at her, deep into the wide, frightened blackness of her eyes.

'Rann. . . .' His name was wrung from her lips. She half raised her hand to detain him.

'Come *on*, what's keeping you?' Le's light footsteps pattered along the corridor towards the door, impatient to be gone.

'Coming!' Rann answered her this time. With a last inscrutable look at Storm he turned away, and reached out a long arm and pulled the door wide, motioning her to precede him. Mechanically she obeyed. With a fixed smile on her face for Le's benefit, she moved quickly past Rann, walking jerkily, puppet-like, with trembling limbs, because the time to join the celebrations had come, and perforce she must go along with the others, no matter that her heart had never felt less like celebrating, and only beat to mourn its irretrievable loss.

CHAPTER ELEVEN

'YOUR orchid matches your skirt.' Le's eyes flew to the flower on Storm's shoulder, and her eyes smiled, a secret, knowledgeable smile that made Storm uneasy, remembering the siri bud.

I'll make Le tell me about the orchids, later, when we're alone, she promised herself. There was no time now, and in any case she did not want to ask about the flower while Rann was within earshot. The embarrassment of learning about the siri bud from him was an experience she did not wish to repeat, but this time he could not shout at her for wearing the flower, since he had chosen it and fixed it on himself.

Le's own orchid matched her blouse. It was a deep, soft pink, and she wore it on her shoulder in the same way that Rann had fixed Storm's own. It was a pity the other girl did not wear it in her hair, Storm mused. The flower would have looked lovely against the long brown mane which Le had left loose for the occasion.

Storm glanced about her interestedly as they reached the village. The elders, at whose invitation they were present, had grouped themselves crosslegged on rush mats in a position of vantage on one side of the big central clearing in the middle of the ring of huts. One large rush mat in the very centre of the group was unoccupied.

'We've got reserved seats for the show,' Krish quipped, and led the way with Rann. Le stepped in behind her husband. That, too, was probably customary, Storm thought tartly. In spite of her Western education, Le seemed content to accept the position, on this occasion at least, one step behind her husband. Perhaps it was in deference to the feelings of the village elders. Storm had not noticed her do other than walk side by side with Krish before. They usually walked hand in hand, she remembered enviously.

She fell in beside Le, and realised too late that her move brought her into the same position, one step behind Rann. For a rebellious moment she felt tempted to increase her pace and step out beside him. The position rankled, rasping at her independent spirit, but even as she started to stride out Rann stopped, and began to address the village elders in a ringing tone. It was so unexpected that it took Storm by surprise, and she only saved herself from crashing into his back by putting out her hand and fending herself off. She must have given him a considerable push, but he remained rock-steady, giving no sign that he felt the pressure of her hand against his back.

'He's got no feeling at all,' she muttered to herself unjustly as he continued to speak without a pause. He stopped with a gesture, and waited, and after a moment one of the men in the group—he looked like the oldest— replied in what was an obvious exchange of courtesies. Storm waited with some apprehension. Would she be expected to speak to them as well? Le would be able to, because she spoke the language, but. . . .

'Do whatever you see the locals do.'

Rann's recent advice came back to her with a rush of relief. It should hold good for this occasion, as well as any other, she thought thankfully, and stole a glance at Le. The other girl made no attempt to speak, she noticed. Perhaps that, too, was a male prerogative, she decided waspishly. Male chauvinism was obviously something that was not exclusive to the West. With an effort she masked her feelings, and mirrored Le's silent smile to their hosts, and hoped her impatience did not show as Rann and Krish sat down one on either side of the rush mat without waiting for the girls to sit down first.

'Surely we're not expected to sit behind them, as well as walk behind them?' Storm asked herself furiously. There would be no point in coming at all, if they had to sit behind the men, who were both much taller than Le and herself. 'We shan't be able to see a thing!'

Le put an end to her indecision by slipping gracefully down on to the mat at Krish's side. She kicked her sandals off, and tucked her feet under her lungyi, then leaned confidently back against her husband, her hand searching for, and finding, his. Storm felt a pang go through her as she watched them.

'Slip your sandals off, you'll be comfier,' Le advised her, and grinned at the expression on Storm's face. 'Once the formalities have been observed, everyone reverts to normal behaviour,' she read her thoughts with deadly accuracy, and Storm felt herself go pink. To cover her confusion she lowered herself on to the rush mat beside Le, but pride would not allow her to emulate the other girl's behaviour. Instead she slipped her sandals off and tucked her knees under her chin, spreading the full material of her skirt down to her toes, and curling her arms round her legs to give her the support she needed, holding herself apart from Rann, emphasising her independence, and trying to ignore the bleakness that washed over her at the feeling of isolation the separateness brought in its train.

'The drums will stop in a minute, they're only used to call everyone to the feast.'

'Thank goodness,' Storm muttered ungratefully. The insistent, throbbing summons was beginning to give her a headache, and she longed to put her hands over her ears as the noise rose to a crescendo, rendering speech impossible. She half turned away from Rann, presenting her shoulder to him, and fixed her eyes on the crowd, resenting the fact that still her inner vision saw only Rann, so close beside her, and yet so far away. With dull eyes she recognised the baby's mother at the other side of the clearing. She, too, had an orchid fixed to her shoulder, Storm noticed. To force her thoughts away from Rann she started to count the women who wore orchids. They were almost like a badge, she thought curiously. Wearing one herself made her feel as if she belonged to a club. Unaccountably she found the sensation pleasant. She took it out and examined it, savouring the feeling of oneness that it brought her. Oneness with the gathering, but not with Rann. To him she was still an unwelcome intruder. But the feeling of belonging persisted, and she hugged it to her for comfort, where no other comfort existed.

The drums stopped with an abruptness that left an even louder silence behind them. 'Now the real show begins,' Le explained in a low voice, as a hush of expectant excitement settled on the circle of onlookers, and infected Storm too, so that she leaned forward, eager to see whatever came next.

'The musicians make their own instruments, from the wild bamboo, and reeds from the river.'

There were about a dozen musicians. One man raised his pipe to his lips, and a sweet, high note floated across the silence, singularly mournful for all its beauty, seeming to seek for something, though she could not imagine what. Storm moved uneasily, strangely stirred by the single note. Others joined in, swelling the sound, and the drums followed, but muted now, serving only as a background to the pipes. The instruments might be home-made, Storm decided, but the music they produced belonged to all who held music in their hearts. She listened captivated as the sound flowed round her, now lively, with the bright notes tripping over each other in their eagerness to be heard; now quietening, until the music was a mere thin thread of sound that finally rose in a wild, triumphant climax that startled her, with its suddenness, and gripped her with a strange excitement she was unable to explain.

Rann explained it for her. He spoke deliberately, over her shoulder, and his voice thrilled through her, crystallising the excitement, and she quivered at the sound of his voice as the reeds quivered at the behest of the musicians who drew from them music they had not the power to produce alone.

'The music portrays the various stages of the hunt,' he initiated her into its language. 'The first long note was the cry of hunger.' No wonder it was so mournful! Against her will Storm found herself listening with growing attention as he went on, 'The jerky, syncopated bit that followed was the quest for food. Then came the sighting of the prey; the long, patient stalk, and finally,' he paused, and added with underlying emphasis, 'and finally the capture.'

An odd note in his voice made Storm turn round and look at him, and immediately wish she had remained with her back towards him as his eyes locked with hers, gripping her with a strange, mesmeric power, so that she could not look away. It was as if some chord deep within him vibrated to the compelling tempo of the music, the wild abandon of the notes echoing the primitive instinct of the hunter that lies unchanged beneath the surface sophistication of every man. Storm caught her breath as the music rose again, encompassing them, carrying them along on the compelling magic of its sound.

'The dancers are beginning their mime now.'

Le spoke, and it was like being torn apart from herself. With an effort that nearly cost her her consciousness, Storm wrenched her eyes away from Rann's. Her breath came in panting gasps, as prey must pant, running from the pursuer until it has no strength left to run any more. She trembled violently, as prey must tremble with fear, knowing its fate to be inevitable, and surreptitiously she wiped drenched palms against her skirt to dry them, and tried in vain to subdue their urgent need to find themselves captured and held by Rann.

'Don't let the sight of the spears bother you, they're only being used for show tonight.'

Le's laughing voice dragged her back to her surround-

ings, to the long blades held high and menacing in the
movement of the mime. Firelight flickered on the glisten-
ing dark faces of men whom she scarcely recognised as the
oozies she had seen washing their animals in the pool.
Gentle, smiling men, who before her very eyes became
transformed into fierce hunters, portraying with consum-
mate skill a tradition as old as the jungle itself. In spite of
her own preoccupation, the actress in Storm thrilled to
the superb performance by people who had never received
a day's stage training in their lives, and yet played out
their heritage in unselfconscious mime that had no need
of the spoken word to hold their audience enthralled.

'After the hunt comes the feasting,' Le continued
happily in her role of impromptu announcer.

'And after the feasting. . . .' Krish began with a mischievous look at his lovely young wife.

'Hush!' She silenced him with a swift, admonishing
finger against his lips, which he promptly kissed, and
captured in his hand. 'Behave yourself,' Le scolded smilingly.

'I don't think I'll risk having anything to eat.' Storm
tried to ignore the emptiness that watching the happy
couple together left in her own heart.

'You must eat something, or you'll offend the elders,'
Rann told her decisively. 'It needn't necessarily be meat,'
he conceded, checking the angry refusal that sprang to
her lips. 'When they bring the food round, I'll choose
something for you. If you eat what I give you, you'll come
to no harm.'

Maybe not gastronomically, Storm thought bitterly.
Rann himself had caused her more harm than any
amount of food was capable of doing. He had destroyed
her desire to continue her career, wrecked her confidence
in her own talent, and removed her heart from her keeping. And now he was dictating to her what she should,
and should not, eat!

'I'll choose my own,' she retorted stubbornly, but when
it came, the bewildering array of meat, fruits and various
concoctions to which she was unable to put a name, at-
tractively laid out on banana leaves, and offered by two
young, smiling girls, looked and smelled delicious. She

hesitated uncertainly, the memory of her recent dietary indiscretion, and its painful outcome, still too sharp to allow her to take another risk.

If only the girls had gone to Le and Krish first! She could then have watched what they chose to eat, and followed suit—and reasserted her independence from Rann. But they had come first to herself, as guest of honour, and she could not keep them waiting. She looked across to Le for help, but Krish's dark head was bent over his wife, and Le's face was upturned, whispering something to him, and she had eyes only for her husband, leaving Storm with no alternative but to turn to Rann.

She hated having to ask him. She hated him, for the quick glint in his eyes that said she should have left the choosing to him in the first place, as he had told her to, and she accepted with an ill grace from his hand the slice of sweet melon, and the mysterious something that was wrapped in a piece of banana leaf, folded over the food to keep it moist, and serving at the same time as a wrapper and a handy plate. She unfolded the leaf and regarded the contents dubiously.

'It's rice, made into a sweetmeat. There's nothing in it to upset you.'

It was not the sweetmeat that upset her, it was the accidental contact with his hand as she took it from him, the slight, electric touch of his fingers that jerked her heart into a wild, uneven beating that made her doubt if she could swallow the food if she tried.

She bit into a piece experimentally. It was sticky, and spiced, and although the taste was strange to her Western palate she found it pleasant, and the melon a refreshing coolness afterwards. She noticed Rann had taken a similar assortment for himself, and ate his share with gusto. He glanced up as if he sensed she was watching him, and noted her half-emptied banana leaf. He smiled without speaking, and resumed his meal, and without quite knowing how it happened Storm discovered herself eating with him in a companionable, happy silence, no longer a stranger at the feast, at loggerheads with Rann. It was as if their minds had called a truce while they were at the celebrations, and she relaxed, and accepted another piece of melon from him, and smiled back her thanks. If only it could always be like this, she wished wistfully, and knew that it could not. When the feast was over, and the celebrations nothing but a memory, they would revert to their constant battle of wills until it was time for her to leave on her journey to the coast, and go out of his life for ever.

Her heart echoed the mournful lament of the pipe at the thought, but before it could descend into the familiar blackness into which it seemed to spend its days since she had met Rann, the music began again, and the gaily chattering crowd put aside their feasting for the moment and grew silent. Storm did not need anyone to interpret the music for her this time. It spoke for itself, questing across the clearing like a lost breeze, seeking, and lamenting as it sought. A young girl slipped into the arena and sank gracefully to the ground. She wore a half opened siri bud fastened in her hair.

At first she sat motionless, with her feet tucked under her, statuesque in the uncertain light from the fires. The music grew louder, and more insistent, and the girl began slowly to sway, bending like a young reed in the breeze to the rhythmic beat of the music. The half-opened siri bud in her hair proclaimed the reason for the fluid, seeking movements of her slender hands and arms, which pleaded with eloquent gestures to the forest and the river, the wide dark skies above her, and the dusty earth below, to help her to find the one she sought.

Storm had seen such dancing only once before, in the South Sea Islands, and it came as a total surprise to find it here, among the wild jungle of the Kheval Province. Hand dancing was the description that came to her mind, but this was something more. Without her moving from her sitting position on the ground, from the waist upwards the girl's supple body became a poem of movement.

If only I'd brought my camera with me, Storm wished fervently, then felt glad that she had not. This was something to be felt, not to be photographed. To be absorbed, and experienced, and shared, and ever afterwards relived in colourful memory that made photographs superfluous.

With eloquent grace the girl gave life to the music, and

Storm felt her imagination captured by the vivid inter-
pretation of her dancing. It drew her, hypnotised her,
claiming her mind and her emotions, identifying her with
the girl's desperate seeking, and knowing the ultimate
despair because she had found Rann without having to
seek, and lost him even as she found.

I wish I hadn't come. The dancer's lonely searching
grew unbearable, and Storm's throat ached with sympathy for her plight, until a shadow flitted through the
firelight, and hope rejuvenated the dancer. With quick,
eager movements her hands followed the man's progress
round the circle, beckoning until he was drawn to her
from the shadows. He sank to the ground in front of her,
sitting a short distance away from her, and together they
began to dance out their courtship ritual, the universal
pattern of pursuit and flight, advance and coquettish re-
jection, with an artistry that would have brought a
London audience to its feet in homage to the performers.

Unconsciously Storm felt herself begin to sway. The
pulsating rhythm of the music beat through her senses,
and claimed her for its own. The artist in her reached out
to join the dancers, living every movement with them,
acting out the pent-up expression of her own frustrated
longing, and all the while agonisingly conscious of Rann,
so close to her that she could touch him, and so hopelessly
out of her reach.

The drums died into silence, and the pipes became a
thin whisper of sound, hardly audible across the clearing,
until they, too, died away, and with a final movement of
graceful surrender the girl reached out gently fluttering
hands towards her partner, and became still.

Impulsively Storm turned to Rann. His features were
darkly shadowed by the dying fires, his expression hidden
from her. She gazed up at him with eyes that were soft
with an echo of the dancer's pleading.

'Rann?'

Her lips parted in a soundless whisper, and her hands
reached out to him, beseeching him. Surely he must understand their message, and respond?

'It's time to go.'

With a single lithe movement he rose to his feet, and

bending, caught her fingers in his own, but it was not to
hold her, as the young performers held each other, dancing out their joy at finding one another. With a quick,
decisive pull, he raised Storm to her feet, and promptly
released her.

'I want to stay,' she protested, 'the dance is still going
on.'

'We mustn't outstay our welcome,' he insisted, and with
a grave word to the elders he drew her away from the
clearing, out through the ring of huts, away from the firelight and the music, across the dark empty space between
the village and the bungalow. Storm shivered, suddenly
fearful of the darkness, longing to run back to the firelight,
but Rann kept his hand under her elbow, obliging her to
walk alongside him.

'I can walk on my own.' She shrugged herself free from
his hold, angry at being forced to leave the celebrations
just as she was beginning to enjoy them; resentful that the
fragile camaraderie between herself and Rann should be
so abruptly shattered, and bitter that the music which
stirred her to such an emotional response should leave
him apparently untouched.

'He's hard. Unfeeling,' her heart complained, not for
the first time. The music still rang through her mind,
refusing to release her. Surely if they had remained for
even a little while longer, its message must have reached
Rann, too?

'What did you think of our local jamboree?'

She became conscious that Le and Krish were with
them, leaving the celebrations too. Her angry protest died
on her lips, and she wondered dully why they had chosen
to come away. They belonged to the Province, so they
must belong to its people, which gave them the right to
remain. But Le did not need the music to help her, because she had Krish. Storm stumbled, her eyes blinded by
the darkness, and the sudden rush of tears that blotted
out what little light there was.

'There's something in my shoe.' Instinctively she bent
to hide her face, using the first excuse to hand, even
though the others could not see any better in the darkness
than she could herself.

'We'll go on, I want to put my orchid in water,' Le called out cheerfully, and passed them by, hand in hand with Krish, and swung up the steps to the veranda.

'Hold on to me for a moment while you shake out your shoe.' Instead of walking on with Le and Krish, Rann paused and grasped Storm's arm to support her while she shook out the non-existent foreign body in her sandal, and nearly succeeded in unbalancing her altogether as her head reeled under the havoc caused by his closeness and his firm, hard grip that sent electric tingles down her arm and threatened to make her drop her sandal from suddenly nerveless fingers.

'A lot of the women at the feast had got orchids fastened to their blouses.' Storm spoke quickly, catching at the first subject she could think of to steady herself, trying to detain Le, trying to steel herself against the magnetism of Rann's touch.

'They're a safety measure.' Le leaned over the veranda railing above them, pausing in her search for a container for her orchid.

'A safety measure?' Storm frowned. What could an orchid guard its wearer against?

'They say, "don't touch",' Le laughed, enjoying her puzzlement. 'When a man gives a woman an orchid, it tells the world she's his property, and warns off any would-be suitors. It saves a lot of misunderstandings, if any young swain becomes over venturesome in the excitement of the celebrations,' she chuckled, and tripped lightfooted after Krish to put her flower in water.

It might save some misunderstandings, Storm told herself furiously, but it caused a lot of others. The major misunderstanding was in Rann thinking he could publicly label her as his woman. Le's unfortunate choice of words grated like sandpaper on her already overwrought nerves, and her anger boiled over at Rann's effrontery. With a quick wriggle she thrust her foot back into her sandal and began to pull at her orchid with fingers that shook.

'Do you want to put yours in water?' Rann's voice came from above her head in the darkness, reaching her through a fog of anger that floated like a mist in front of her eyes. 'The fastening of the pin's probably stuck.' He misunderstood her frantic fumbling. 'Let me undo it for you,' and he reached out towards the flower on the shoulder of her blouse.

'Don't touch me!' With the swiftness of a catspaw she struck his hand aside. 'Go and pin your labels on someone else!' she hissed at him furiously. 'I don't want to keep your orchid, in water or anywhere else. If I'd known what it stood for, I wouldn't have worn it in the first place. You can have it back!'

With a mighty tug she tore the flower from her shoulder. The slender stem snapped under the pressure, but the pin remained stubbornly closed, and the force of her pull ripped the thin material of her blouse in a jagged tear, but she did not care. The very feel of the flower against her shoulder was a humiliation. Deliberately she closed her mind to the obvious protection it had afforded her.

'Keep your flower!' she cried furiously. 'I won't be branded as a mere possession, by you or by anyone. I'm not your woman, and I won't be labelled so!'

And never will be, her heart lamented, as with a strangled sob she flung the orchid blindly in his direction, and turning, stumbled up the veranda steps, and fled for the sanctuary of her room.

CHAPTER TWELVE

'IT looks like the beach at Brighton, on a bank holiday!' Storm hung over the rail of the veranda beside Le, and stared fascinated at the kaleidoscope of colour and movement going on along the river bank below. 'I wouldn't have believed there were so many people in the Province,' she marvelled.

'The market canoes travel together for protection,' Le answered lazily. 'They have to contend with a lot of natural hazards on their journey from the coast, and if a canoe capsizes, or they meet with a storm, it's a good thing to have someone else around to help.'

The hazard she had met with on her journey was Rann,

and there was no one else around to help. With an immense effort Storm kept her eyes fixed on the busy scene in front of her, making them look at the colourful piles of merchandise, the colourful clothing of the vendors; the busy activity on the water, as more canoes arrived and jockeyed for an advantageous mooring, when all the while she could see, without even having to turn round and look, Rann still sitting with Krish at the breakfast table behind her, indulging in a second, leisurely cup of coffee instead of, as was his wont, hastily swallowing one in order to be off to attend to the work with the oozies, at the site, or with the endless messages that seemed to come into the wireless room at all hours of the day or night.

He's behaving as if he's human for once, she told herself tartly. For some reason she had not expected Rann to take the day off the same as everyone else. It came as a disconcerting surprise to find him still in the bungalow when she quit her room for breakfast, deliberately late in order to avoid him.

Would he say anything about the events of the evening before, that had kept her tossing late into the darkness of the night, her ears bombarded by the seemingly endless sounds of celebration still taunting her from the village, accompanied by the never-ending patter of the night dew on the roof of the bungalow until, when she felt as if she would scream if the noise continued for a moment longer, she dropped at last into a restless sleep, only to be tormented by wild dreams of herself dancing for Rann, beckoning him, but never able to lure him to her side, and when she arose with the daylight, heavy-eyed and unrefreshed, she was unprepared to meet the object of her dreams who, she saw resentfully, looked as alert and clear-eyed as if the doubts and yearnings that wrecked her own rest had never disturbed a moment of his.

She hesitated, but before she could turn back and regain her room, and wait for Rann to go out, Le noticed her and called out a cheery, 'Good morning!' and there was nothing Storm could do but go forward and join them at the breakfast table, and pretend she did not care if Rann did say anything. Pretend she had forgotten the unforgettable.

She addressed her own, 'Good morning,' to the table at large, summoning up the reserves of her willpower to make it sound as cheery as Le's greeting, and Rann responded along with the others, casually, as if he had genuinely forgotten the evening before, and instead of feeling relief at the unexpected reprieve, Storm hated him for his easy ability to put aside what had passed between them.

'I can't sit here eating toast, while all that activity's going on along the river,' Le burst out impulsively. 'I must go and watch. Come and join me,' she begged Storm, 'it won't look so dreadfully rude if you leave the table too.'

'We'll forgive you,' Rann smiled indulgently, but he smiled at Le, and not at Storm, and she felt suddenly cold. It was like standing in the shadow, while the sun shone somewhere else. She rose restlessly, thankful for the excuse to leave the table, thankful to turn her back on Rann.

'Just look at that canoe, it's a wonder it doesn't sink with all those bales of cloth in it.' Storm joined the other girl with alacrity.

'Aren't the colours marvellous?' Le enthused. 'We're all going down to have a closer look later on.' She mistook the reason for Storm's eagerness to join her at the veranda rail.

'You've got masses of clothes already, without buying more dress material,' Krish protested, in a voice that said he knew he was fighting a lost cause.

'Just one piece, for special occasions,' Le coaxed. 'There's one man who comes with some very special cloth,' she told Storm enthusiastically, 'it's hand-embroidered, and very lovely.'

'And very expensive,' Krish mourned resignedly. 'Perhaps he won't come this year,' he hoped unrepentantly.

'He's just coming upriver now,' Le triumphed. 'There he is,' she pointed to a tall canoeist who energetically poled his craft against the current while he kept a sharp lookout for a space on the bank in which to land.

'Surely he doesn't pole all the way here from the coast

in that manner?' Storm regarded the man in the canoe
with awed astonishment as he balanced skilfully on one
leg, and with his other leg wrapped round the long pole,
he used the implement more as a stilt than as a punt-
ing pole, and literally 'walked' the canoe along the
water.

'It's the accepted method hereabouts,' Krish replied.
'It's a wonderful way of building up your muscles,' he
teased Storm, 'why not try it? We could have a contest, to
see who could do it without falling into the river.'

'Not I,' Storm refused to be drawn. 'I don't want my
muscles to bulge like his,' and she cast an unenthusiastic
look at the sinewy members of the loincloth-clad canoeist.

'It'd be a lovely excuse to buy a length of pretty
material to hide them,' Le twinkled, joining in the
banter.

'That's out, too,' Storm retorted ruefully. 'I haven't got
anything I could use for barter.' She had abandoned her
basket when the elephant charged her, and had not had
the heart to go back to collect it again afterwards. 'All
that I've got, except coin of the realm, is a caseful of
clothes, and it'd be like taking coals to Newcastle to try to
use those as barter here.' It was a pity, she thought wistfully, the glimpse she had caught of the hand-embroidered
cloth as the canoe drifted past below the veranda bore
out Le's description. It was indeed lovely.

'That doesn't matter,' Le assured her, 'the traders are
people from the coast, they'll take. . . .'

'If we're going to have a look at their merchandise, we
might as well go while it's still reasonably cool,' Rann
interrupted, and rose abruptly from his chair to join them
at the rail.

'Wait while I get a hanky,' Le begged, and promptly
disappeared towards her room, and Storm was left to guess
at what the traders would take in exchange for their
goods.

'I won't ask Rann,' she vowed stubbornly, 'I'd rather
do without the material.' Krish vanished after his wife,
and she was left with Rann leaning beside her over the
veranda rail. No doubt wishing I'd ask him, so that he
could snub me, she fumed, and searched round in her

mind for something to break the silence between them. If I don't speak, he might, about last night, she panicked, and blurted out,

'It seems hotter than ever this morning.' When in doubt, talk about the weather. The advice held good even here, she thought with a surge of desperate amusement.

'There's a storm brewing.' Krish returned in time to hear what she said. There had already been a storm of a different kind the evening before, she thought waspishly, but Krish was not to know that.

'I hope it passes us by.' Rann followed the warden's anxious glance at the sky. 'The last thing we want now is a sudden build-up of water and storm debris behind that last layer of rock that's still to be cleared at the site.'

'Perhaps it'd shift it for you, if a heavy storm broke?' Le suggested hopefully.

'I hope it doesn't,' her husband retorted fervently. 'It'd send a tidal wave of water and goodness knows what else, all along the one waterway. A storm normally raises the water level of the two arms of the river quite considerably. Imagine the results if a mass of water and dead tree trunks, and all the rubbish a storm usually collects from the jungle, suddenly descended on to the one waterway, particularly with this crowd gathered here,' he gestured towards the busy scene below them, that turned the river bank into a crowded band of colour for a couple of hundred yards on either side of where they stood, except for a clear space several yards all round the godown. Even today Rann had not relaxed his vigilance, Storm saw, and felt a surge of impatience. With all these people about, the poachers were hardly likely to try to break into the store. Rann himself had said the villagers had no cause to like the poachers, so their presence alone should be sufficient deterrent. Surely he could relax just for the one day?

'The canoes are moored right at the bend of the river,' Krish voiced his concern out loud. 'They'd be in the most vulnerable spot on the waterway, if a sudden flood came down. The weather *would* do this to us, just when we're nearly finished at the site, and have all the market canoes on our hands as well,' the warden grumbled.

'There's too much rock still left for it to move, even under a heavy storm,' Rann said decidedly, and added as Krish still looked concerned, 'If it'll ease your mind, we can warn the traders about the possible danger, and then if it starts to rain they'll pull their canoes and their wares well away from the river. If you two girls want to go and see the market we might as well start off now, and get it over.' He swung down the steps as if he was impatient to be done with the chore.

'If he doesn't want to come with us, why does he bother?' Storm asked herself angrily. Rann seemed to regard dallying among the market as a waste of his valuable time. No one would miss him, she assured herself uncharitably, and knew that was not true. Le and Krish were too absorbed in each other to be upset by his absence, but if Rann was not with them, the colour would be gone from the market place for her, the reason for wanting to see it would be vanished. She idled behind him with Le and Krish, unwilling to walk beside him, pausing when he paused to speak to one of the traders, obviously telling him to pass the word round about the danger presented by the impending storm.

A pile of gourds blocked her way, and she stopped to admire them; shook her head smilingly to the hopeful patter of the vendor of metal cooking pots and steel hair combs, and shuddered away from a pile of dried fish hung from poles, unpalatably orange in colour, and seeming to attract as many flies as it did customers. Equally doubtful, but attracting less insects, was a stall offering sweetmeats wrapped in the now familiar torn off square of banana leaf.

'It's the local equivalent of jellied eels,' Krish laughed as they caught up with Rann eventually beside a vendor who was just tipping his wares on to a square of cloth spread out on the ground.

'Don't be tempted by the sweetmeats,' Rann warned her sharply.

'Would I be so silly?' Storm flashed back. Did he not think one disastrous mistake was enough?

'That's for you to say,' he retorted, but the look on his face said she had already been silly once, and suffered for it, and he would not put it beyond the bounds of possibility for her to be just as silly again.

Why did I have to give him a question to answer? she berated herself vexedly. It was like banging a tennis ball at him. All she got back was a return stroke so hard she could not even field it.

'Look out!' Krish drew her to one side as Rann spoke to the vendor. 'You're stepping on the end of his market stall.'

'Sorry!' Storm apologised quickly, and added with swift envy, 'Life is so simple here.' She meant without the complication of Rann, but she did not say so out loud. The market people come and set up their stalls, simply by spreading a piece of matting on the ground, and piling their goods on top. They don't have to obtain permits, or licences, there's no paperwork, and no complicated fixtures and fittings to be erected before they can begin to trade. She gazed about her at the brown, intent faces of the crowd, busily haggling over their barter, even shouting at one another, and then parting with smiles all round, vendor and purchaser alike content with their bargains. It was so very like the market places of the West, except for the absence of strain on the faces of the people—the absence, she discovered observantly, of any sense of urgency such as was so commonplace at home, and brought with it tension, and frustration, and impatience, and a dozen attendant unwelcomes in its train. Here, people had time to spare, time to live. Suddenly even the jungle seemed to present less of a threat than before. To most of these people it was home, and would be regarded as no more of a hazard by them than would the city streets she herself was accustomed to. Probably less, she deduced shrewdly, since charging elephants would be much less frequent than were the multiple crashes that made everyday headlines from the motorways.

'What's more, they're sure of their customers,' Krish followed up her train of thought. 'When a market only appears once a year, and there aren't any other shops around, the traders can be sure of getting rid of any produce they bring with them.'

'Surely all these people can't be from our own village?'

Unconsciously Storm identified herself with the local people, unaware of Rann's sharp glance in her direction as her words reached his ear.

'Some of them come from many miles away,' Krish confirmed. 'Word gets around that the market's coming, the drums pass on the news of which day to expect it, and every village within miles up sticks and treks towards the spot. Some of them have been two or three days on the way.'

'And they've got the same journey back, carrying whatever they've bought,' Storm marvelled.

'It's the highlight of their year, remember,' Krish pointed out. 'Just as it's the ruination of me,' he groaned, spotting Le enthusiastically haggling with the trader of the hand embroidered cloth.

'It looks as if she's going to choose the yellow material.' Storm watched the proceedings with interest. 'Why don't you buy her a bracelet to match it?' she suggested to Krish. 'This man's got some—look.' The man whose 'stall' she had stepped on had a dazzling mixture of circlets for sale. 'Go on, admit defeat and buy her one,' she urged him teasingly.

'Whose side are you on?' Krish grumbled. 'You choose one for her. I'm no good at colours. Any I choose either don't match, or they're entirely the wrong shade, or what I call pink, Le calls red. . . .'

'This one will go beautifully with that yellow material she's looking at,' Storm assured him. She bent to pick up the bracelet, and smilingly indicated to the trader that the warden was responsible for the purchase. The man straightened up from spreading out his wares at the same time that Storm rose to her feet, and for a moment they looked directly into one another's faces. Storm's smile faded in a puzzled frown as she stared at the trader. Something elusive tugged faintly at the back of her mind as her eyes met his blank, unsmiling stare, but before she could capture whatever it was Le called out eagerly,

'Do come and help me to choose, Storm,' and with an abrupt movement the man turned his back on her and started to haggle with Krish.

'You go on, while I settle for this.' Krish took the

bracelet she had chosen and urged her in his wife's direction with a grin. 'At least if you help Le to choose the material, I shan't get the blame afterwards if it doesn't work up as she hopes,' he chuckled.

'I don't know whether to have the yellow, or the peacock blue,' Le wailed.

'Have them both,' Rann teased.

'Don't encourage her,' Krish protested.

'You've got a yellow lungyi,' Storm reminded her, 'the one you lent to me.'

'Then it'll have to be the peacock blue,' Le decided. 'Now I'll have to start to haggle all over again.' She recommenced her bargaining with undiminished enthusiasm, and the two men drifted away, past experience warning them that it would be some time before her purchase was completed.

Storm remained to listen, using it as an excuse not to go with Rann. 'I think I like the peacock blue better than the yellow anyway,' she reassured Le. 'Oh, my goodness!' She stopped as a sudden thought struck her. 'The yellow bangle,' she breathed below her breath. 'I must tell Krish to change it.' She tapped Le on the arm. 'I'll be back in a minute,' she said, but already her friend was back in full swing, bartering with the trader, both of them enjoying the procedure too much to be interrupted.

'Krish!' Storm called after him, and the two men paused in their strolling and looked back. Storm avoided Rann's eye, and hurried up to the warden. 'The yellow bracelet won't be any good to go with the peacock blue material,' she explained her errand breathlessly.

'Women!' the unfortunate husband exploded. 'The minute you do one thing, they change their minds and want another. You can't rely on them for two minutes together. . . .'

'Except to do the wrong thing at the most inconvenient moment,' Rann put in in a barbed aside, and Storm sent him a glare that should have shrivelled him on the spot, but to her chagrin it merely widened the grin on his face, and she tightened her lips and deliberately turned her back on him to urge Krish,

'The trader would change the bangle for you if you

went back, I'm sure. You've only just bought it from him, so he can't possibly have forgotten you in this short time, and I know he had a peacock blue one, I saw it when I picked up the yellow one from his pile.'

'Pretend it's Le's birthday, and buy her the two,' Rann laughed unsympathetically.

'You're all of you ganging up on me,' Krish complained. 'It's all right for you,' he grumbled at Rann, 'you're still single.'

'And blessedly unhampered,' Rann agreed, and Storm scowled.

'He can stay that way, for all I care,' she muttered to herself. 'Who'd want him anyway?' and winced as her heart reminded her painfully,

You do. You always will. . . .

'Let's find the trader with the bangles.' She quietened it hastily before the sudden sting in her eyes should get out of hand, and urged Krish back along the direction from which they had come.

'The man was somewhere around here,' she began doubtfully.

'You must be mistaken.' Rann strolled along with them. 'He's not here now.'

'I can see that for myself,' Storm flashed angrily. 'And I'm not mistaken. The man was only a few paces nearer to the river bank than the sweetmeat stall, and those poles of revolting fish.' Did Rann think she had no sense of direction at all? she asked herself hotly.

'Storm's right.' She cast Rann a triumphant glance as Krish backed up her statement. 'I noticed the fellow used coconuts to weigh down the corners of his mat,' the warden went on. 'The nuts are still here—look.'

'In that case, perhaps he's coming back,' Storm began, but Krish shook his head.

'No, this other man here,' he indicated the trader on the sweetmeat stall, who called to them across his pile of merchandise, 'he says the man with the bangles packed up in a hurry and took his cloth full of wares, as soon as he'd sold me the yellow bracelet. Apparently he went off down river in a canoe.'

'What a shame,' Storm sympathised, 'I'm sure that

bracelet would have been a perfect match for Le's peacock blue material.'

'Oh well,' Krish shrugged philosophically, 'he's saved me from having to buy another one,' but he looked disappointed just the same.

'Since he's left his coconuts behind, you might as well use them for barter, as you've got nothing else.' Rann stooped swiftly and gathered up the nuts, and piled them into Storm's arms.

'I can't take these,' she began indignantly. The nuts did not belong to Rann. She did not want to accept them from him, even if they did. She did not want to accept anything from Rann. For a brief, unrepentant moment she felt strongly tempted to take the nuts by their whiskers and one by one hurl them back at him. But only for a moment. Sanity, in the presence of Krish and the market crowd, prevailed before her fingers had done more than curl round the beard of the first nut, and Rann said gravely,

'Coconuts are acceptable barter, and quite valuable if there's anything special you'd like from the market?'

She could not check her quick glance in the direction of the embroidered cloth. Vexedly she knew that Rann had seen her look, and drawn his own conclusions, but it was too late to do anything about it. Le had finished her bargaining, and was coming towards them with her material draped over her arm, and an expression on her face known to every dressmaker who has suddenly come into a windfall of something extra special, and is dreaming of ways of making it up. Le smiled happily, and spoke, but her mind must have been as far away as her expression, because she used her native tongue, an unusual slip on her part. Since Storm had been staying in the bungalow, both the warden and his wife were meticulous in their use of the English language in her presence, a courtesy small in itself, but typical of the wholeheartedness of their welcome. To Storm's surprise, Rann answered Le in the same language.

'He doesn't have Le's excuse,' she criticised him silently. She felt affronted by his deliberate use of words she could not understand. It was an insult, she told herself angrily.

Rann had never tried to make her feel welcome, in the way Le and Krish had, although he had been responsible for her remaining at the bungalow in the first place. Perhaps he was grasping at this further opportunity, using the local dialect to remind her that she was still, to him, an outsider.

'Now you've got something to barter with, you simply must have some of this material,' Le urged her. 'I'll come with you, and help you to choose. I can't resist another look,' she twinkled at Krish wickedly.

'I shan't be able to bargain, the same as you,' Storm still hesitated, reluctant to use Rann's unexpected gift, but tempted by the opportunity to possess some of the material, which would never come again. When the market arrived next year, who knew where she might be? She only knew that it would not be here. 'I can't speak the language.' She shot a barbed glance at Rann, condemning him silently for his discourtesy in using it in front of her.

'I'll haggle for you,' was his disconcerting reply, and she immediately wished she had looked in the other direction, instead of at Rann. Perhaps he thought her look was a silent invitation to speak for her? Her cheeks went hot at the thought, and she opened her mouth to speak, to tell him she did not want the material, or the coconuts, or his help in interpreting the language, but Le spoke first, and said eagerly,

'Take back the coconuts, Rann, you'll need them if you're going to do the haggling.' She smiled at him, a mischievous, lilting sort of smile, as mysterious to Storm as the words the two exchanged a moment before, but Le's fingers were gripping her hand, urging her to release the coconuts to Rann and go with her towards the vendor and his fascinating bales. Reluctantly Storm released the nuts. Rann would never know how close he was to receiving them back in a far more forceful manner, she thought with a sudden inward grin, and turned quickly to go with Le in case it should surface, and he should guess.

'The black material would be perfect, with your black hair and eyes.' Le stood with her head on one side, watching as the trader repeated the performance he had just given for her benefit. 'With that silver thread embroidery, it would make an exotic evening gown. Just imagine,' she sighed, 'with a silver bag and sandals, and perhaps a silver bracelet. . . .'

It had to be the black. The coloured materials were beautiful, but for her, the black was perfect, as Le said. It was surely worth more than four coconuts? There must be hours of work on the embroidery alone. The silver thread shimmered in the sunshine as the man let the stuff flow over his arm to show her the pattern. She gazed at it, and her heart contracted. The entire cloth was embroidered with silver butterflies—some with their wings folded, at rest, some in flight, large ones, small ones. The shimmer of the sunlight on the thread made them seem to move, as if they were about to fly away, as the butterflies in the clearing had flown, and leave only the darkness of the black material behind for her. Without conscious thought she put out her hand to stop them from flying away. She could not bear the prospect of the blackness without them. Had Rann seen them? she wondered. She dared not turn round to look at him, standing just behind her, waiting for her to choose before he started to bargain with the trader. He spoke, in English this time.

'Le's right, the black *is* perfect for you.' He turned and spoke to the trader, who folded the material quickly and put it into Storm's outstretched hand, and a small spark of rebellion rose inside her because he had not waited for her to say yes, that was the material she wanted. He had taken the decision for her, and he had no right. . . . Or perhaps he thought he had the right, because he had given her the coconuts? But the spark died away because she could not utter the words to bring it into flame. Her throat was choked with her need to keep the butterflies, and her total inability to ask Rann if he had noticed them too, in case he had not, or if he had, in case he did not remember what they stood for.

'There are butterflies too, remember?'

She folded the length of material over her arm carefully, tenderly. The silver embroidery thread was slightly stiff, with a faint scratchy feel against her bare skin. Rann started to bargain with the trader, using the local dialect, and the butterflies became silver embroidery again, and Krish complained,

'I'm hungry.'

'Let's go and get something to eat. I didn't realise how long we'd been among the stalls. Rann will come along when he's finished.' Le urged her away, among others who were evidently hungry too. Storm became conscious that the fierce bargaining that made the morning noisy just a short time ago had died away, and traders and customers alike squatted happily on the ground and began to devour their midday repast. A ripe odour from the orange-coloured fish rose from a number of cooking fires, and she wrinkled her nose at the smell.

'Don't worry, Gurdip won't give us fish.' Krish laughed at her expression.

Gurdip gave them melon, and curry, and cool iced fruit, and Storm hurried through her toilet beforehand, and was hardly finished and changed into a dress when Le gave a quick knock on her door and begged,

'Do me up at the back. Krish has disappeared, and the zip on this blouse is so fine I can't manage it on my own.'

'You've got your yellow lungyi on,' Storm noticed, as she obligingly closed the back fastening on the blouse. It was the same lungyi that Le had lent to her, but now she had her own clothes back she preferred to wear them. After tripping over the long cotton skirt with such disastrous effects, she did not feel secure in a lungyi any more.

'I put it on so as not to disappoint Krish,' Le smiled. 'He's given me the yellow bracelet to match it.' She held her arm out and inspected it happily. 'It's nice that we've both had a present today,' she said contentedly.

'I still don't know who to thank for mine,' Storm confessed ruefully, 'Rann or the trader.' The latter had vanished, and she did not particularly feel like thanking Rann. 'Four coconuts are the oddest present I think I've ever had. By the way,' she added curiously, 'what did Krish use to purchase your material with? He hadn't got anything with him that he could exchange, so far as I could see.' And yet he had bought the bracelet, and the material. 'I still can't believe that four homely coconuts could purchase such exquisite material,' she marvelled.

'Krish used money, of course.' Le looked surprised at
her question. 'I told you, the traders from the coast will
accept money. It's only the villagers who live in the jungle
who have to use goods for barter. The traders sell the
villagers' goods in the coast towns, so they get cash for
them in the end.'

Le had started to tell her, but Rann had interrupted
before she could finish. Deliberately? If she had known,
she could have used her own money, she still had some
currency left over from her holiday.

'But the coconuts?' Storm looked her bewilderment.
'Rann said. . . .'

'Rann paid for your material in cash, the same as Krish
paid for mine,' Le laughed at her innocence. 'He didn't
want you to know, that's why we spoke to one another in
the local language,' she apologised. 'I asked him what on
earth he meant by dumping a load of old coconuts on
you. He said he told you they were valuable as barter,'
she giggled. 'He asked me to take you away when you'd
chosen your material, so that he could pay for it without
you knowing. And you came like a lamb, all unsuspect-
ing,' she chuckled.

'I'd never have chosen the material, if I'd known!'
Storm stared at the other girl, appalled. 'It must have
cost the earth!'

'It did,' Le confirmed her fears with cheerful frankness.

'He'll have to take it back. I won't accept it.' Storm's
eyes flashed angrily. Rann had deliberately misled her,
made her look a fool. No doubt he was laughing with
Krish even now, at the ease with which she had fallen for
his trick. Perhaps he thought the material paid her for
finding his wretched ivory. 'I'll give it back to him,' she
vowed fiercely, 'I'll. . . .'

'You mustn't give it back to him.' Le's eyes widened in
dismay. 'I promised Rann I wouldn't tell you. I'd hate
him to think I'd betrayed his confidence,' she begged
Storm's silence.

By the same token, she could not betray Le.
Reluctantly, Storm followed the other girl on to the veranda as Gurdip sounded the bell for the meal.

'I won't take his material. I won't even thank him for

it,' Storm muttered to herself furiously. 'I'll find some way
of giving it back to him, without letting him know that
Le told me.'

'It'll make a lovely souvenir when you go home,' Le
said, and unconsciously showed her the way.

'When I leave here for the coast, I'll leave the material
behind me.' It was the perfect solution, she decided with
satisfaction. 'Rann will find it after I've gone. He'll know,
then, what I think of his gift, and of him.'

She took her seat next to him at the table, just as the
first spear of lightning crackled across the sky, forerunner
of the gathering storm that struck an echo in the wild
tumult that raged in her own rebellious heart.

CHAPTER THIRTEEN

'I RECKON this storm's going to hit us at about dark
tonight,' Krish predicted as a second spear of lightning
followed the first, and a rumble of faraway thunder
followed immediately upon it.

'I wish to goodness it would break. The heat's frightful,'
Le complained.

'It doesn't seem to have affected the activity in the
market,' Storm remarked. Gurdip had thoughtfully
placed the lunch table close to the veranda rail so that
they could watch the colourful bustle while they ate. She
was grateful for his consideration. It provided a much-
needed distraction while she swallowed a meal she no
longer had any appetite for, and tried to ignore Rann
sitting next to her, his gift of material looming unspoken
between them, as explosive as one of the lightning flashes,
waiting to burst like the hovering storm, and only needing
a word or a gesture to trigger it off.

'The gourds seem to be selling well.' The trader had
only a few left of his original large pile.

'They make ideal containers for dry stores, such as rice,'
Le gave her the clue to their popularity.

'The girl who was doing the hand dancing at the celebration in the village last night seemed to want an awful lot of them,' Storm remembered.

'She'll need a lot of everything,' Le smiled, 'that was her betrothal dance last night. She's setting up a new home.'

'You mean the dancing was for real? No wonder. . . .' Storm stopped. No wonder the girl's dancing had been so expressive. No wonder it had reached out and touched an answering chord in her own heart. The dancer was in love. And so, Storm thought wretchedly, and so am I. But there the likeness ended. Resolutely she closed her mind to the difference between her own lot, and that of the young dancer.

'The couple would be married after we left last night,' Le explained. 'It's a very private affair, with only the people actually belonging to the village being present at the ceremony.'

That must have been why Rann insisted upon them leaving when they did. It gave her a small sense of satisfaction to know that he had been obliged to leave as well. But why hadn't he explained the reason to her? He knew she wanted to remain. If he had told her why they had to leave, she would not have been so vociferous in her protest at being obliged to come away. She would have understood. But he had not bothered to explain, and his high-handed indifference to her feelings stirred her ready anger against him.

'The girl's parents agree the bride price with the boy's parents,' Le went on dreamily.

'For four coconuts, perhaps? They're supposed to be valuable.' Storm could not resist the jibe. She spoke softly, so that only Rann could hear her, and he slanted a swift glance at her, but his expression remained inscrutable, and she bit her tongue and wished she had not spoken, because she had promised Le. . . . The other girl chattered on happily, unaware of the barbed interchange.

'When everything's been amicably agreed, the couple declare their intentions to the elders of the village, and receive their blessing, and everything's settled, and the feasting can begin. Today, both families will be helping with building and thatching a new hut for the happy couple.'

'I saw the girl collecting a whole variety of things at the market, but I didn't realise why.' Storm tried not to let the envy sound in her voice, and hurried on, as if she was not particularly interested in the newlyweds, 'I recognised several of the local people there. The baby's mother was one, she had a metal cooking pot, and some of the women who were weaving baskets were exchanging them for that awful fish.'

'You see, you're already a local yourself,' Le teased her. 'When you begin to recognise one person from another, it means you belong.'

'I must admit everyone did look alike when I first arrived,' Storm confessed.

'Everyone always looks alike to a newcomer from another race,' Le agreed cheerfully. 'Krish and I had just the same trouble when we went to England. There seemed to be an absolute sea of white faces at the college, and no means of telling one from the other,' she remembered ruefully.

'We had one advantage over Storm,' Krish reminded her. 'At least the people had different coloured hair. There was black, ginger, blonde and mousy,' he grinned, and Storm burst out laughing, a rich chuckle of amusement that brought Rann's eyes swiftly to her face, but their expression was hidden from her because she was looking towards the warden and Le.

'I first learned to recognise the women of the village by their hair,' she confirmed merrily.

'They've all got straight brown hair here, so how . . .?' Krish looked his puzzlement.

'They do it up in different styles, the same as women do all over the world,' Storm enlightened him gravely.

'Oh, hair-styles.' Krish looked lost among such feminine mysteries, and Storm took pity on him.

'I still don't find it easy to tell the men apart,' she comforted him. 'Although the man who was selling the bangles. . . .' She trailed to a halt, and her frown returned. 'There was something about his face . . . I can't place him,' she puzzled, still unable to catch the elusive something that tugged at her memory.

'You're hardly likely to have met up with any of the traders from the coast before,' Le said practically. 'Perhaps the man just looked like one of the locals here. Maybe he'd got pockmarks or something?' she suggested helpfully. 'A lot of the older people were marked by smallpox, before modern medicine reached the interior. It could be something like that which struck a chord somewhere for you.'

'I don't think so,' Storm began doubtfully.

'The man wasn't scarred, I saw him myself,' Krish put in definitely. 'He haggled with me over your yellow bracelet, so I had time to have a good look at him.'

'Scars . . . that's it!' Storm breathed. 'I know, now, where I've seen him before.'

'But he wasn't . . .' Krish insisted.

'I know he wasn't scarred, but that's why I recognised him,' Storm burst out. 'I'm getting incoherent,' she realised, and drew in a deep breath and started again. 'Maung Chi was scarred. You told me yourself how he got his injuries. And the man with the bangles was one of the men who were with Maung Chi when they brought us to the bungalow after the plane crashed. I knew I'd seen him before,' she vindicated her earlier claim.

'Are you sure of that?' Rann's spoon dropped with a clatter on to his dish, and he leaned forward, his face intent, and his meal forgotten.

'Of course I'm sure.' Storm's frown darkened, and she snapped angrily, 'I shouldn't have said so if I wasn't sure.' She was not an irresponsible child, to say something for effect in order to gain attention, she told herself wrathfully. She could not complain about the attention she was receiving now. Three pairs of eyes were riveted on her face, and an air of sudden unease blew like a cold wind across the table.

'If I'd had the chance of a longer look at him, I'd probably have recognised him before this, but he'd vanished when we went back. Even if he left his coconuts behind,' she threw at Rann tartly.

'When you first saw him, did he see you, too?' Rann did not respond to her sally, and there was something in his tone that made Storm answer his question without demur.

'Yes, he did. Krish asked me to choose a bangle to match the yellow material that Le was looking at. I picked one out of the pile and held it up for the man to see, and indicated that Krish would pay. I must have looked at him fairly hard, because I knew I'd seen him somewhere before, and couldn't at that moment think where. He saw me staring at him, probably looking puzzled, and he turned his back on me and started to bargain with Krish. And then when Le chose the peacock blue material- instead of the yellow, and we went back to try to change the bangle, the man was gone.'

'Hoping, no doubt, that you'd think no more about him if you didn't see him again,' Rann said thoughtfully.

'The sweetmeat trader said he'd gone off down river in a canoe,' Krish remembered.

'Probably to report to Maung Chi,' Rann nodded. 'It means they're still keeping close to the village,' he frowned. 'Carry on eating, I'll be back soon.' He rose and left the table, and a questioning silence behind him that Storm broke with an impatient,

'Surely he doesn't imagine the poachers will try to raid the godown, with all this crowd about?'

The wireless room received Rann without any explanation of what he was about to do, and he vouchsafed none when he returned a few minutes later in time to hear her remark.

'This morning gave us evidence that the poachers have infiltrated the crowd,' he reminded her curtly.

'The crowd's nowhere near to the godown,' she pointed out with asperity. 'You doubled the guard on the hut, and there's a clear space all round it. With such a crowd about, the poachers wouldn't dare to try to break in.'

'If they made a concerted rush on the hut, the resultant confusion among the crowd would be to their advantage,' Rann interjected, in no way impressed by her reasoning. 'No one would know who was trader, and who was poacher, in the mêlée, and there are enough canoes lying about unattended to make it easy for them to steal what they need, load up and get away, particularly if they grabbed some of the rifles and ammunition from the hut as a deterrent to any wouldbe apprehenders.'

He sounds as if he's organising a raid on the godown himself, instead of trying to prevent one, Storm thought disparagingly. He's asked all the questions, and got all the answers ready beforehand. She studiously ignored the tactical sense of such thinking.

'We've got no means of telling how many of the market traders are genuine, and how many belong to the poachers,' Krish put in gloomily.

'There's one way of finding out,' Rann disagreed, and turned to Storm. 'You recognised one of the men who was with Maung Chi. Maybe you could recognise the others.' He did not wait for her to reply, but reached out and took her by the hand, and drew her to her feet. 'We're going on a walkabout among the market,' he announced, 'to see if you can recognise any of the others among the crowd.'

If he had asked her, instead of telling her, she would not have minded so much. It was the authoritative way he spoke, expecting her to comply meekly with his order, that made her temper boil over.

'I'm far too hot to go wandering about the market place,' she mutinied, and sat down again defiantly. The heat was intense. The high humidity made even her thin sleeveless dress stick to her with a clammy embrace, and the effort of answering him back made trickles of perspiration feel their way with maddening persistence down her back. She wriggled irritably against the clinging material, and watched snakes' tongues of lightning flicker across the sky almost non-stop as the looming storm built up an atmospheric pressure that leaned on the parched earth until Storm felt she could have screamed with the tension. She screamed at Rann instead.

'Go and look yourself, if you want to, but count me out in this temperature!' she defied him shrilly. 'If you're so concerned for your ivory, you should have got the authorities to remove it to a place of safe keeping when you first found it. When *I* first found it,' she corrected herself waspishly.

'The only helicopter in the area has been seconded to work in the 'quake zone until now, it had other things to do that were more important. It won't reach here for another couple of days.'

Could anything be more important than what Rann wanted? she asked herself sarcastically, and said aloud, 'Then get the oozies to help you to look for your poachers. The men aren't at work today, so they won't have anything to do. They're more used to the heat than I am.'

'The oozies can't help, or I'd have taken them along.' Rann left her in no doubt who he would prefer to help him in his task. 'You're the only one who's able to recognise the other poachers, because you're the only one who had a good look at them. You'll come with me if I have to drag you,' he told her determinedly.

'And what if I won't?' she flared angrily. They were quarrelling openly now. The heat, and the tension, cracked apart the carefully built-up walls of restraint, and loosed the flood of pent-up resentment and frustration in a spate of angry words. 'What if I *do* see the poachers, and recognise them, and don't tell you?' She played her trump card triumphantly. 'How are you to know, if I don't tell you?' she jeered, taunting him with the knowledge that she had the upper hand, and there was nothing he could do about it. 'You can't make me tell you, any more than you can make me recognise the men,' she flung at him vindictively.

'If I can't make you, perhaps this will.' Rann's face went white under his tan, and his eyes glowed with a force of fury that stopped the words in her throat, and turned her own cheeks the colour of his as he spun towards her, and bending down he grabbed her with both hands and lifted her from off her chair as if she was no heavier than a child, and pulled her stumbling with him to the veranda rail. With one hand he held her there, while with the other he gestured angrily towards the crowd of people milling below them, their meal finished, and going about the business of trading with renewed enthusiasm.

'Look at them,' he gritted, in a voice that if she had not been so angry herself would have frightened her into compliance. 'What do you think will happen, if the poachers do try to raid the godown, and any one of those people down there accidentally gets in their way? Remember, they're the same men who deliberately used fire to drive a wounded elephant into a village full of women and children, merely to create a diversion to cover their first raid.'

'They're hardly likely to be able to produce another wounded elephant, just like that,' she retaliated sharply. That was stretching credibility too far, even for Rann. 'And they'd have to get into the godown before they could arm themselves with the rifles.'

'They already carry elephant guns,' Rann reminded her harshly. 'Do you think they'll stop short of using them, if anyone gets in their way? You've seen the scars Maung Chi carries, so you know what damage a charge from a gun of that calibre can do. Do you want to be responsible, if that happens to her?' He pointed to a small girl, toddling happily in the sunshine, and beaming at the bright new bracelet that adorned her chubby arm. 'Or her?' The young dancer of the night before looked up from the crowd and saw them standing together at the veranda rail, and smilingly acknowledged Rann's courteous salute. She was lovelier than ever in the clear light of day. Storm's heart gave a painful twist at the sight of her. Nature had endowed her with all the peerless beauty of her race, and as she turned to smile at them she seemed to glow, with the special, shining aura that only love can bestow.

'Do you want to risk it happening to them?' Rann demanded of Storm harshly, and when she did not immediately answer, 'Well, do you?' he shouted.

She did not. The disfigured face of the Burman swam across her mental vision. It had hardly been recognisable as a face at all, on one side. For a moment, as she remembered, the bright colours of the market darkened in front of her eyes, and she clung to the rail for support.

'There's no time to lose,' Rann pressed her remorselessly.

'I'll go and get my hat, and then join you.' She stumbled to her room. The hat was on her dressing table, and she groped her way towards it, and her fingers searched blindly for the familiar dry rush brim.

'Are you coming?'

He intends to make sure I don't go back on my word, she realised irritably as he called to her from just outside her door.

'I said I'd come, and I will.' She erupted through the door to join him on a surge of exasperation. It helped her to keep pace with him as he hurried her down the veranda steps, his hand under her elbow, urging her on.

'You don't need to keep me captive, I shan't disappear,' she snapped, and then felt contrarily glad that he kept it there in spite of her protest, as they became submerged in the crush of the market. The seller of fish was still there, his stock replenished from his canoe, doing the same brisk trade as before. Likewise the man at the sweetmeat stall. But the seller of gourds was gone. Had he sold all his stock, and decided to go home? Storm wondered. But Le said the market people always travelled together for protection, so why had he not waited? For the first time, a prick of fear sent an icy trickle along her spine, and instinctively she shrank closer to Rann.

'Well?' he questioned her quietly, from close to her ear, and his hand left her elbow and rested on her shoulder. Did he sense her sudden fear? Or did he, more likely, think that even now she might turn back, and was ready to prevent her if she tried?

'No.' She spoke equally softly, and shook her head. Her growing ability to recognise individuals helped to make her sure of her answer.

'Watch the customers, as well as the traders,' Rann warned, and she nodded.

I feel a bit like a detective, she thought without humour, and found she did not much like the feeling. It was not in her nature to be suspicious, and she tried without success to play her way into the part, as if she was on stage, and this was merely an act that would soon come to an end. But her efforts lacked conviction, and she felt ill at ease among the hitherto friendly-seeming crowd, wary of everyone she met, afraid, except for the reassuring presence of Rann at her side.

'Try this on.' To her surprise he stopped beside a stall of trinkets. Her eyes flew apprehensively towards the vendor's face, and she felt rather than saw Rann's questioning look. She gave a slight shake of her head and made to move on, but he kept a detaining hand on her arm.

'Try this on.' He picked up a finely chased bracelet, and caught at her hand to see if it would fit.

'You don't have to pay me for my services.' She refused it swiftly, and clenched her fist into an unaccommodating ball so that he could not slip the bracelet over her fingers. 'Put—it—back!' She forced the words out through teeth clenched as tightly as her fist when he persisted. 'I won't be bought!' Since he had practically blackmailed her into accompanying him, it was adding insult to injury to attempt to reward her for her efforts as well. First the material, and now the bracelet. . . .

'I'm not trying to buy your services,' he growled back in a low voice. 'I'm acting normally, and you must do the same. If you carry on like this, everyone in sight will begin to suspect something's wrong. At least try to look as if you're interested in having the bracelet.' His low-toned warning cut through her anger like a lash. For a second or two it did not register, and she stared up at him, furious and uncomprehending. Vital seconds, in which her hand went limp, and allowed him to deftly straighten her fingers and slip the bracelet over her hand and slide it up on to her wrist, where it gleamed dully, mocking her because he had given it to her for the sake of appearances, and not because he wanted to make her a gift.

'I'll leave it behind along with the material when I go.' She would take it off the moment she got back to the bungalow, and not wear it again. It would be easy enough for her to roll it into the embroidered cloth, for Rann to find when she had gone. The decision made her feel slightly better, and she summoned up years of stage discipline to produce a brilliant smile of thanks, which should even convince an unbeliever, she thought humourlessly.

'That's better.' From his grudging tone, it obviously did not convince Rann, and she smarted under his curt response. He made a hopeless audience, she told herself critically. Or was it her own acting that was at fault? The uneasy possibility crossed her mind like one of the rumbles of thunder, that growled threats above them, and momentarily loomed closer and more frequent.

'Don't daydream, you might miss seeing something important,' Rann bade her sharply. He seemed to have an uncanny ability to sense the workings of her mind, and his curt order brought her back to her surroundings with a jolt. 'Keep your eyes on the crowd,' he commanded, but she turned them on him instead, flashing angrily:

'I've looked at the crowd until I'm dizzy, and there's nothing there to see.'

'Are you absolutely sure?' His eyes bored into hers, probing, searching, trying to assess whether she was telling the truth or not.

He still doesn't trust me, she thought. His mistrust hit her like a blow, and in spite of the heat her face went chalk white. After all this, he still doesn't trust me!

'Of course I'm sure.' Her voice cracked with anger. 'I promised you I'd look, and I have. I must have looked at every person in the market, twice over,' she exaggerated bitterly. 'There's such a crush that it's almost impossible to tell one person from another, and now I'm absolutely melting, and I want to go back to the bungalow.' Her face shone with perspiration, even her hair felt damp, and she scrubbed her handkerchief impatiently across her forehead, with no noticeable effect except that the small cambric square came away as limp and damp in her hand as she felt herself. 'There's no need for us to go any farther,' she mutinied, 'we've come to the very edge of the market. It doesn't extend into the village itself.'

'We'll walk through the village as far as the pool, just the same, in case any of the traders have gone among the huts.'

Rann was taking caution to the absolute limit, she decided furiously, and half turned in defiance to retrace her steps. Immediately his hand came out to detain her, and she stiffened, but before she could speak a group of people split off from the crowd and wandered towards them, and Storm bit back the angry words that tripped on the edge of her tongue, and reluctantly turned with him and walked between the village huts, across the clearing where the dancer had so expressively acted out her destiny the night before, and so to the edge of the now deserted pool.

'There's a new hut,' she exclaimed. It had not been there last night. The rush thatch stood out, pale against its smoke darkened neighbours.

'It's the home for the newlyweds.' Rann's voice was as expressionless as his face. 'They've built it too close to the water,' he added critically.

'Maybe that's where they wanted it,' Storm retorted sharply. What right had Rann to criticise? It was pleasant beside the pool, cool and peaceful on the edge of the river. It was an ideal spot for the new hut. She turned away, suddenly unable to bear the sight of the bright new home.

'We're wasting our time here, there's no one in the village.' The inhabitants were all in the market, the newlyweds among them, collecting goods to use in their new home. 'We needn't have come this far after all,' she accused him.

'We had to make sure.'

Was he making sure, or was he simply being domineering, forcing her to go with him to the limit of the village? To the limit of her endurance in the breathless, enervating heat. She felt angrily convinced it was the latter, especially when she observed, as they struggled back through the crowd,

'There are more canoes arriving. If we walk along the river bank, we can have a look at them, as well,' and Rann replied indifferently,

'There's no need. Now we've started, we might as well carry on the way we're going,' and he continued to propel her in front of him through the crush of the market crowd, when there was a much clearer path along the edge of the river bank, where they could have walked in comparative comfort. People pressed about her on every side, hemming her in. The merciless heat bore down upon her, and Rann's hand forced her to keep on walking. Desperate with heat and exhaustion, she turned on him like a tigress when at last they gained the sanctuary of the bungalow.

'What is it you want of me?' she asked him wildly, and without giving him time to answer, rushed on, 'First you tell me to have a look at everyone I see in the market, in case I recognise the poachers. When I look, and tell you they're not there, you don't believe me, and when more canoes arrive, you tell me not to bother. I've had enough!' she declared furiously. 'When the helicopter arrives to take away the ivory, I'm going with it, whatever you say.' Wherever the helicopter went, it would be better than remaining here with Rann. 'It's not my battle,' she declared forthrightly, 'and I see no reason why I should be involved.'

The battle she fought was a personal one, with herself, and not with ivory poachers, and it was a battle, she realised with black despair, that she had lost before it was hardly begun. With a strangled sob she flung away from him across the veranda.

'Fight it yourself!' she choked, and fled, her hasty steps pursued by a crashing roll of thunder that drowned her words and shut out the sunshine, until the bright market scene they had just left became shadowed in a darkness almost as black as the cloud that had taken possession of her own spirits.

CHAPTER FOURTEEN

THE heavens opened.

One second there was nothing but the thunder and the lightning, and the next, a deluge descended that seemed as if someone had unzipped the clouds and dropped their entire contents on the cowering earth in one mighty sheet of water. It emptied the market place of customers, and left the traders crouched under hastily erected tarpaulin shelters on ground that steamed like a cauldron. The wildest stage fantasy could not have produced such a weird effect. Storm stared, fascinated.

'I've never seen rain like it before,' she marvelled. A billion drops, each one of which would fill a thimble, drove through the forest with a throbbing roar like the beating of an army of tiny drums, and she stared out from the veranda, both exhilarated and frightened at the unleashed savagery of the elements.

'The weather can certainly put on a show at this lati-
tude, when it wants to,' Rann joined her at the veranda
rail.

'This one's a first-nighter,' she agreed, and heard her
own words with a feeling of detached disbelief. She was
actually agreeing with Rann! Suddenly, the wildness of
the storm became a link between them, fiercer than her
own resentment, stronger than her own anger against him,
the natural forces reaching a pinnacle of violence that left
her own emotions becalmed by comparison.

'Even the storm that crashed our plane wasn't so bad
as this.' She grasped at the link, holding on to it as an
anchor in a drowning world.

'It wasn't the storm that crashed your plane, it was
sheer lack of maintenance,' Rann responded flatly. 'Fuel
lines don't burst at the first clap of thunder.'

Did he have to contradict everything she said? Her brief
calm vanished. First he disbelieved her when she said she
could not recognise any of the crowd in the market place.
Now it was the plane. It simply isn't possible to hold a
normal conversation with him, without arguing, she
fumed, her taut nerves over-reacting like the tempest outside, in a flash of spirit that denied his words, and challenged his right to utter them, because,

'You weren't there, so you can't possibly know,' she
flashed. 'I was in the plane, and it was the storm that
crashed it,' she insisted stubbornly.

'I know Mac,' was all he answered, indifferently.

As if knowing the pilot disposed of all argument, she
thought furiously. Rann was the absolute limit! On every
conceivable occasion he set himself up as judge and jury,
and expected everyone else to accept his pronouncements
without question. So far as her heart was concerned, he
was executioner as well, she acknowledged bitterly.

If only the noise would stop! Since her arrival at the
bungalow the persistent, nightly patter of the dew on the
roof drove her to distraction, but the rain was far worse.
Several hours later, Storm felt as if her nerves were reaching breaking point.

If it goes on for much longer, I'll scream, she told herself
desperately, and then, I'd have to, if I wanted to be heard

above the din! The endless drumming of the rain on the roof, and the almost ceaseless rumble of thunder, doubled in intensity by the echoes thrown back from the high escarpment farther up in the hills, where the site work was being carried out, made normal speech impossible, until the incessant waves of noise began to take on the form of a physical assault.

'I feel as if a thousand hammers were banging around in my head.' She voiced her plaint amid a temporary lull, and Le looked across at her sympathetically.

'I feel the same,' she grumbled, and added, 'You'd think the rain would have cooled the air a bit, but it seems hotter than ever.' She fanned herself languidly.

'It's the combination of high humidity and atmospheric pressure that's making it so unbearable,' Rann explained. 'It'll lift when the storm clears away, and the sun comes out again.'

He's got an answer for everything, Storm thought resentfully, and shot a barbed glance in his direction. The heat did not seem to affect him, or if it did he made no sign, and his very coolness added to her impatience.

'I'm tired of sitting here watching the rain.' Le got up restlessly. 'We might as well all go to bed, and hope the storm blows itself out by the morning.'

'We'll need an early start tomorrow.' Krish got up as well. 'It'll be a tricky business to remove that last barrier of rock at the site, if the flood waters have built up to any extent behind it.'

'The barrier should hold.' Rann repeated his earlier assertion with undiminished confidence. 'It's the bottom half of the landslide, so there's a good broad base for any flood water and debris to push against. It'll take more than a storm to shift it.'

'We'll have to find a means of draining away the dammed-up water behind it, without letting it out in a rush and flooding the whole area,' Krish said concernedly.

'We'll go up there together, tomorrow, and have a look to see how it can be done.'

Rann was even contradicting himself now! Storm heard him incredulously. It was he who had said either he or Krish must always be present in the area of the godown until the ivory was removed. She opened her mouth to tell him he was contradicting himself, then shrugged limply. It was too hot to argue, and the effort of shouting above the noise of the storm would make it even hotter. And if there was an argument, by some means or another Rann would win. She gave up the unequal contest, and with a 'Goodnight' which she did not care if he heard or not, she followed Le's example and went to bed. But not to sleep. The heat built up to intolerable proportions in the enclosed room until even the flimsy mosquito netting seemed to take on the duties of an oven door, holding it in. Restlessly she flung the netting aside and got up.

I might as well get dressed, she decided. The rain was not so heavy now. It still pattered on the roof, and the thunder still rolled, but it seemed to be farther away instead of directly overhead. Storm sponged her face and hands, and felt slightly better as she slipped into her trouser suit and sandals and reached for her watch.

I wonder what time it is? she thought. It did not seem to be quite so dark. She could see the hands clearly enough for her to make out that it was gone midnight. She crossed to the window, and discovered it was moonlight. A weak sliver of silver light pierced the clouds, lending a ray of hope to the sodden world below, and with a resurgence of energy Storm snapped her watch bracelet closed, and opened her bedroom door. It would be cooler on the veranda. There, at least, what air there was would circulate more freely than in her room. She felt confident of being undisturbed. She had heard Rann's bedroom door close shortly after Le and Krish retired, and Gurdip slept in his own home in the village. She closed her bedroom door quietly behind her, and crossed soft-footed to the veranda rail, and leaned her arms gratefully along the damp wood. The flotilla of canoes rocked gently on the river, each with its tarpaulin shelter keeping its sleeping owner dry. The space between the bungalow and the village huts, that a few short hours before had been full of colourful life, now lay silent and deserted, a sea of mud shining wetly under the fitful moon.

I can't fight any longer. Wearily, Storm bowed her forehead on her arms. She felt drained, mentally and physically, by the humid heat, by the burden of un-happiness that lay on her spirit like a leaden weight, sub-merging her in a cloud of despondency at the hopeless inevitability of it all. A roll of thunder echoed her feelings, and she gave a sigh and raised her eyes to the distant sweep of the jungle-clad escarpment where the landslip lay. She had never been there, but she felt as if she knew every inch of it by heart from Krish's enthusiastic descriptions of the work being carried out there.

She probably would never go there now, she mused. Would never see the site that was the author of her mis-fortunes, for if it had not been for the desperate urgency of the work Rann would doubtless have allowed her to hire men and a canoe to take her to the coast, if only to be rid of her unwelcome presence. And she would have thrown herself back into her work, and except perhaps for an occasional wistful backward glance, would have for-gotten Rann in time. But because she had stayed, because Rann had made her stay, it was too late. When the heli-copter came to take away the ivory, she would travel with it, but she would take with her only an empty shell, and all that was worthwhile, her mind, her heart and her spirit, would be left behind in this remote jungle outpost.

She felt no bitterness, not any more. Just an empty blankness, that nothing in the future, and nobody but Rann, could ever fill. Forked tongues of lightning played across the sky over the escarpment, and she watched them with dull eyes. It was better to watch them than to do nothing, and now there was nothing else for her to do. To occupy herself she began to time the flashes of lightning and the rolls of thunder, to give herself some idea how far away the storm had travelled. Two flashes split the clouds, and died away. A third. The fourth was a sheet of flame, not a forked flash as the others had been. Storm stared, alertness coming back. The sheet had come from the bottom of the escarpment, not from the sky, as it should have done. Even as the oddness of it struck her, a dull roar followed the sheet of flame, that could have been mistaken for thunder, and she knew that it was not.

She did not pause to question how she knew. Even before her mind had fully time to comprehend what it

was she had seen, her feet carried her across the veranda
floor on wings, along the corridor past her own room, and
skidded to a halt outside Rann's bedroom door.

'Rann! Rann, wake up!' With both clenched fists, she
hammered a tattoo on his bedroom door. 'Rann. . . .'

'What is it? What's the matter?' His hair was tousled
with sleep, but his eyes were keenly alert. He reached out
both hands and caught at her fists, stilling their hammer-
ing, and demanded,

'What's wrong? Tell me!' he gave her a slight shake as
she paused to gulp in breath before she could blurt,

'It's the lightning. It flashed from the escarpment, not
from the sky. It shouldn't flash from the mountain.' She
sobbed in her need to tell him, to make him understand
fears that she scarcely understood herself. 'The thunder
that followed it wasn't thunder, and the market people
are sleeping in their canoes on the river. . . .' The words
poured from her in an incoherent jumble, desperate, anguished words that made no sense, but somehow had to
make Rann understand. She stammered to a halt as her
mind began to register the implications of the words, and
stopped them in mid-flow. She stared up at him speech-
lessly, her eyes pleading for her, begging him to understand.

'Krish!' He raised his voice and shouted. Storm jumped,
not expecting it, and then Krish was with them, with Le
behind him, disturbed by the noise she had made.

'The rock barrier on the site's been blown.' Swiftly,
unerringly, Rann grasped the essentials, and summed up
the situation. 'We've got to warn the canoe people to get
off the river, the flood will reach them any second now.'

Blessedly, Rann understood. Storm felt herself go weak
with relief. Unbelievably he believed her, and did not
argue, nor stop to ask time-wasting questions.

'You said the barrier would hold up against the flood
waters?' Le cried bewilderedly.

'Maung Chi must have used the dynamite the pilot
stole from the godown. Nothing else could have shifted
that rock pile.'

His mercurial mind latched on to the cause of the flash,
and its consequences, swiftly assessing the danger, and the

action he must take to mitigate it, even as he tugged a pair of slacks over his pyjama trousers and thrust his feet into shoes.

'Let's go, Krish. There's no time to lose.' For a brief second Rann paused, holding Storm, looking down at her with those unfathomable green eyes. 'Stay here,' he commanded her brusquely. 'Stay in the bungalow, you'll be safe here.' Then he was gone. With an agile spring he vaulted the veranda rail, ignoring the steps as being too slow. She heard the mud squelch under his feet as he landed, saw his body jack-knife under the force of the fall, and springing back on to his feet again, running even as he rose. Running towards the river, and shouting at the top of his voice as he ran, calling in the local dialect that she did not understand, and now would never need to learn.

'The searchlight, Le. Turn on the searchlight!' Krish called back over his shoulder to his wife as he followed Rann, and Le grabbed Storm urgently by the arm.

'Help me,' she begged. 'I can't manage the searchlight on my own, it's too heavy.' She ran towards the wireless room and flung open the door, and unquestioningly Storm followed her. 'Push it outside, on to the veranda.' It was incredibly heavy, even though it was on wheels. The cable tangled with their feet, and tripped them up, but they gritted their teeth and pushed, and once it was started it rolled more easily under its own momentum, the weight helping to take it along.

'Be careful,' Le gasped, 'we mustn't let it run down the steps.'

'Switch it on, I'll stop it rolling.' Storm pushed Le back towards the wireless room, and without pausing to think she flung herself in front of the heavy piece of machinery, and braced her feet against the floorboards, grateful for the rubber soles of her sandals that gave her a hard grip. The lamp pressed against her back, the corners of the fixture digging in, but somehow she managed to hold her ground, and it stopped rolling and stood still, and after an endless minute of waiting a brilliant beam of light cut across the clearing towards the river. It caught at the running figures of Rann and Krish, and outlined the silent canoes.

'The canoe men must be deaf.' A wall of water bore down on them from the mountainside above, and still they slept peacefully on, oblivious of the danger. Instinctively Storm glanced at her watch. It seemed a million years since she first saw the flash in the mountains. Her mind registered detached surprise that it was less than five minutes ago. Five minutes, and a tidal wave of water travelled towards them, at what speed?

'They've heard!'

Abruptly, frenzied activity split the silence of the river. Figures appeared on the canoes, gesticulating and shouting, in response to the shouts of Rann and Krish. The effect was that of a newly stirred ants' nest, Storm thought dazedly. One moment, nothing, and then, bedlam. The canoeists nearest to the shore jumped out of their craft on to the bank. Storm saw Rann and Krish bend to pull a canoe on to land, then turn to help the next one, gesturing to the owner of the first to do likewise. The figure of a man ran across the clearing to help. It must be the guard from the godown, and with the three of them under Rann's guidance helping to pull a canoe here, unblocking a tangle of craft there, two-thirds of the flotilla were beached in less time than Storm thought it could have been possible.

They'll never get all the craft ashore in time, she thought anxiously. In spite of their Herculean efforts, there were still a round dozen of the canoes on the river.

'I wish they'd come ashore themselves.' Le's husky voice was high with terror. 'Did Rann and Krish *have* to go out on to the farthest canoes, to chivvy the traders in?' she wailed.

'It looks as if they're trying to make the men abandon their canoes that are still on the water. Rann seems to be helping the one man to bring his merchandise ashore.'

'What does the merchandise matter? If they stay there much longer, they'll never make it to the bank in time themselves. I can hear the water coming already,' Le cried frantically. 'Look at the canoes!'

Storm did not want to look. The forerunner of the flood caught at the craft still left on the water, and tossed them in the air like corks. Figures jumped from one canoe to the other, using them as stepping stones as the owners abandoned their craft and fled for the safety of the bank.

'Krish!' Le screamed.

'He's safe, Le. He's just jumped ashore.' Storm caught a glimpse of the Warden following the traders, saw his final desperate leap on to terra firma. 'Krish is safe, Le.'

But Rann was not. Instead of racing for the shore along with the others, the trader Rann had gone to help stooped down, as if to pick up some of his merchandise from the bottom of his canoe, to bring along with him. The craft was the farthest from the shore, right out in the middle of the wide river, and the first wild wave of water caught it, and lifted it high in the air. The white beam of the searchlight caught the two figures, outlining them like puppets on the wildly tossing craft. Storm saw Rann grab the trader, his arm rose as if he knocked something from out of the man's hand, probably the sack of merchandise, then he literally hurled himself and his companion out of the canoe, and jumped for the craft next to it with a marathon leap.

'I daren't look,' Storm whispered faintly, but her eyes refused to tear themselves away from the two figures, caught in the glare of the searchlight like a spotlight on a stage. It lit up something else as well. A huge, tidal bore of water and debris which rounded the bend of the river in a solid wall, and bore down upon the remaining canoes with a roar that blotted out Storm's wild cry,

'Rann! Rann!'

Her staring eyes caught the mass of debris in the forefront of the giant wave, a tangled mixture of branches and tree trunks, rocks and creeper, and all the flotsam and jetsam of the jungle, gathered up and used as a battering ram by the water that poured down a river designed at best to carry only half the flow. It smashed down on to the stranded canoes with a sound that would haunt Storm for the rest of her days. Within seconds, all but two of the canoes were reduced to matchwood. Before her horror-filled eyes, one of these was sucked under the roaring water as if into the maw of some wild beast of prey, and the other became caught up in the tangle of branches among the mass of debris, and hung there like abandoned washing, carried helplessly along with the flood.

Storm moaned softly as she watched it go, out of sight round the river bend, and felt her heart die within her as it disappeared. It did not seem to matter that it died. Rann was no longer there to leave it with, when she went away. She did not know which of the canoes he had been in when the bore of water hit them. She had lost sight of him in the chaos of water, and debris, and splintered wood. But that did not seem to matter either, now. The outcome was the same.

Slowly she prised her clenched fingers from off the veranda rail. All that she most wanted to hold on to in life was gone, so there was no point in holding on to the veranda rail any longer. Her eyes were still aware of her surroundings, although the rest of her seemed mercifully numb. The river bank looked as if it had been hit by a bomb. Yards away from its proper course, the water had flowed out in a huge wave as it rounded the bend of the river and washed those canoes that had been beached closest to the water, higgledy-piggledy on top of the ones farther away. Branches and boulders lay among them, adding to the confusion, and to the damage. One of the canoes wore a hat of pale-coloured thatch. It looked silly, wearing a hat. A giggle that was half a sob rose in Storm's throat as she looked at it. The giggle died, and left only the sob, as it dawned on her dazed mind what the 'hat' must be.

The young couple's new hut. The roof of their hut had got pale coloured thatch. She remembered the paleness stood out against the smoke-darkened thatch of the established huts. Rann had criticised the builders for putting it too close to the water. The flood must have caught up with it, and carried it away. Slowly the numbness left her, and a burning anger rose in her against the men who could do this thing, who could deliberately, and knowingly, go to such lengths for personal gain. The face of the young dancer swam in front of her eyes, full of beauty, full of promise. Promise that would now never be fulfilled. It joined with Rann's face, crystallising her anger.

I must know, she thought. Her legs trembled, and her
feet felt like lead, but she had to find out if. . . . She dared
not allow herself to think what she wanted to find out.
She forced herself to her feet and made them carry her
down the veranda steps, and on to the slippery mud
below. She did not hear Le's anxious call,

'Storm?'

She only heard the music of the pipes, thin, and high,
and sweet, and saw the pale straw thatch that made a hat
for a broken canoe.

The traders straggled back among their craft, to examine the wreckage of their belongings. They bewailed
their losses with loud voices, but Storm hardly heard
them. With urgent steps she forced her feet to hold her
upright on the slippery mud. There was a man beside the
canoe she was making for. He looked at her strangely
when she reached it, but she did not notice that, either.
All she could see was the 'hat' of pale-coloured thatch.
She reached out and tried to turn it over, off the end of
the canoe, but the water soaking it made it too heavy for
her to lift unaided. Desperately she pushed with all her
strength, and dimly she became aware that other hands
helped her to push. Slowly their combined strength tipped
the thatch over on to its side. It fell into the mud with a
dull squelch, and Storm went weak with relief. There was
nothing—nobody—underneath the pathetic cone. She
swayed, and hung on to the edge of it for support, but her
strength left her, and she wondered dully how she could
manage to drag herself back to the bungalow. The light
from the searchlight got in her eyes and blinded her, and
she wished crossly that someone would switch it off.

Crash!

The crash of splintering glass echoed across the clearing
at the same instant that the light went out. There was a
second of darkness, and eerie silence, then Le's frightened
voice calling her name across the clearing.

'Storm? Storm, come back! There's a raid on the
godown. . . .'

CHAPTER FIFTEEN

THIS was why Maung Chi dynamited the escarpment. This was his second 'diversion'. Thoughts raced through Storm's mind as bedlam erupted round her. Running figures appeared from all directions.

'Storm!'

She could hear Le calling, but the sudden change from brilliant light to semi-darkness momentarily blinded her, and her straining eyes could not see in which direction the bungalow lay. Exerting all her willpower, Storm made herself stand still and closed her lids, trying to make her eyes adjust to the change.

I must get back to the bungalow. One thought became paramount in her mind. Rann had told her not to leave the bungalow. He'll be furious. And then she remembered, and her eyes flew open again, because with them closed they saw again the wall of water, and the splintered canoes. . . . Blindly she started to stumble towards where she thought the bungalow must be, slipping and sliding on the mud.

'Look out . . . oh!' Her cry of warning came too late. The running figure collided heavily against her, righted himself, and ran on. Off balance, she skidded wildly on the greasy surface, and her flailing hands caught for support at the dim outline beside her.

The thatched roof of the new hut! She grasped at it, and held on, letting it take her whole weight that her sliding feet refused, and forgot until she felt the thatch begin to move that it was cone-shaped, and that it lay upon its side. It had been too heavy for her to lift unaided off the canoe, but now its shape, and the slight slope of the river bank, combined to start it rolling.

'Ugh!' Before she could regain her balance it deposited her on her hands and knees in the mud. What had been surface dust before the rain was now a good inch of black slime. It oozed between her fingers, soaked through the knees of her slacks, and only by using all her muscle power was she able to prevent herself from falling flat on her face. With an exclamation of disgust she pushed herself back on to her haunches, and felt something round and hard under her hands.

A canoe pole? She heaved it up from the wet surface as an idea occurred to her. It might help her to keep her balance until she could get back to the bungalow. She raised her head and glanced round her, and discovered that her eyes had adjusted to the change of light, and she could see fairly clearly now, sufficiently to make out Le's figure, faintly outlined against the veranda rail, still trying to locate her.

'I'm coming.' She tried to call out, but her voice sounded faint, and cracked. She swallowed, and tried again, only to have her call drowned by an outburst of shouting from the area of the godown. A glint of moonlight showed a mêlée of fighting bodies, in which half the market appeared to have joined.

The quicker I get back to the bungalow, the better.

For the first time, a sense of her own danger penetrated Storm's mind. The traders who had come to examine their beached canoes had fled, either to join the pitched battle that raged in front of the store hut, or to take themselves off to a place of safety until it was all over, leaving her alone among the wrecked canoes and debris on the river bank. Storm shivered. The beam of moonlight strengthened, shedding an eerie light over a scene that looked as if it had come from another planet, of which she was the sole inhabitant except for one other person.

'Maung Chi!'

There was no mistaking the running figure who burst from the mêlée in front of the godown, and came racing towards her. She had only seen him once, but his face was emblazoned on her mind. Fear pierced through Storm like a knife at the sight of him, and Rann's words repeated their warning in her ears,

'Either of you would make an excellent hostage.'

The poacher was running directly towards her. He did not appear to have seen her yet, but in another minute . . . another few seconds. . . . Her pale-coloured trouser suit was much the same shade as the new thatch, and both were liberally daubed with mud, which made a temporary camouflage. Swiftly she looked round for a hiding place, but there was nothing, and short of flattening herself in the mud and hoping the poacher would not actually run over her, there was no adequate cover, except for the thatched roof. No sooner had the idea occurred to her than she ducked inside the pale-coloured cone, and curled herself up into a tight ball as far into the back as she could crouch.

Perhaps he would run straight past.

She held her breath as the running feet pounded closer. Perhaps Maung Chi would not be looking at thatched roofs, he would be intent only on escape, perhaps on stealing one of the least damaged of the canoes. The river was still a frightening turbulence, but the worst of the flood had passed, and to a desperate man it would be navigable, and the Burman must be used to handling a canoe.

'Stop!'

A voice cut across the uproar, clear, and commanding. Subconsciously Storm's mind registered the fact that it shouted in English. She winced. Rann would shout in English. But that was impossible. It must be Krish. She risked a peep round the edge of her hiding place, and ducked hastily back again. Other men were running with Maung Chi, and she blinked as the strengthening moonlight washed palely on the burdens they carried under their arms.

Tusks!

Ivory, that commanded a fantastic price from those who were prepared to support a black market in order to make carved trinkets for tourists. But that was not the real price of the ivory. Rann, and the innocent trader he had gone to save, had paid the real price, the ultimate price, for the tusks which the poachers were making off with now. So too had the unfortunate animals on Krish's game reserve, that soon, if Maung Chi and people like him had their way, would become extinct, something that only the very old would remember having seen, and children would know only from picture books. A heritage destroyed for pecuniary gain.

At the sight of the tusks something seemed to snap in
Storm's mind. What she had declared to be only Rann's
battle suddenly became her own. Thoughts of Rann, and
the young dancer's proud new home, now a pitiful wreck
at her feet, all became jumbled together in a white-hot
tide of fury. It flooded through her, and wiped away every
vestige of fear for her own personal safety. With an im-
pulsive leap she forsook her hiding place and jumped out
directly in the path of the running band of poachers. It
was doubtful who was the most surprised by her action,
Storm herself or the men she confronted, a slender,
outraged, muddy figure, crying vengeance for the things
which they had done.

'You shan't get away with the tusks!' The callous greed
and the sheer wanton waste of it all took her by the throat.
She wanted to weep at the waste. Her heart already wept
for Rann, but her eyes were dry, and hard, and blazing
with anger as she faced the poachers. She did not know or
care whether they understood her words, her fiery confron-
tation was condemnation enough.

'You shan't have the tusks!' she cried, and lunged at
their running feet with the long canoe pole.

They were too tightly bunched, and running too fast,
to avoid it. Her sudden, unexpected appearance in front
of them turned their startled eyes on to Storm, and they
forgot to look where they were going. Maung Chi was the
first to trip over the pole, and the others saw it too late to
save themselves. With wild oaths the entire raiding party
measured their lengths in the mud, scattering tusks in all
directions. It was beautifully simple, and all over in a
matter of seconds. Before the poachers had time to scramble to their feet, other men caught up with them. Men
who looked like market traders, but who behaved more
like——

'Policemen!' Storm breathed. The quick authority of
their actions proclaimed them for what they were, and
events clicked into place in her mind like the pieces of a
jigsaw puzzle as she watched them. Now she knew what
the radio message was that Rann had put out. He had
foreseen the raid, although he could not have known what

tactics the poachers would use. When the newcomers joined the market, he knew who they were, which was why he had walked her back through the crowd instead of along the river bank, to identify them. She felt sick as she remembered the way she had railed at him when they got back to the bungalow. This, too, was why he had made plans to go to the work site with Krish; he knew the police would be left behind in charge.

Slowly Storm moved away. She might as well go back to the bungalow now, there was nothing left here for her to do. She had done her best for Rann, and for the game reserve. The knowledge would be some consolation to take with her, when she went away. Somewhere, wherever he might be, she hoped Rann would know she had done her best, and forgive her for shouting at him. Her foot touched something in the mud, and she looked down. It would be ironic if she herself tripped over another canoe pole. The thing at her feet was shorter than a canoe pole, fatter, and curved. A tusk. She shuddered away from it, all the anger, and the protest, and the wild spirit of defiance that had temporarily bolstered her courage, draining away from her, and leaving her empty and shaking. A wave of faintness swept over her, and she staggered, scarcely aware of her surroundings, holding on to consciousness only because, somewhere in the dim recesses of her mind, she knew that she must return to the bungalow and stay there, because Rann had told her to.

'Storm? Where are you, Storm?' Through a darkening haze she heard a voice calling her name.

'Here! Here I am. . . .' Her voice did not seem to belong to her. It called out, answering the other voice. Her feet slipped wildly in the mud as she tried to turn in the direction from which it came. She lifted up one foot and took a step, and brought it down on something long and thin and round. The canoe pole rolled under her sandal, and with a muffled cry she flung up her arms and pitched forward into blackness.

She was floating in somebody's arms. It was an odd sensation. She savoured it lazily. It was different from floating on water. Not so smooth, but much pleasanter. It had a comforting, secure feeling about it. She seemed to be going up, along with the arms, as if whoever owned them was walking up steps. And then they lowered her down. It seemed a waste of time to go up, only to be lowered down again afterwards. Something soft and flat received her, and the arms withdrew their support. She felt lonely and bereft without the arms. She tried to tell them so, but all her voice seemed capable of producing was a low murmur.

'She's coming round.' Someone spoke, then footsteps walked away, and there was a sound like the closing of a door.

Round where? she wondered hazily. Round the bend of the river? It must be, because she felt water splashing on her face. She tried to turn her head to shake it off, but something gripped her chin, and more water came, only it was warm, not cold as river water should be. It splashed over her nose and mouth, and she brought up her hands to try to brush it away.

'Keep your hands away, they're still covered in mud.'

There was no mistaking the feel of a wet, soapy flannel. It evoked memories of long-ago nursery days, but she was grown-up now, not a child any more, and it was an indignity to be washed, when you were grown-up. She opened her eyes wide to protest to the washer, and looked up straight into the stern, tanned face of—Rann.

His eyes bored down into her own. They were green, and very much alive. And furiously angry. That he was angry with herself, he left her in no doubt.

'I told you to stay in the bungalow!' he shouted at her, raising his voice to make sure it penetrated her returning consciousness, and that she understood clearly his anger.

His hair glistened with wet. It was plastered flat against his head, as if he had run impatient hands across it to squeeze out the worst of the water, and left the rest to dry as best it might on its own. He had not quite succeeded. One tawny lock disengaged itself from the rest and fell across his forehead, lending itself as a drain to drip wet drops of river water across his cheek, and down his lean, uncompromising jaw. Storm let her eyes watch the drips slowly running down, while her mind began to register what it still hardly dared to believe.

He's alive! Rann's alive. . . . The words sang in her heart with a wild, joyous refrain, forcing her to believe the unbelievable.

'Look at the state you're in!' He towelled her face roughly, and started on her hands, scrubbing at the mud, soaping and swilling with angry concentration. She longed to clasp his fingers in her own, to stop them at their work and hold them, but the soap was slippery, and his hands slid away from her clutch. She resented the soap. It did not matter that her hands were muddy. Rann was muddy, too, as well as wet, and his slacks gaped in a large tear across the one knee. Storm struggled upright on the bed, stung into full consciousness.

'You're in the same state yourself, and worse!' she realised. He had no right to shout at her for being in such a mess, when he was in an even worse one himself.

'It wouldn't have happened, if you hadn't left the bungalow.'

Did he mean her bedraggled condition, or the raid on the godown? 'You can't blame me for the raid on the godown,' she retaliated with a flash of her old spirit. How like a man, to blame a woman for something that had nothing to do with her! 'If I hadn't warned you about the flash on the escarpment, the flood would have done a lot more damage than it did, and the consequences would have been a lot worse. If I hadn't tripped up the poachers, you'd have lost the ivory.' Without quite knowing how it happened, she found herself sitting up and shouting back at him, and everything was as it had been before, they were together, and they were quarrelling, and nothing had changed. Miraculously, Rann was alive, and instead of crying her joy to the world she was shouting at him, railing at him, just as she had done before.

'I wasn't blaming you for the raid,' he waved aside her justification impatiently. 'I was blaming you for being silly enough to risk your life, by leaving the bungalow and going out there. What on earth possessed you?' he demanded angrily.

'I went because . . . because. . . .' She gulped to a halt. How could you possibly explain to a furious man that you had disobeyed him and left the safety of the bungalow, because a canoe had worn a thatched hat? She still did not know if. . . . Her mind jinked away from learning what she did not know about the pathetic thatched cone. 'It didn't seem to matter at the time,' she finished lamely.

'Didn't seem to matter? You risked your life, and it didn't seem to matter?'

'I saw the huge wave of water hit the canoes, and then I lost sight of you. I thought . . . I thought . . . that's why nothing seemed to matter any more.' Storm faltered to a halt. To her dismay, the flood seemed to have invaded her eyes. She blinked hard, trying to hold it back, but her long, curling black lashes proved of no more avail than had the river banks, and the flood spilled over and rolled down her newly washed cheeks, washing them again.

She put up a hand to brush the wetness away, but somehow her fingers found their way to Rann's face instead, and brushed away the drips of river water that still ran down his jaw. 'I thought you'd been drowned. . . .' A sob choked back the words, and the flood of tears ran faster still as she lived again that awful moment when her heart died within her, and the rest of her life turned into an empty waste of time. 'When I saw Maung Chi and his men with the tusks, and knew what they'd done to get them, knew what it meant to you. . . .' Stammering, she tried to explain. 'I had to stop them, somehow,' she finished simply.

'And risk your life in the process?' A scowl still darkened his tanned face as he ground out, 'Your warning saved everyone else's life, and then you go and deliberately risk your own!' He glared at her ferociously, but for once she did not heed his glare. Instead, her mind latched on to his words.

'But the young couple . . . the new hut . . . I found the thatched roof.' For the first time since she had found the pale-coloured thatch, hope began to rise in her.

'The young couple got out in time. So did the rest of the village. There isn't even a pi-dog missing, thanks to you. If you'd been asleep in bed instead of star-gazing over the veranda rail, if you hadn't realised what the flash meant, and raised the alarm in time. . . .' His face darkened further still as he looked at what might have been.

'If you hadn't understood, and shouted at the market traders, they wouldn't have been able to get ashore in time. Even then, one man almost delayed too late.'

'He wanted to bring his merchandise ashore with him.' Suddenly the scowl vanished, and Rann laughed, and the tension between them vanished, though Storm did not join in the laughter, not yet. The blackness of desolation was too recent, too close, she had not had time to adjust. 'The trader wanted to bring his merchandise ashore with him,' Rann grinned. 'When the branches of that dead tree scooped up the canoe we were in, and carried us with it round the bend of the river, he had time to wish he'd put his life before a few trinkets.'

'It was your life he risked, as well as his own. I still can't believe. . . .' Storm gazed up at him, her eyes enormous in her white face, hardly daring to look away in case even now she should wake up and discover it was all a dream, and Rann was not really there at all.

'Neither can I,' he sobered, 'it was a sheer fluke that saved us. An eddy of water washed the dead tree on to the bank as the wave took the bend of the river. I grabbed the trader and we jumped for our lives before the undertow sucked the whole lot back into the river again, and away.'

'So Maung Chi lost, after all,' Storm breathed. 'Nobody was hurt.' Her heart rejoiced for the young dancer. 'The damage can be repaired, and you've got your ivory back.'

'All the ivory in the world isn't worth harming a single hair of your head.'

Suddenly she was in his arms. He caught her to him, hungrily, and his voice was rough with emotion. With gentle fingers he stroked her hair, making sure that each precious strand was safe. 'I couldn't bear to lose you,' he muttered hoarsely. 'If any harm had come to you, my life would have been ended, too.' With urgent arms he strained her close, his lips demanding her own with a longing that would take a lifetime to satisfy, and then hunger for more, and all the pent-up strain and uncertainty and heartache was released on a flood of feeling that was stronger than any river flood, and more devastating than any explosion.

'Don't ever frighten me like that again.' His lips left her mouth and buried themselves in her hair. 'Don't ever leave me.' He closed her eyes with passionate kisses, so that she could not see the way to leave him, demanded her promise from the soft fullness of her parted lips, and when it came, low on her quivering breath, he sealed it with fire along the long, slender column of her throat.

'I love you ... I love you,' he groaned, and strained her to him, pledging his love with hoarse, broken words so utterly unlike the words of the Rann Moorcroft she had known hitherto, the confident, masterful, man of teak. 'Storm darling, say you'll marry me?' he pleaded. 'I'll go anywhere, do anything, but don't go away. Don't ever leave me. . . .'

She had known the agony of uncertainty, and could not bear to see him suffer, too. 'I'll never leave you.' Tenderly, still hardly daring to believe, she clasped her hands behind his head, drawing his face down again to meet her own, whispering promises that only she could give. With gentle fingertips she brushed away the drops of river water that still escaped and ran across his forehead, because now they had found one another, nothing must ever come between them again, not even drops of river water.

'I won't be able to get to the coast for a day or two, to buy you a ring. The police want the helicopter trip to take the poachers into custody.'

'I'll wear your bracelet instead.' A ring was not important. It was like icing on a cake, sweet to have, and lovely to look at, but unimportant beside the new-found certainty of their love. 'You can give me an orchid to wear in the meantime,' she teased him mischievously.

'I'll bring you a fresh one every day, until the helicopter can make room to take us to the coast. We can be married by special licence, at the Consulate.'

'But we'll come back here afterwards?'

'Will you mind too much? We can find a home on the coast, if you'd rather. I've got to remain in the Province for another year, until my contract here is finished. I can't let the firm down, they took me on to give me an insight into the teak extracting business, because I wanted to learn all aspects of the raw material we handle before I accepted a partnership in the family timber business back home.' Unconsciously he revealed the determination and commitment that scorned to take the easy path, and spoke eloquently of the mature strength that she had mistakenly believed to be hardness, that would support her and shelter her for the rest of their lives.

'I'd rather live here, in the bungalow. It's where we first met.' Shyly she begged to be allowed to come back.

'I thought you hated the jungle?'

'I feared it, at first,' she admitted candidly, 'but not any longer.' Not with Rann beside her. 'It's got butterflies too, remember?' she reminded him softly.

'It's got more, much more,' he assured her eagerly. 'I'll show you pools where waterlilies grow, high up in the hills, and where the weaver birds build their nests. . . .'

'You must show me the work site, too.' She still had not seen the work site, that had played such a leading role in bringing them together.

'There won't be a lot more work to do on it now, except for tidying up,' Rann said thankfully. 'The dynamite must have cleared the last rock barrier right away, and set the other arm of the river flowing again.'

'How can you tell? You haven't had time to go up there yet.'

'Because our arm of the river here has subsided so quickly, after the initial flood,' he replied confidently. 'It couldn't have calmed down so soon if it had been carrying a double load of water. We didn't dare to risk using explosives ourselves, because of the flooding, and the risk to the villagers, but now it's been done, and the river's flowing into the game reserve again, the animals will follow the water, and drift back to their own grazing grounds without any urging from us. Krish will stay here and superintend the finishing off of the work on site, and I'll be free to take some leave.'

The glow in his eyes as he looked down at her brought the soft, rosy colour to warm her cheeks, deeper where his lips pressed against them, widening her mouth into a smile. 'So decide where you'd like to go for our honeymoon,' he urged her. 'We could go to the coast, and the beaches where you spent your holiday, if you wanted to. You said you enjoyed it there.'

'And be among crowds of people, and shops full of tourist trinkets, carved from ivory?' Storm shook her head vehemently. 'Let's leave Krish and Le in your bungalow, here. . . .'

'Our bungalow,' he insisted, and deepened her colour still further.

'Our bungalow.' It had a lovely sound. 'We could borrow their bungalow on the game reserve. We'd be there to watch the animals come back.'

'It sounds a perfect way to spend a honeymoon.' Tenderly Rann sealed his approval of her choice, in a way that precluded speech for quite a time.

At last—'I must warn the helicopter pilot to make room for four, instead of one,' he remembered, and laughed softly at her puzzled,

'Four?'

'Krish and Le will want to come with us, to be best man, and maid of honour, and witnesses all in one. The pilot will bring them straight back here afterwards, and then drop us off on the reserve.'

'What will happen to Mac, the pilot of the plane?' Mention of the helicopter pilot suddenly reminded her of Mac. From the warmth of her own happiness, she could feel compassion for him now.

'I've already put in a good word for him. He'll be up on a charge of shooting an elephant without a licence. It'll carry a heavy fine, but not a prison sentence.'

'He may not be able to pay.' Storm's forehead puckered. 'He lost his job when the plane crashed.'

'That's been taken care of, too. There's another job lined up for him in the sawmills on the coast, if he wants it.' Rann smoothed the pucker away. 'Whether he'll settle down for long is another matter.'

'I didn't steal his gold hunter.' It was important that Rann should believe her, that nothing should be allowed to come between them.

'Mac never owned a watch, let alone a gold hunter. That was nothing but a red herring, to sidetrack me from questioning him.' He laughed her fears away, and then suddenly his face became serious again, and he looked down at her sombrely.

'What's more important, will *you* like *your* change of job?' he questioned her anxiously. 'If you marry me, it'll mean you giving up the stage, and your career.' The torment in his eyes, and the sudden tremor that shook his voice, told her what her answer meant to him, and warned her not to tease.

'*When* I marry you, not *if*,' she corrected him firmly. 'I don't want to spend the rest of my days acting out the stories of other people's lives. I want to live my own.' She rejected her career without regret.

'You dreamed of becoming a star. You would have been, except. . . .'

'I'd rather have reality than any dream.' Eagerly her lips sought his, stilling his doubts, and drinking deep draughts from the life-giving well of his love. For a long, timeless minute they clung together, fusing their present and their future in a strong, unbreakable bond, that lit bright stars in Storm's dark eyes, that from now on would shine only for Rann.

Harlequin Plus
THE LURE OF IVORY

For centuries man has been braving the dark interior of Africa in search of the male elephant and its magnificent tusks. Stripped of their rough outer layer, the tusks reveal a fine-grained smooth core. Soft and creamy white, or sometimes hard and reddish brown, this precious ivory core has been used by man from prehistoric times to the present for fashioning everything from crudely carved tools to beautiful works of art.

Although ivory can be found in the tusks of other mammals, including extinct ones—the USSR is noted for its mammoth tusks found preserved in Siberian glaciers—it is the majestic African elephant with its average one-hundred-pound tusks that has most successfully captured the imagination—and greed—of men. Until the late 1800s, the ivory trade was controlled by the Arabs, the only ones who dared enter the heart of Africa to hunt elephants. But with the arrival of European hunters, armed with guns and fast rail transportation into the interior, the elephant herds began to disappear from the continent.

The ivory trade in Africa almost ended with the near extinction of the elephant, leaving museum collections of inlaid furniture and religious statues as testament to the heights ivory workmanship once reached. Today ivory is still exported from Africa, but on a much smaller scale, and it is mainly mass-produced into cheap trinkets in India. The days of great ivory carvings may be long gone, but the elephants can now roam free in the darkest jungle recesses or in the shelter of African game reserves.

Harlequin Romances

The books that let you escape
into the wonderful world of romance!
Trips to exotic places...interesting
plots...meeting memorable people...
the excitement of love.... These are
integral parts of Harlequin Romances —
the heartwarming novels read by
women everywhere.

Many early issues are now available.
Choose from this great selection!

Choose from this list of Harlequin Romance editions.*

*Some of these book were originally published under different titles.